Louis Couperus

Majesty

A Novel

Louis Couperus

Majesty
A Novel

ISBN/EAN: 9783337031848

Printed in Europe, USA, Canada, Australia, Japan

Cover: Foto ©Andreas Hilbeck / pixelio.de

More available books at **www.hansebooks.com**

MAJESTY

A NOVEL

BY

LOUIS COUPERUS

TRANSLATED BY

A. TEIXEIRA DE MATTOS
AND
ERNEST DOWSON

NEW YORK
D. APPLETON AND COMPANY
1895

MAJESTY

CHAPTER I

I

LIPARA, a city white as marble; long, white rows of villas on a Southern blue sea; endless, elegant esplanades on the front, with palms whose green lacquer shimmered against an atmosphere of vivid blue ether; and above it drifted heavily, fraught with storm and with tragedy, a sombre sky full of grayness, like a danger in the firmament. And that gray sky was full of mystery, was full of destiny, of strange destiny; it precipitated no thunder, but remained hanging over the city; it only cast pale shadows over the pallor of its palaces, over the width of its squares and streets, over the blueness of its sea, its harbours, where

the ships, upright, still, anxious, shot up their tall
masts.

White, square, massive, in the greenness of the
Elizabeth Parks, in the more intimate mystery of
its own great plane-trees—the park of the celebrated plane-trees of Lipara, trees of renown—
lay the Imperial, the Emperor's palace, quasi-
Moorish, with white, pointed arcades; it lay as
the very civic crown of the capital: one great
architectural jewel, separated from the city, in
whose midst it lay, by all that park verdure.

The Empress, Elizabeth of Liparia, sat in the
private drawing-room of her apartments in the
right wing; she sat with a lady-in-waiting, the
Countess Hélène of Thesbia. The windows were
open; they opened on to the park; the celebrated
plane-trees rose there, knotty with age, wide-
spreading, anxious, motionless with their trimmed
leaves, between which a dull green twilight shimmered down upon the lawns which ran out, rolled
soft and smooth, into the distance, like velvet
tightly stretched, drawn out endlessly into a
violet perspective, with just there the one
strident white patch of a statue.

A great silence buzzed its strange sound of
stillness in from the park; it buzzed around the
Empress. She sat there smiling; she listened to

Hélène reading ; she endeavoured to listen, she did not always understand. A nervous dread haunted her, surrounded her, as with an invisible net of meshes unbreakable. This dread was for her husband, her children, her eldest son, her daughters, her youngest boy. This dread crept along the carpet beneath her feet ; it hung from the ceiling over her head, stole round about her through the whole room. This dread was in the park ; it came from afar, from the violet perspectives ; it swept over the lawns and climbed in through the open windows ; it fell from the trees, it fell from the sky, the gray, thunder-laden sky. This dread quivered through Lipara, through the whole of Liparia, through the whole empire ; it quivered in, in to the Empress, filling her whole being. . . .

Then Elizabeth drew a deep breath and smiled. Hélène had looked up to her at a certain sentence with a light stress of voice and eyes, pointing the dialogue of the novel ; this made the Empress smile, and she listened afresh. The anxiety remained in her, but she extinguished it with much acquiescence, acquiescence in what was to happen, in what must happen.

The novel that Hélène was reading was " Daniële Cortis," a work that was in vogue at court because the Princess Thera had liked it. The Countess read carefully and with great expression; the arabesques of the Italian came forth from her lips with the elegance of very pointed Venetian glass, flowery and transparent. And the Empress wondered that Hélène could read so beautifully and did not seem to feel the anxiety which yet stole about everywhere like a spectre.

There was a knock at the door leading from the anteroom; a lackey opened, and a lady-in-waiting appeared between the hangings with a courtesy.

" His Highness, Prince Herman. . . . " she announced in a voice that hesitated a little, as though she knew that this hour of the afternoon was almost sacred to the Empress.

" Ask the Prince to come in," replied the Empress; her voice with all its haughtiness sounded friendly and attractively sympathetic. " We have been expecting the Prince so long. . . ."

The door remained open, the lady-in-waiting disappeared, the lackey waited at the hangings, immovable, for the Prince to come. His firm tread sounded, approaching quickly, through the anteroom, and he entered pleasantly, friendliness on his healthy red face, the pleasure of meeting again in his large gray eyes, from which shone a black pupil. The lackey closed a door behind him.

"Aunt!"

The Prince, with both hands outstretched, stepped towards the Empress. She had risen, as had Hélène, and she moved a step towards him; she took both his hands, and allowed him to kiss her heartily on both cheeks.

Hélène courtesied.

"Countess of Thesbia. . . ." and the Prince bowed.

"So you have come at last!" said the Empress, with jesting discontent. She shook her head, but could not but look kindly at his pleasant, handsome, healthy face. "Why did you not telegraph for certain when you were coming? Othomar would then have gone to the station, but now . . ."

She shrugged her shoulders with a regretful smile, as much as to say that now it could not be helped that his reception had only been a casual one. . . .

"But, aunt," said Herman—the tone of his voice seemed to say that he would never have demanded this of Othomar—"I have been excellently received; General Ducardi, Leoni, Fasti, our worthy minister, and Siridsen . . . "

"Othomar will be sorry all the same," said the Empress; "he is out driving now with Thera.

Thera is driving her new bays. I can't understand why they went; it is sure to rain!"

The Empress resumed her seat with an anxious look at the weather outside; the Prince and Hélène sat down likewise. A cross-fire of inquiries after the two families was kindled between the Empress and her nephew; they had not seen each other for months. There was much to be discussed; the times were full of disaster, and the Empress showed a long telegram which the Emperor had sent from Altara about the inundations. Her fingers which held the message quivered.

She was still a woman of remarkable beauty, in spite of her grown-up children. But the charm of her beauty was apparent to very few. In public that beauty assumed a stiffness as of a cameo; fine, clear-cut lines; great, cold eyes, without expression; a cold, closed mouth; before people her slender figure assumed something stiff and automatic; she even showed herself thus before the more intimate circles of the court. But when she was seen, as now, in the seclusion of her own drawing-room, with no one except her nephew, whom she loved almost as much as her own children, and one little lady-in-waiting whom she spoilt, then, in spite of the dread which she repressed deep down in her heart, she became another woman. In her simple gray silk—she was in slight mourning for a relation—what was stiff and automatic in her figure changed into a gracious suppleness of carriage and movement, as spontaneous as the other was studied; the cameo of her face animated itself; a look almost of melancholy came into her eyes, and, above all, a laugh about that cold, rigid mouth was as a gleam of sympathy that rendered her unrecognizable to one who had seen her for the first time stiff and austere.

Prince Herman of Gothland was the second son of her sister, the Queen of Gothland. A great, sturdy fellow in his undress uniform as a naval lieutenant, with the healthy, Germanic fairness of the House of Gothland: a firm neck, broad shoulders, the swelling chest of a gymnast, the determined quickness of movement of a lively nature, more than sufficient intelligence in his large gray eyes with the black pupils, and with now and then a single pleasant, soft note in his baritone voice: a note that caused a momentary slight surprise and made him sympathetic when it sounded gently in the midst of his virility. And now that he sat there, easily, simply, pleasantly, and yet with a certain dignity that did not permit him an absolute excess of joviality; now that he spoke, with his sweet voice, of his father, his mother, his brothers and sisters, and asked after his uncle, the Emperor Oscar of Liparia, asked after Othomar, Thera—now, yes, now he aroused in the Empress a delicate feeling of family sympathy, something of a secret bond of blood, a very solid support of relationship amid the isolation of their highness-ships, the highness-ships of Liparia and Gothland. Over there, at the other side of Europe, far, far away from her, and yet so near through the magnetism of this delicate feeling, she felt Gothland lying as one great plain of love, whither she could allow her thoughts to wander. She was no longer giddy with melancholy and dread that she was so high together with those who loved her, for she was not high alone; in her highness she leant against another highness, Liparia against Gothland, Gothland against Liparia. It brought moist tears to her eyes, it brought a melancholy that was like happiness into her breath. The spectre of dread had disappeared. She could have embraced her nephew; she would have liked to tell him all that; his presence alone already gave her this feeling, a feeling of comfort and of strength; she had not known it for months.

II

The door was opened; the lackey stood stiff
and upright, with a rigid look, that stared straight
before him, in the shadow of the hangings.   Princess Thera and Othomar entered; the Princess
went up blithely and kindly to her cousin, they
kissed; Othomar also embraced Herman, with a
single word.   But in comparison with the natural
utterances of the Empress and of Thera, this
single word of the Duke of Xara sounded studied
and smilingly cold, not intimate, and with an un-
necessary air of etiquette.   It did not conceal a
translucent insincerity, a transparent show that
made no effort to simulate sympathy, but seemed
quite simply what at this moment it could not
but seem: a salutation of affected kindness between two cousins of the same age.   Prince
Herman was accustomed to this; there was no
intimacy between him and Othomar, and this was
especially striking when they saw each other the
first time again for months: it affected the
Empress keenly, disagreeably.

The conversation turned once more upon the
inundations in the North.   The Empress showed
her children the latest telegram, the same that she

had shown to Herman; it mentioned new disasters:
still more villages swept away, towns harassed
by the swollen and overflowing rivers, after a
month of rain that had resembled the Flood. It
had caused the Emperor to proceed three days
earlier to the Northern governments, but they were
now every moment at court expecting his desire
that the Crown Prince should replace him there,
as he himself was to return to Lipara on account
of the Cabinet crisis.

The Crown Prince discussed all this a little
coldly and formally. He was a young man of
twenty-one, slender and of short stature, very
slightly built, with delicate, melancholy features
and dull, black eyes, that generally stared straight
before him; a young moustache tinted his upper
lip as with a stripe of Indian ink. He drooped his
head a little on his chest, and then had a way of
looking up from under his eyelids; he generally
sat very quiet; his hands, which were small and
broad but delicate, both rested evenly upon his
knees, and he had a trick of carrying his left hand
to his eyes, and then—he was a little short-
sighted—just peering at his ring. He was tightly
dressed in the blue-and-white uniform of a Captain
in the Lancers, the uniform that he generally wore
in public: its silver frogs lent a certain breadth

to his slenderness; on his right wrist he wore a narrow bracelet of dull gold.

"This is the first letter," said the Empress; "read it out, Thera. . . ."

The Princess took the letter. The Emperor wrote:

"It is heartrending to see all this, and to be able to do so little. The whole district to the south of the Zanthos, from Altara to Lycilia, is one expanse of water; where villages stood there now float the remains of bridges and houses, trees, accumulations of roofs, dead cattle, carts, and household furniture, and as we were going along the Therezia Dyke, which, God be praised! still stands firm at Altara, a cluster of corpses was slowly washed straight before our feet in one gigantic embrace of death. . . ."

The Crown Prince had suddenly turned pale; he remained sitting in his usual attitude: he peered at his ring, with the trick that was his habit. Thera read on. When the Crown Prince looked up he met his mother's eyes. She nodded to him with her eyelids without being seen by the others, who were listening; he smiled—a smile full of heartbreaking melancholy, and answered her with the same invisible quiver of the eyelids; it was as though he understood that gentle greeting, and drew a scrap of comfort from it for a mysterious sorrow that tacitly depressed him within himself, that lay on his breast like an oppression of breath, like a nightmare in his waking life.

But Prince Herman was already talking about the ministerial crisis; it was momentarily expected that the Authoritative Government, rendered powerless since the new elections in the House of Representatives with its majority of Constitutionals, would proffer its resignation to the Emperor. The question, as always, was that of a revision of the Constitution, which the Constitutionals desired, and the Authoritatives — taking the side of the Emperor—opposed. The Empress Elizabeth sighed with a sigh of fatigue; how often had not this question of a revision of the Constitution, which in Liparia always meant an extension of the Constitution and a restriction of the Imperial authority, come looming up during their twenty years' reign as a personal attack upon her husband! Resembling his long line of Liparian ancestors, hereditarily autocratic, Oscar could never forgive his father, Othomar XI., for allowing a Constitution to be formed in his more Liberal reign. And now, at this crisis, it was no small thing they asked, the Constitutionals. The

House of Nobles, hereditary and Authoritative, the Emperor's own body, which cancelled every proposal of a too Constitutional character sent up from the House of Representatives, was no longer to stand above them, hereditary, and consequently, because of its hereditary nature, invariably Authoritative: they wanted to make it elective! Even Othomar XI., with his modern ideas in favour of a Constitution, would never have suffered this attack upon one of the most ancient institutions of the empire, an attack which would shake Liparia to its foundations. . . .

While Herman was debating this, casually, his words lightly touching this all-important question, it seemed to Othomar as though he were turning giddy. A world passed through his head, rushing with rapid clouds through his imagination, and out of these clouds visions loomed up before him, pale-red, quick as lightning, terrible as a kind of apocalypse, the end of the universe in an explosion of dynamite. Out of these clouds there flashed up for an instant a scene, a recollection of the history of his Imperial inheritance: one of the Emperors of Liparia murdered centuries ago by one of his favourites at a court festival. Revolutions in other countries of Europe, the French Revolution, flickered up with

a blood-red reflection; the strikes in the quick-
silver mines of the Eastern governments grinned at
him out of them, out of the clouds, the world of
clouds that stormed through his thoughts. . . .
And so many more, so many more, all so rapid,
with the rapidity of their lightning-flashes; he
could not understand them, the ruddy lightning-
flashes; it all just flickered through him, and
then away: it flickered away, far away! . . .
And it seemed strange to him that he was sitting
there, in his mother's drawing-room, with the
stately park swarming behind the plate-glass
windows, with tints of old mediæval gold-leather,
now, in the lower gleam of the sun-rays; with his
mother opposite him, so sweet, so daintily gentle
in the intimacy of this short, uninterrupted meeting; his cousin talking, and his sister answering,
and the little lady-in-waiting listening with a
smile. . . . How strange to sit like that, so
easily, so peacefully, so serenely, in the seclusion
of their palace, as though Liparia were not
shaking like an old, infirm tower! Yes, they
were talking about the crisis, Herman and Thera,
but what did talking do? Words, nothing but
words! Why this endless stringing together of
words, beautiful, empty words, which a sovereign
is obliged to string together and then utter to his

subjects, now on this occasion, now on that?
No, no, they were not in his province, speeches!
For what, after all, were they supposed to express,
this or that? What was right, what was just,
what was right and just for their Empire, this or
that? How could one know, how could one be
certain, how could one avoid hesitating, seeking,
feeling, blindfolded? Even if he had a thousand
eyes all over the empire, would he be able to see
everything that should happen? and if he were
omniscient, would he always be able to know
what would be right? The Constitution—was
it right for a country to have a constitution or
not? In Russia—was it right in Russia? A
republic—would a republic be better? And who
was right? Was his father right in wanting to
reign as an absolute monarch, with his hereditary
House of Nobles, in which he, Othomar, now
remembered his admission, as Duke of Xara, at
his eighteenth year, with the Ducal crown and the
robes and chain of the Order of the Imperial Orb?
Or was the House of Representatives right?
would it be a good thing to place a restriction
upon absolute sovereignty? It was a difficult
puzzle to decide. . . . The inundations: " It is
heartrending to see all this, and to be able to do
so little. . . . An expanse of water all the way to

Lycilia, a cluster of corpses in the embrace of death. . . ."

It lightened.

Dull, heavy rumblings rolled through the sky; fat drops fell as hard as liquid hail upon the leaves of the plane-trees; the whole park seemed to quiver, dreading the break in the clouds that was to come. Hélène rose and closed the window.

Then Othomar heard a strange sound : Syria . . . . Had they ceased talking about the House of Nobles ? Syria, Syria. . . .

"The King and Queen were to have come next week, but they have now postponed their visit," said the Empress.

"Because of the inundations," added Thera. "They are first going to Constantinople; I only wish they would remain with the Sultan. . . ."

"This visit seems to me at least to be something of an infliction," said Herman, laughing; "and how long do they stay, aunt ? "

The Empress raised her shoulders to express that she did not know : the approaching visit of the King and Queen of Syria pleased neither her nor the Emperor, but it was not to be avoided . . . . But she did not want to say much on the subject before Hélène, and replied :

"All the court festivities are now postponed, Herman, as you know, because of these terrible disasters. You will have a quiet time, my boy. You had better go with Othomar to Count Myxila's. . . ."

Count Myxila, the Imperial Chancellor, was that day keeping his sixtieth birthday. He was the Emperor's principal favourite. That morning he had been to the Empress to receive her congratulations. The Crown Prince was, by the Emperor's desire, to appear for a moment at the reception at the Chancellor's palace.

Prince Herman looked towards Othomar inquiringly, as though he were expecting him too to say a word.

"Of course. . . ." the Duke of Zara hastened to say; "Myxila will rely upon seeing Herman. . . ."

III

When at half-past ten in the evening Othomar and Herman returned from the Chancellor's palace in a downpour of rain, it was known among the Empress's entourage also that the ministry had resigned; the princes had met the ministers at Count Myxila's; the crisis had

thrilled through the outward worldliness of the
reception like a threatening ague. Also there
was a telegram from the Emperor for the Duke
of Xara :

"I charge Your Imperial Highness to proceed
to Altara to-morrow.—OSCAR."

The telegram did not come as a surprise, but
was the natural consequence of the resignation of
the Government and the return of the Emperor;
for the Emperor did not wish to leave the scene
of the disasters without the consolation that the
Heir Apparent was about to replace him.

After a moment spent with the Empress, Othomar withdrew to his own apartments. He sent
for his equerry, Prince Dutri, and shortly and in
few words consulted with him; after which the
equerry hurried away with much ado. In his
dressing-room Othomar found his valet, Andro,
who had been warned by one of the chamberlains, and was already occupied in packing up.

"Don't pack too much," he said, as the valet
rose respectfully from the trunk before which he
was kneeling; "it would only be in the way. . . ."

So soon as he had said this, he was really unable to say why. Nor did the valet seem to take
any notice of it; kneeling down again before the
trunk, he packed up what he thought fit. It

would be quite right as Andro was doing it, thought Othomar.

And he threw himself into a chair in his study. One of the windows was open; a single pedestal lamp in a corner gave a dim light. The furious downpour raged outside; a humid whiff of wet leaves drifted in.

The Prince was tired, too tired to call to Andro to pull off his tight patent-leather boots. He wore the white-and-gold uniform of a colonel of the Throneguards, the Imperial body-guard; the chain of the Order of the Imperial Orb hung round his neck; other decorations studded his breast here and there. Before his eyes there still whirled the reception at the Imperial Chancellor's; in his brain there buzzed, together with the rain, the inevitable conversations about the crisis, the Government, the House of Nobles. He saw himself the Crown Prince, always the Crown Prince, always too condescending, too affable, not sufficiently natural, not simple, not easy, like Herman, and he saw Herman moving easily through the rooms of the Chancellor's palace, asking quite simply to be introduced to the ladies, now by Count Myxila and again by an equerry. And he envied his cousin, who was a second son. Herman did not cause the atmosphere around him at once to freeze, as did he with the cold Imperial look of his Crown-Princedom.

He saw the ministers, the ministers who were about to resign, each with his own interests at heart instead of those of Liparia. He suspected this from their humble attitudes before him, the Crown Prince, when he had spoken to all of them . . . . He felt that they were only playing a part, that there was much in them that they did not allow to transpire, and he suddenly asked himself why, why this should all be so, why so much show, nothing but show. . . . And he suffered now, deep in his breast; the tightness of his bestarred uniform oppressed him. . . .

He saw the old Countess Myxila, and some other ladies, whom he had seen courtesying amid the crackling of their trains and the sudden downward glitter of their diamonds, whom he had seen flushing with pleasure because the Duke of Xara had taken notice of them. And the wife also of the High Marshal, the Duchess of Yemena, who had been absent from court so long in voluntary exile at her estate in Vaza, he saw her approaching, conducted by Prince Dutri. For he did not know her; when formerly she had been at court he was a boy of fifteen, undergoing a strict military education, seldom with the Empress, and never at the court festivals; at that period he never saw the Duchess.

Now, in the twilight of the lamp, with the weather raging outside, he saw her once more, and she became as it were transparent in the lines of the rain; she looked strange through the rain, as through a curtain of wet muslin. A tall woman, with a voluptuous form, half naked under the white radiance of her diamond necklace, that is how she approached him, her hair blue-black with a gleam in it, her face a little pale under a thin bloom of rose powder: so she came nearer, slowly, hesitating, in her yellow-gold figured satin, edged with heavy sable; so she bowed before him, with a deep, reverential courtesy before the Imperial presence; her head sank upon her breast, the tiara in her black hair shot forth rays, her whole stature curved down as with one serpentine line of grace in the material of gleaming gold that shone about her bosom and seemed to break over the thick folds of her train with a filagree of light. He had spoken to her. She rose from the billows of her reverential grace; she replied, he forgot what; her eyes sparkled upon his like black stars. She had made an impression upon him. He thought it was because he had heard her

much spoken of as a woman with a life full of
passion : a thing that was a riddle to him.   His
education had been military and strictly chaste,
his youth had remained uncorrupted by the easy
morality of the court, perhaps because his parents,
after a long and secret separation, known to none
but themselves, had come together again from a
need of family life and mutual support ; the
Empress Elizabeth had forgiven the Emperor
Oscar and submitted to his infidelities as inevitable.   Round about him Othomar had never had
occasion to observe the life of the senses.   At the
University of Altara, where he had studied, he
had never mingled, except officially, in the diver-
sions of the students ; he had always remained
the Crown Prince, not from haughtiness, but
because he was unable to do otherwise, from lack
of ease and tact.

And something in the Duchess had made an
impression on him, as of a thing unknown.   He
felt in this woman, who courtesied so deeply
before him with her sphinx-like smile, a world of
emotion and knowledge which he did not possess ;
he had felt poor in comparison with her, small and
insignificant.   What was it that she possessed
and he not ?   Was it an enigma of the soul ?
Were there such things, soul-enigmas, and was it

worth while to try to penetrate them ? Such a woman as she, was she not quite different from his mother and sisters ? Or did his equerries, among themselves, speak of his sisters too as they spoke of the Duchess ? And that life of passion, that life of love for so many, was that then the truth ? Did they not slander her, the equerries, or at least, did they not make truth seem different to what it was, as they always did in everything ? as if the truth must not always be made to seem other to a prince than to a subject?

He felt fatigued. And he remained sitting, endeavouring in vain to drive from him the whirl of the strange figures of that reception seen through a transparency of rain. Before him, as though in his room, they all walked through one another—the ministers, the equerries, Count Myxila, and the Duchess. . . .

A knock, a chamberlain.

" Prince Herman asks whether he may intrude on Your Highness for a minute."

He nodded yes. Prince Herman entered after a moment.

" You are always welcome, Herman," said Othomar, and his voice sounded cold in spite of himself.

" I have just come to ask you something," said

Herman of Gothland. "I would much like to go with you to Altara to-morrow; but I want to be certain that you don't mind. I would not have asked it of my own accord if my aunt had not spoken of it. What do you think?"

Othomar looked at Herman; Othomar did not like his cool voice.

"If you do so out of sympathy, because you happen to be at Lipara, by all means. . . ." he began.

"Let me tell you once more: I am doing this principally because of . . . . your mother."

His voice sounded very emphatic.

"Do it for her, then," replied Othomar gently. "It will give me great pleasure if you go with me for my mother's sake."

Herman realized that he had been unnecessarily cool and emphatic. He was sorry. The Empress had asked him to accompany Othomar. He had hesitated at first, knowing that there was a lack of sympathy between Othomar and him. Then he had yielded, but had not known how to ask Othomar. His usual ease of manner had forsaken him, as always, in Othomar's presence.

"Very well, then. . . ." Herman stammered clumsily.

Othomar put out his hand.

" I understand your intention perfectly.
Mamma would like you to go with me, because she will then be sure that there is some
one there whom I can trust in everything. Isn't
that it ? "

Herman pressed his hand.

" Yes," he said, glad, contented, with no annoyance that Othomar had had the best of this
conversation, very delighted that his cousin took
it like this. " Yes, just so ; that's how it is.
Don't let me detain you now, it's late. Good-
night. . . ."

" Good-night. . . ."

Herman went away. It was still pouring with
rain. Othomar sat down again ; the chilliness of
the rainy night pressed coldly in and fell upon his
shoulders. But he remained staring motionlessly
at the toes of his boots.

Andro entered softly.

" Does Your Highness wish me to. . . ."

Othomar nodded. The valet first closed the
window and drew the blind, and then knelt before
the Prince, who, with a gesture of fatigue, put
out his foot towards him and rested the heel of
his boot on his knee.

IV

The downpour ceased during the night; but it rained again in the morning. It was seven o'clock; a sultry moisture covered the colossal glass dome of the station, as though it had been breathed upon all over. The special stood waiting; the engine snorted with short, powerful pants like a dissatisfied, tired beast. A great multitude, a buzzing accumulation of vague people filled the glass hall; a detachment of infantry—two files, to right and left; the uniforms dark-red and pale gray; above, a faint glitter of bayonets—drew two long stripes of colour diagonally through the sombre station, cut the crowd into two, and kept a broad space clear in front of the Imperial waiting-room.

Dissatisfaction hovered over the crowd; angry glances flashed; rough words crackled sharply through the air, and curses; a contemptuous laugh sounded for an instant in a corner.

There was a long wait; then a cheer was heard outside—the Prince had arrived in front of the station. The waiting-room became filled with uniforms, glistening faintly in the morning light; short, low conversations took place.

Othomar entered with Herman and the Marquis of Dazzara, the Governor of the residential capital, the highest military authority, whose rich uniform stood out against the simpler ones of the others, even against those of the Princes; they were followed by adjutants, Liparian and Gothlandic equerries, aides-de-camp. The Mayor of the town, the managing-director of the railway stepped towards Othomar and saluted him; the Mayor lost himself in long phrases before the two Princes.

" Why has the approach to the platform not been forbidden to the public ? " asked General Ducardi of the director. The Adjutant-General had taken a look at the platform through the lace curtains, curious about the humming outside.

The director shrugged his shoulders.

" That was our first intention ; it was done in that way when the Emperor departed," he replied. " But a special message was sent from the Imperial urgently to ask us not to shut off the platform ; it was the Duke of Xara's wish."

" And how about all those soldiers ? "

" By command of the Governor of the capital. An aide-de-camp came to tell us that a detachment of infantry was to come as a guard-of-honour."

" Was that aide-de-camp also from the Imperial ? "

" No, from the Governor's Palace. . . ."

Ducardi shrugged his shoulders; an angry growl made his great gray moustache quiver. He went straight up to the Crown Prince.

" Is Your Highness aware that there is a detachment of infantry outside ? " he said, interrupting the Mayor's long sentences. The Governor heard him and drew nearer.

" A detachment ? . . . No. . . ." said Othomar, in astonishment.

" Did Your Highness not command it, then ? " Ducardi continued.

" I ? No," Othomar repeated.

The Governor bowed low; he was made nervous by the powerful voice of the General, who spoke loudly.

" I thought," he said, urbanely, but mumbling, stammering—and he tried to be at once humble before the Prince and haughty towards the General—" I thought it would be well to safeguard Your Highness against possible . . . . possible unpleasantness, especially as your Highness desired. . . . desired that the platform should remain open to the public. . . ."

Othomar looked out as Ducardi had done;

he saw the infantry drawn up, and the crowd behind, angry, murmuring, gray, threatening.

"But, Excellency," he said, aloud, to the Governor, "in that case it would have been better to shut off the platform. This is quite wrong. The town police would have been sufficient to prevent any crowding up."

"I was afraid of. . . . of unpleasantness, Highness. Troubled times, the people so discontented," he whispered, fearing to be overheard by the equerries.

"Quite wrong," repeated Othomar, angrily, nervously excited. "Let the infantry march off."

"That's impossible now, Highness," Ducardi hastened to say, with an unhappy smile. "You understand that that can't be done."

The conversation had been carried on aside, in a half-whispering tone; yet they seemed to listen. Every eye was gazing on the group surrounding the Princes; the rest were all silent.

"Then let us prolong this regrettable situation as little as possible," said Othomar, and his voice quivered high, young, and nervous in his clear throat.

The doors were opened; Othomar, in his hurry, stepped out first; the equerries and aides-de-

camp did not follow him at once, as they had to
make way for Prince Herman, who happened
to be a little behind. Herman hurried up to
Othomar; the others followed.

The Princes made a movement of the head to
left and right as though to bow; but their eyes
met the rigid, round eyes of the soldiers, who
presented arms with a flash; they saluted and
walked on to their compartment a little quickly,
with an unpleasant feeling in their backs.

Under the colossal glass roof of the station,
behind the files of soldiers, the crowd stood as
still as death, for the humming had almost ceased;
there was no curse nor scornful word heard, but
also no cheer, no vivat sweet to the ears of
princes.

And the faces of those vague people, separated
by uniforms and bayonets from their future ruler,
remained staring rigidly with dull, hostile eyes,
with firmly-closed lips, full of forced restraint.

The Princes from the windows waved their hands
to the dignitaries, who stood on the platform bowing, saluting. The locomotive whistled, shrieked,
tore the close atmosphere of humidity under the
dome; the train left the station, drove into the
early morning, which was lighter outside the glass
arch; glided, as it were, over the rainy town

upon viaducts, canals, streets, squares beneath
it; further on, the battlements and steeples of
the palaces and churches; the two marble turrets
of the Cathedral, with the doves nestling in the
Renaissance arabesques of the lacework of its
steeples, standing out pale-white already against
the sky growing blue; then, in the centre of the
town—green and wide, one oasis—the Elizabeth
Parks, the white mass of the Imperial, and behind
that the gigantic bend of the quays, the harbour
with its forest of masts, the oval curve of the
horizon of the sea—everything wet, glittering,
raining in the distance.

Othomar looked sombrely before him. Herman
smiled to him. "Come, don't think about it any
more," he advised him; and, laughing, added,
"Our poor Governor has had his appetite spoilt
for dinner to-day."

General Ducardi muttered an inward curse.

"Monstrously stupid. . . ." Herman heard
him mumbling afterwards.

"I wanted to show them," said Othomar, suddenly. . . . he was about to say, "That I am not
afraid of them." He threw a glance around him,
he saw the eyes of Prince Dutri, his equerry,
fixed upon him like a basilisk's, and let his voice
change from proud to faint-hearted; sadly he

concluded. . . . "that I love them and trust them
so completely. Why need it have turned out
like this? . . ."

His voice had sounded faint because of Prince
Dutri; but it displeased the General. He first
glanced aside at his Crown Prince and then at
the Prince of Gothland; he drew a comparison;
his eye continued to rest appreciatively, approvingly, with soldierly pleasure on the smart
naval lieutenant, broad and strong, his hands on
his thighs, bending forward a little, looking after
the white capital which was receding before his
eyes through the slanting rainbeams. . . .

After four hours' travelling, Novi, in the province of Xara. The train stops; the Princes and
their suite alight, consult clocks, watches. They
are surprised, they walk up and down the platform for half an hour, for an hour. Prince Herman engages in a busy conversation with the
station-master. It rains unceasingly.

At last the special from Altara is signalled. It
glides in and stops; the Emperor Oscar steps
from the Imperial compartment. Generals and
adjutants follow him; their uniforms, the Emperor's included, have lost something of their
smartness, and hang in tired creases over their
shoulders, like clothes worn a long time. The

Emperor, still young, broad, and sturdy, and only just turning gray, walks with a firm step; he embraces his son, his nephew, brusquely, hastily. The Imperial party disappear into the waiting-room; Ducardi and one of the Gothlandic officers follow them. The interview, however, is a short one; after ten minutes they reappear on the platform; quick words and shakes of the hand are exchanged; the Emperor steps into his compartment again, the Crown Prince into his. The Prince's train waits until his father's passes it, with a last wave of the hand; then it too rides away. . . .

Care lies like a cloud upon Othomar's forehead. He remembers his father's words; in a desperate condition, our fine old city. The Therezia Dyke may be giving way—so little energy in the Municipal Council; thousands of people without a roof to cover them, fleeing, spending the night in churches, in public buildings. And his last word:

" Let them go to St. Ladislas. . . ."

Othomar reflects; all are silent about him, depressed by the after-sound of the Emperor's words, which have painted the disaster anew, brought it afresh before their eyes: the eyes of Ducardi, who knows himself to be more ready with the

sword than with sympathy in cases of inundation;
the eyes of Dutri, still filled with the mundane
glamour of the incomparable capital.   Something
of their self-absorption begins to be silent; a
thought of what they are about to see crosses
their minds.

And Othomar reflects.   What shall he do,
what can he do?   Is it not too much that is
asked of him?   Can he combat the stress of the
waters?

"Oh, that rain, that rain," he mutters, and
silently clenches his fist.

Five hours' more travelling.   The towers of
the city, the crenulated outline and huge plateaus of St. Ladislas, with its bastions, shoot up
on the horizon, shift to one side when approached.
The train stops, in the open country, at a little
halting-place; the princes know that the Central
Station is flooded; the whole railway manage-
ment has been transferred to this halting-place.
And suddenly they stand in the presence of the
smooth, green, watery expanse of the Zanthos,
which has emptied itself; one sea of water, broad
and even, hardly rippled, like a quieted anger.   A
punt is waiting, and carries them through ruins
of houses, through floating household goods.   A
dead horse hooks on to the punt, a musty odour

of damp decay hovers about. At an overturned
house men in a punt are engaged in fishing up
a corpse; it hangs on their boat-hooks with slack
arms and long, wet hair, the pallid, dead head
hanging backwards; it is a woman. Herman
sees Othomar's lips quiver. Now they float
through a street, deserted, tall houses of a poor
suburb. This part has been flooded for days.
They alight in a square; the people are there;
they cheer. Louder and louder they cheer, moved
by the sight of their Prince, who has come to
them across the water to save them. A group of
students shout, call out his name and vivat, and
wave their coloured caps.

Othomar shakes the Mayor, the Minister for
Waterways, the Governor of Altara, and other
dignitaries by the hand. His heart is full; he
feels a sob welling up from his breast.

From among the group of students one steps
forward, a big, tall lad.

" Highness ! " he cries. " May we be your
guard-of-honour ? "

Etiquette hardly exists here, although the
dignitaries look angry. Othomar remembers his
student days, not yet so long ago, presses the
student's hand; Prince Herman too, and the
students are excited, and cry again, " Vivat,

vivat, and vivat Othomar, and vivat Gothland!"

Behind the square the city is considered to be
in distress, a silent distress from yet greater
danger threatening ; the old coronation-town, the
town of learning and tradition, the sombre monument of the Middle Ages ; it looks gray against
the white Lipara, which lies laughing over yonder,
and is beautiful with new marble on her blue sea,
but which does not love her sovereigns so well as
she does, the dethroned capital, with her gigantic
Roman cathedral, where the sacred Imperial
crown with the Cross of St. Ladislas is pressed
on the temples of every Emperor of Liparia.
Though her masters are faithless to her, and
have since centuries lived in their white Imperial
over yonder, and no longer in the old castellated
fortress of the country's Patron Saint, she, the old
city, the mother of the country, remains faithful
to them with her maternal love, and not because
of her oath, but because of her blood, of her heart,
of all her life, which is her old tradition. . . .

But, like his father, Othomar was not this time
to go to the Castle of St. Ladislas ; the fortress
lay too high, and too far from the town, too far
from the disasters. Open carriages stood in
waiting ; they stepped in, the students threw

themselves on horseback; the Princes were to take up their residence in the palace of the Cardinal-Archbishop, the Primate of Liparia, in the Episcopal, which, together with the Cathedral and the Old Palace, formed one colossal, ancient, gray mass, a town in itself, the very heart of the town.

They rode quickly on. The people cheered; they looked upon them as a train of deliverers who, they thought, would at last bring them safety. Between the departure of the Emperor and the arrival of the Prince a depression had reigned, which, at the sight of Othomar, wound itself up into sickly enthusiasm.

It became suddenly dark, but not yet through the sun's setting—it was five o'clock in the month of March in the South—it became dark because of the clouds, the ships in the sky carrying in their tense, bowl-shaped, giant sails water which was already recommencing to trickle down in drops. Under that gray sky the cheering of the people rose up in a minor key, when suddenly, as though the swollen clouds were bursting open with one rent, a flood dashed down in a solitary perpendicular sheet of water.

Othomar sat with Herman and Ducardi in the first carriage.

" Would not Your Highness prefer to have the
carriage closed ? " asked the old General, helping
the Prince on with his cape.

Othomar hesitated ; he had no time to answer
the General ; the crowd increased, became
thicker, cheered ; and he bowed back, saluted,
nodded. The heavy rain dashed straight down.
The hard rainbeams ran down the Princes' and
the General's backs, into their necks, soaked
their knees. The crowd stood sheltered under
an irregular roof of umbrellas, as though grouped
together under wet, black stars, filled the narrow
streets of the old city, pressed in between the
outriders and the carriage : the coachman had to
drive more slowly.

" Won't you have the carriage shut ? " Herman
repeated after Ducardi. Othomar still hesitated.
Then, and he himself thought his words a little
theatrical, and did not know how they would
sound, he answered aloud :

" No, do not let us be afraid of the water ; they
have all suffered from the water here."

But Ducardi looked at him ; he felt something
quiver inside him for his Prince. . . .

The carriage remained open. In one of the
landaus following, Prince Dutri looked round
furiously to see how much longer the Duke of

Xara meant to let himself be soaked with rain, and his suite with him. In the narrow, high streets near the Cathedral they had to drive almost at walking pace, right through the cheering of the crowding populace. Soaked to the skin, the Crown Prince of Liparia with his following arrived at the Cardinal-Archbishop's; they left a trail of water behind them on the staircases and in the corridors of the Episcopal.

V

In fresh uniforms, a short dinner with the high Prelate; a few canons and abbés sit down with them. The room is large and sombre, barely lighted with the feeble glimmer of candles; the silver gleams dull on the dressers of old black oak; the frescoes on the walls—sacred subjects —are barely distinguishable. A silent hurry quickens the jaws, the conversation is carried on in an undertone; the lackeys, in their sombre livery, go about as though on tiptoe. The Cardinal, on either side of whom the Princes are seated, is tall and thin, with a refined, ascetic face, and the steel-blue eyes of an enthusiast; his voice issues from low down in his throat, like

that of an oracle; he says something of the
Lord's will, and makes a submissive gesture with
both hands, the fingers just spread out, as Jesus
does in the old pictures.   One of the abbés, the
Cardinal's secretary, a young man with a round,
pink face and soft, white hands, laughs rather
loudly at a joke of Prince Dutri, who, sitting next
to him, tells a story about a countess in Liparia
whom they both know.   The Cardinal throws a
stern look at the frivolous secretary.

After the hurried dinner, the Princes and their
suite ride into the town on horseback, cheered
wherever they go.   The water already comes
close up to the Cathedral and the Archiepiscopal
Palace.   Groups of men, women, and children,
in sobs, flow together towards the Prince, as he
rides across the dark squares; they carry torches
about him, as the gas is not everywhere lighted;
the ruddy flames look strange, romantic, over the
ancient dark mass of the walls, are reflected with
long streaks of blood in the water that lies in the
narrow lanes.   A large house of many stories and
rows of little windows appears to have suddenly
gone under; a sudden mysterious pressure of
water, filtering up from the foundations through
the masonry of the cellars, making its treacherous
way through the least crack or crevice.   The

inhabitants save themselves in little boats, which row with little red lights through the black, watery town ; a child cries at the top of its voice. They are poor people that live there in hundreds together, heaped up as in boxes. The Princes alight, and get into a boat, go to the spot, and it becomes known who they are ; they themselves help an old woman with three children, wet to their waists, to climb on to a raft ; they themselves give them money, call out orders. And they point to the old fortress of St. Ladislas as a refuge. . . .

But a cry arises, further on, not clearly perceived at first in the darkness of the evening, then at last, distinctly audible ·

" The Therezia Dyke ! the Therezia Dyke ! . . ."

The princes want to go there; it is not possible on horseback ; the only way is in boats. Prince Herman himself grasps the sculls; in the following boat Dutri asserts to Von Fest, one of the Gothlandic equerries, that taken all round, Venice is more comfortable. . . .

" The Therezia Dyke ! the Therezia Dyke ! . . ."

The dyke lies like the black back of a great, long beast just outside the town, on the left bank of the Zanthos, and protects the whole St. Therezia district, the Eastern portion of the town,

which lies tolerably high, from the river, which
generally overflows in springtime. The boats
glide on over the water-streets; it is possible to
land on the Therezia Square; lanterns are burning; torches flare, ruddy scintillations dart over
the water. The square is large and wide; the
houses stand black round about it, and surround it in the night with their irregular lines
of gables and chimneys, with the massive pile of
the Church of St. Therezia, whose steeples are
lost in the dark sky; in the centre of the square
rises a great equestrian statue of a Liparian
Emperor, gigantic in bronze immobility, stretching out its arm over the petty swarming of the
crowd, grasping a sword.

Othomar and Herman have sent their three
equerries, Dutri, Leoni, and Von Fest, for whom
horses have been found and saddled, to the dyke,
which protects a whole suburb of villas, factories,
and the St. Therezia railway-station against the
waters of the Zanthos, which has already poured
forth its right bank over the country, and is
drowning it. The Princes stand in the middle
of the square on the steps of the pedestal of the
statue; they wanted to go on further, but the
Mayor himself has begged them to remain there;
further on there is mortal danger threatening at

every moment. . . . All that could be done
has been done; there is nothing more but to
wait.

Quarters of an hour, half hours, pass by. This
waiting for terrible news calms them; they hope
afresh. The officers ride to and fro; the villas
and factories yonder are deserted: a whole town
lies empty, forsaken. Prince Dutri assures them,
turning his horse, which he has ridden out of
breath, that the embankment will hold firm; after
he has spoken with the Princes, he is surrounded;
it is the occupiers of the villas, the manufacturers,
who overwhelm him with questions, fortified by
the self-assurance of the Imperial equerry. Dutri
gallops off once more.

Now the doors of the church are opened wide,
quite wide; at the end of the perspective, between
the pillars, the little lights glitter on the altar; a
procession files out slowly: a mitred bishop,
priests, acolytes, singing, and carrying banners,
and swinging clouds of smoke from their censers;
behind the upraised crucifix, the relics of St.
Therezia, in their antique shrine of mediæval
gold and crystal and precious stones, round or
roughly cut; it is borne under a canopy, and in
the shimmering gleam of candles it glitters and
shines like a sacred jewel, like a constellation,

across that sombre square, through that black night of disaster; flicker the giant emeralds, sparkles the precious chased gold, and before the Most Holy the crowded populace draws back on either side, and falls down upon its knees. This is the fifth time that day that the procession goes round, that the relics are borne on high, to exorcise the calamity. It passes the statue, the Princes kneel down ; the Latin of the chant, the gleam of the relics in their shrine, the cloud of the incense passes over them with the blessing of the bishop. . . .

The procession has brought stillness to the square, but one now hears a murmur as from afar. . . . The crowd seems to surge as though in one wave, nobody is now kneeling; the very procession is broken up and confused. Through the throng rushes the report : the dyke has given way ! . . .

One cannot yet believe it, but suddenly from above the fort of St. Ladislas, that spreads its ramparts about the castle, a shot thunders out and vibrates over the black city, and shakes through the black sky as though its rebound were breaking against the lowering clouds. A second shot thunders after it, as with giant cymbals of catastrophe, a third . . . the whole town knows that the Zanthos has broken the dyke.

The whole square is in confused motion, like a swarm of ants; bands of tardy fugitives still come thronging in, poor ones now, and indigent, who had not been able to fly earlier, who had been still hoping; through the crush Prince Dutri, panting, cursing, on horseback, terror in his eyes, endeavours to reach the statue; the distant murmur as of a sea comes nearer and nearer. Men scatter along the streets, on foot or in boats; the disordered procession, with the glitter of the shrine of its relics, seeming to reel on the billows of a human sea, spreads itself towards the church.

" Is not even the square safe ? " asks Othomar. He can hardly speak, his chest seems cramped as it were with iron, his eyes fill with tears, an immense despair of impotence and pity suffuses his soul.

The Mayor shakes his head.

" The square lies lower than the suburbs, Highness ; you cannot remain here any longer. For God's sake go back to the Episcopal in a boat ! . . ."

But the Princes insist on remaining, though the murmur becomes louder and louder.

4

"Go into the church in that case, Highnesses; that is the only safe place left," the Mayor beseeches. "I beg you, for God's sake!"

The square is already swept clean, the torch-bearers lead the princes to the steps of the church; the Zanthos comes billowing on, like a soft thunder skimming the ground.

Inside the church the organ sounds; they sing, they pray all through the night. And the whole night outside it remains chaotically black, murmuring gently. . . .

When the first dawn pales over the sky, which begins to assume in the distance tints of rose and gray, pale opal and mother-of-pearl, Othomar and Herman and the equerries step out on to the steps of the church.

The square stands under water; the houses spring up from the water; the statue of Othomar II. waves its bronze arm and sword over a lake that ripples in the morning breeze.

From the Therezia Square to the Cathedral Square everything is under water.

VI

To Her Most Gracious Imperial Majesty,
Elizabeth, Empress of Liparia.

The Episcopal, Altara,
—— *March*, 18—.

My adored Mother,—Your letter reproaches
me with not writing to you the day before yesterday, without delaying; forgive me, for my
thoughts have so constantly been full of you.
But I felt so tired yesterday after an oppressive
day, and lacked the strength to write to you in
the evening. Let me tell you about myself now.

You describe to me the terrible impression
made at Lipara on receipt of the telegram from
here about the breach in the Therezia Dyke, and
how none slept at the Imperial. We too were up
all night, in the Therezia Church. No such
fearful inundation has been remembered for fifty
years; at the time of that which my father
remembers in his childhood, the Therezia Square
was not flooded, and the water only came as far,
they say, as the great iron-factory.

How can I describe to you what I felt that
night, while we were hoping and waiting, hoping

in turn that God and His Holy Mother would ward off this disaster from us, and waiting for the catastrophe to burst forth! We stood on the pedestal of the equestrian statue, unable to do anything further. Oh, that impotence about me, that impotence within me! I kept on asking myself what I was there for, if I could do nothing to help my people. Never before, dearest Mother, have I felt this feeling of impotence, of inability to counteract the inevitable, so possess my soul, until it became entirely filled with despair; but neither have I ever so thoroughly realized that everything in life has its two sides, that the greatest disaster has not only its black shadow but also its side of bright light, for never, oh! never, have I felt so strongly and utterly through my despair, the love for our people; a thing that I did not yet know could exist in our hearts as a truth, as I then felt it quivering through me; and that love gave me an immense melancholy at the thought that they all of them, the millions of souls of our empire, will never know, or if they did know, believe that I love them so, love them as though my own blood ran in their veins. Nor do I wish to deceive myself, and I know well that I should never have this feeling at Lipara, but I have it here, in our ancient city, which gives us all her sympathy. I feel here that I myself, like our Altarians, am more Slav than Latin, like our Southerners in Lipara and Thracyna ; I feel here that I am of their blood, a thing that I do not feel over there.

No doubt much has been said and written in the newspapers about the want of tact of the Marquis of Dazzara, with his foolish guard-of-honour at the station at our departure ; however that may be, I felt great sadness in the train, to think that, in spite of their having come there to see me leave, they did not seem to love me. I know you will once more disapprove of this as a false sensitiveness on my part, but I cannot help it, my dear Mother : I am like that, and I am over-sensitive to sympathy in general, and to the utterances of our people in particular. And for that reason too I love them, very simply and childishly perhaps, but because they show they love me : enthusiasm everywhere, and genuine, unaffected enthusiasm, wherever we go ; and yet what are we able to do for them, except give them money ! I find this sympathy among the lowest of the people ; workmen and labourers, whom, after all, I had never seen before to my knowledge, and to whom I could only just say three or four words of comfort—and I can never find much else to say—it is always the same; and among the soldiers, although they must instinctively feel, in spite of their never seeing me except in uniform, that I am no soldier at heart; among the students, the priests, the civic authorities, and the higher functionaries. Yesterday we went round everywhere, to all the places which have been appointed as refuges; not only the barracks, and shops, and factories, but even some of the rooms of the Palace of Justice, two of the theatres, and the prison, poor souls! And also St. Ladislas. From the Round Tower we had a view of the surrounding country : towards the East there was nothing but water and water, like a sea. My heart felt as though screwed tight into my breast.

We went to the University also. I remembered most of the professors from two years ago, when I was studying there.

It was a terrible scene outside the town. Oh, Mamma, there were hundreds, there were thousands of corpses, laid out side by side on a meadow, as in a morgue, before the burial, for identification. I saw harrowing scenes, my heart was torn asunder : troops of relations who sought, or who, sobbing, had found. A terrible air of woe filled the whole atmosphere. I felt sick, and turned quite pale, it required all my energy to prevent myself from fainting, but Herman put his arm through mine, and supported me as far as possible without ostentation, while a couple of doctors from among the group of physicians to whom I was speaking gave me something to smell. Oh, Mamma, it was a terrible spectacle, all those pallid, shapeless, swollen corpses on the green grass, and above, the sky, which had become deep blue again !

I have informed the Common Council, in accordance with your wish and my father's, that you each of you offer a personal donation of a million florins, and I at the same time presented my own. The whole world seems in sympathy with us ; money flows in from every side, but the damage seems to be a pit, that cannot be filled up. As you say, the donation of our Syrian friends is truly princely and Oriental.

What have I to tell you besides ? I really do not know ; my brain is confused with a nightmare of ghastly visions, and I have difficulty in thinking logically. But I promise you, my dear Mother, to do what I can, and to do it with all my might, and all I ask is that you will send me a single word to tell me that you are not too dissatisfied with your boy. ,

As my father desires, I will stay here another

week; it seems to do the people good to see us, they love us so. They were enraptured when it was announced that after my departure you and Thera were coming to Altara. You with your soft hand will be able to do so much that we have neglected. How they do love us here! And why are we not always at St. Ladislas: though the fortress is sombre, it is bright with their sympathy.

But do not let me write to you so poetically in these days of distress, in which we should be practical. Herman's society does me a deal of good, and I am able to do more when he is by my side. General Ducardi is a fine, indefatigable fellow, as always. The others have all been very willing and practical, and, if I may be allowed respectfully to contradict my father, I am inclined to think that the Municipal Council does what it can. It is true, an English engineer told me that with better precautions and a more thorough supervision the Therezia Dyke would perhaps have held out; however, I don't know.

Herman will accompany me on my journey through the provinces. We shall go to Lycilia and Vaza, and so far as possible to the low-lying districts. These are of course in the worst case.

I have just received the telegrams; the Marquis of Dazzara dismissed, and the Duke of Mena-Doni—I don't like that man—Governor of the Capital! Lipara in a state of siege! And will my father succeed in preserving our House of Nobles by this dissolution of the Representatives?

Dearest mother, His Eminence has just sent to ask me to receive him. I do not want to keep him waiting, and thus close my letter hurriedly ; embracing you with both arms, I subscribe myself, respectfully and fervently,

your son who loves you with all his soul,

your boy,

OTHOMAR.

CHAPTER II

I

THE Government of Vaza, also, lying to the north of the Altara Highlands, the mountain-range of the Gigants, was harassed in parts by the Zanthos. The capital, Vaza, was flooded. In the neighbourhood of the mountain-slopes the province had been spared. There vast terraces of vineyards lay, alternated with forests of chesnut-trees, and walnut-trees, and olives. The glittering white snowline of the mountain-tops surged up against a dazzling blue sky, cut into it with its crests, and bit pieces out of the deep azure with ragged outlines; seemed to whet ice-teeth, gleaming white fangs, against the metal of the firmament like burnished steel. There, twelve miles from the town, stood old Castel Vaza enthroned on its rocks, the castle of the Dukes of Yemena and Counts of

Vaza, surrounded by parks and woods, half castle, half citadel, strong, simple, mediæval, rough in outline, with its four turrets and its square patches of battlements, rounding off the horizon about it on every side, and keeping it aloof. Near at hand, a swarm of villages: in the distance, the towers and steeples, the roof confusion of Vaza; still further, in the circle of panorama that broadly girt the towers, the broad Zanthos, winding down to hurl itself into the sea, and Lycilia, white in the sun with its little squares of houses, set brilliantly on the blue of the water; then a second sea: the mountain-tops which surged away in snowy perspectives and distant mists. And, also glittering in the sun, those strange lakes on the Zanthos: the water that the full river had vomited out, the inundations.

The square castle, enclosing a courtyard in its four wings, has two additional wings built on behind, in a newer style of more elegant renaissance, and looking out on to the park, in which lie the ornamental basins, like oval dishes of liquid silver, set in emerald grass. The fallow deer graze there, dreaming as it were, and graceful, roaming slowly on slim legs: sometimes, suddenly, stretching themselves

out, their heads thrown back, their eyes wild,
they run some distance, a number of them, in
flight from invisible panic; others, calmer, graze
on, laconically, philosophically.

The Dukes of Yemena and Counts of Vaza
are one of the oldest families of the empire,
and their ancestral tree is rooted ages back,
before the time of the first Emperor of Liparia.
The present Duke, Court Marshal and Constable
of Liparia, has three children of his first marriage:
the heir to his title, the young Marquis of Xardi,
aide-de-camp to the Emperor, and two daughters,
young girls still, at a convent.

The Duchess is alone at the castle. She is
sitting in a large boudoir, built out with a
triangular loggia, and looking out on to the
park, the basins, the deer. A breeze is blowing
outside, and the rapid clouds, which, like flaky
spectres, like rays hidden beneath diaphanous
veils, chase one another through the clear blue
sky, trail their shadows, like quick eclipses,
over the park, just tinting it with passing
darkness, which obscures the deer also, and then
lets them gleam brown again in the sun. It
is still outside; it is still in the castle. The
castle lies lonely there; within, the servants
move softly through the reception-rooms and

corridors, speaking in whispers, in expectation of the august visitors.

Lunch is over. The Duchess lies half out-stretched on a couch, and gazes at the deer. She is not yet dressed, and wears a tea-gown, loose, with many folds: old rose broché, salmon-coloured plush, and old lace. When she is alone, she likes plenty of light, from a healthy desire for space and fresh air; the curtains are drawn aside from the tall bow-windows, and the crudeness of the spring sky comes streaming in. But the light does her beauty no good; for although her hair is still raven black, her complexion has the dulness of faded white roses; her eyes, which can be beautiful, large, liquid and dark, look full of lassitude, encircled with pale-yellow shadows, and very clearly visible are the little wrinkles at the side, the little grooves etched around the delicate nose, the lines that have lengthened the mouth and pull it downwards.

The Duchess rises slowly; she passes through a door that leads to her bedroom and dressing-room, and stays away a few moments. Then she returns; with both hands, pressing it to her, with difficulty, she carries a visibly heavy casket, and sets it on the table in front of the

couch. The casket is of old wrought silver with
gilt chasing and great blue turquoises, of that
costly renaissance work which they no longer
make. She selects a little straight, gold key
from her bracelet, and unlocks the casket. The
jewels glisten : pearls, brilliants, sapphires,
emeralds, and catch up on their facets all the
spring light of the sky : blue, white and yellow.
But the Duchess presses a spring unclosing
a secret drawer, and takes from it two packets
of letters and some photographs.

The photographs show the same face of a man
no longer young, a strange face, half dreamy,
half sensual, with much mystery and much
charm. The photographs show him in the
elaborate uniform of an officer of the Throneguards, in fancy-dress as a mediæval knight, in
flannels, and in ordinary mufti. The Duchess's
eyes pass slowly from one to the other, she
compares the likenesses, a sad smile about her
mouth, and melancholy in her eyes. Then she
unties the ribbons of the letters, takes them out
of the carefully preserved envelopes, unfolds them,
and reads here and there, and reads again, and
refolds them. . . .

She knows by heart the phrases that still tell
her of a strange passion, the most fervent, the

truest, the simplest, and perhaps for that reason the strangest that she has ever felt, that has surrounded her with fairy meshes of fire. Though her eyes look out again at the deer—the sunshine streams like fluid gold over the park—between her and the peaceful landscape there rise up, transparent, in tenderly gleaming phantasmagoria, the remembrances of the past, the pictures of that love, and it seems to her as though sparks are dancing before her eyes, as though brilliant arabesques, scintillations of light are swarming everywhere. She lives through the incidents of the past in a few moments; then she draws her hand over her forehead, and thinks how sad it is that the past is nothing more than a little memory, which flies like dust through our souls, which we sometimes endeavour, in vain, to collect in a costly urn. How sad it is that one cannot continue to mourn, though one wish to, because life does not permit it! Nothing but that dust in her soul, and those letters, those photographs. . . .

She locks them away again, and now looks at the jewels. And she looks well into her own heart, sees herself exactly as she is, for she knows that she has been loyal, always, always to him and to herself. Loyal, when

their love broke like a glittering rainbow of
sparkling colours on a wide firmament, and she
refused to continue to see or to exist, and
withdrew from the court into this castle, and
let it be rumoured that a lingering illness was
causing her to pine away, and she mourned,
and mourned, first sobbing and wringing her
hands, then calmer in despair, then . . . The
deer had gone on grazing there, as though they
always remained unchanged. But she. . . .

She had been loyal, always, in her despair;
and also in what followed, in the abatement
of that despair. Then she was most melancholy
of all because despair could abate. Then mournful because she still lived and felt vitality within
her. Then . . . because she began to grow
weary. Because of all this, great despair had
grown into her strange soul, as with the morbid
blossoms of strange orchids. She hated, despised,
cursed herself. But nothing changed in her.
She was weary.

She led a solitary life at the castle. Her
husband and her stepson were at Lipara; her
stepdaughters, to whom she was much attached,
were completing their education at a convent,
of which an Imperial Princess, a sister of the
Emperor, was the abbess.

She was alone, she never saw anybody. And she was wearied. Life awoke anew in her, for it had only slumbered, and she had thought it dead, had desired to bury it in a sepulchre around which her memories should stand as statues. Within herself, she felt herself to be what she had always been, in spite of all her love: a woman of the world, hankering after the glamour of Imperial surroundings, the court-splendour which fatally re-attracts and is indispensable to those who have inhaled it since their birth as their vital air. And at moments when she was not thinking of her despair, she thought of the Imperial, she saw herself there, brilliant in her ripe beauty, fêted and adored as she had always been.

Then she made her stepson, the Marquis of Xardi, spread the rumour that she was convalescent. A month later, in the middle of the winter season, after a great court festival, but before one of the intimate reunions in the Empress's own apartments, she demanded an audience of Elizabeth.

Thus she saw herself, in true, clear truth, and she was deeply mournful in her poor soul filled with desire of love and desire of the world and humanity because life insisted on continuing

5

so cruelly, as in a mad triumphal progress of itself, crushing her memories under its chariot-wheels, clattering through her melancholy with its trumpet-blasts, making her see the pettiness of mankind, the puniness of its feeling, the littleness of its soul, which is nevertheless the only thing it has. . . .

The Duchess locks the twice-precious casket away again. She forgets what is going on about her, what is awaiting her; she gazes, dreams, and lives again in the past, with that enjoyment which one finds in the past when one loses youth.

There is a knock at the door, a lackey appears and bows.

" Excellency, the cook begs urgently to be allowed to speak to you in person. . . ."

" The cook . . . ? "

She raises her beautiful face, dreaming, half laughing, with its profile like Cleopatra's, so Egyptian in its delicacy and symmetry; settles herself a little higher on the couch, and leans on her hand.

" Let him come in. . . ."

Everything returns to her, reality, the day of to-day, and she smiles because of it, and shrugs her shoulders: such is life.

The lackey goes out, the cook enters in his white apron and white cap; he is nervous, and now that his mistress is already compressing her eyebrows because of his disrespectful costume, he begins to stammer.

"Forgive me, Excellency:" and he points with an unhappy face to his apron, his white sleeves. . . .

And he complains that the chief huntsman has not provided sufficient ortolans. He cannot make his pasty; he dares not take it upon himself, Excellency.

She looks at him with her enigmatical eyes; she has a great inclination to burst out laughing at his comical face, his despairing gestures, his outstretched arms, to laugh and to cry also, wildly and loudly.

"What are we to do, Excellency, what are we to do?"

The town is too far away; there is no time to send there before dinner, and, for the matter of that, they never have anything there. Besides, it is really the fault of the steward, Excellency; the steward should have told Her Excellency. . . .

"There are larks," she says.

"Those were to be sent to Lipara to-morrow, Excellency, to his Excellency the Duke!"

The Duchess shrugs her shoulders, laughing a little.

"There is nothing else to be done, my friend. His Imperial Highness the Duke of Xara comes before his Excellency, does he not? Make a chaufroid of larks."

Yes, that is what he had thought of also, but he had not ventured to suggest it. Yes, that will do very well, admirably, Excellency.

She gives another little laugh, and then nods, to say that he can go. The cook, evidently relieved, bows and disappears. She rises, looks at herself standing erect in a mirror, in her lazily creased folds of pink and salmon-colour and old lace, stretches out her arms with a gesture of utter fatigue, and rings for her maid, after which she enters her dressing-room. Does she want to laugh again? or to cry again? She does not know; but she does know that she has to get dressed. . . . Whatever confronted a person, love or ortolan-pasty, the person must dress, dress and eat and sleep, and after that the same again, dress . . . and eat . . . and sleep. . . .

II

Three carriages, with postillions, bring Othomar, Herman, and the others along the broad, winding, undulating road to Castel Vaza. It is five o'clock in the afternoon, and the weather is mild and sunny, but not warm; a fresh breeze is blowing. The landscape is wide and noble; with the windings of the road come changes in the panorama of snow-white mountains. The country is luxuriantly beautiful. The little villages through which they drive look prosperous : they are the property of the Duke. Between Vaza and the castle the land has been spared by the water: the overflowing of the Zanthos has inundated rather the Eastern district. It is difficult here to continue to think uninterruptedly of that dreadful disaster of water and of the condition of Lipara over yonder, which has been proclaimed in state of siege by the Emperor. It is so beautiful here, so full of the life of spring, and the setting of the sun after a fine summer day is here without melancholy. The chesnut-trees waft their fresh green fans, and the sky is still like mother-of-pearl, although a dust of twilight already hovers over it. A lively conversation

is being carried on between the Princes, Ducardi
and Von Fest, who are sitting in the first carriage ; they talk with animation, laugh, and are
amused because the villagers sometimes no doubt
salute them, as visitors to the castle, with a touch
of the cap or a kindly nod, but do not know who
they are.   Prince Herman nods to a fine young
peasant-girl, who stays looking after them with
open mouth, and recalls the delightful hunt of
big game last year when, with the Emperor and
Othomar, he had been the guest of the Duke.
They had not seen the Duchess that time : she
was unwell. . . . General Ducardi tells anecdotes
about the war of fifteen years ago.

And they all find some difficulty in fixing their
faces in official folds when they drive through the
old, escutcheoned gate over the lowered draw-
bridge into the long carriage-drive and are received by the steward in the inner courtyard of
the castle.   This is prescribed by etiquette.   The
Duchess must not show herself before the steward,
surrounded by the whole household of the Duke,
has bidden the Duke of Xara welcome in the
name of his absent master, and offers the Crown
Prince a telegram from Lipara, which the major-
domo hands him on a silver tray.   This telegram
is from the Duke of Yemena ; it says that his

service and that of his son, the Marquis of Xardi,
about the person of his Majesty the Emperor, the
Duke of Xara's most gracious father, prevent
them from being there to receive their beloved
Crown Prince in their castle, but that they beg
His Imperial Highness to look upon this house
as his. The Prince reads the telegram and hands
it to the aide-de-camp, the Count of Thesbia.
Then, conducted by the steward, he ascends the
steps and enters the hall.

Notwithstanding that it is still daylight outside,
the hall is brilliantly lighted, and resembles a
forest full of palm-trees and broad-leaved ornamental plants. The Duchess steps towards the
Crown Prince, and breaks the line of her gracious-
ness in a deep bow. Thus he has already seen
her bow. But perhaps she is still handsomer in
this plain black velvet gown and Venetian lace,
cut very low, her splendid bosom exposed, white
with the vein of Carrara marble, her statuesque
arms bare, a heavy train behind her like a wave
of ink; a small ducal coronet of brilliants and
emeralds in her hair, which is also black, with a
gold-blue raven's glow.

She bids the Princes welcome. Othomar offers
her his arm. Prince Herman, the equerries,
follow them up the colossal staircase, through the

hedge of lackeys, who stand motionless, with fixed eyes that seem not to see. Then through a row of lighted rooms and galleries to a great reception-room, glittering with light from the costly rock-crystal chandelier, in which the candle-light coruscates and casts expansive gleams, and shimmers over the marble mosaic of the floor, and along the ornamental mirrors in their frames of heavy Louis XV. arabesques and the paintings by masters of the Renaissance on the walls.

A momentary standing reception, a little court; in their dazzling uniforms—for it was a delightful drive from Vaza, and the gentlemen had taken time to change into their full-dress uniforms in the town—the equerries and aides come to kiss the Duchess's hand one after the other; except the Gothlandic officers, she knows them all, nearly all intimately; she is able to speak an almost familiar word to each of them, while the gold of her voice melts between her laughing lips, and her great Egyptian eyes look out, strangely dreaming. So she stands for a moment as a most all-amiable hostess between the two princes, she as woman alone amid these officers who surround them, in the midst of a cross-fire of compliments and badinage that sparkles around them.

Then the steward appears, while the doors open
out and the table is revealed brightly glittering,
and he bows before his mistress as a sign that she
is served. The Duchess takes the arm of the
Crown Prince ; the gentlemen follow.

The dinner is very merry. They are an intimate circle ; people accustomed to seeing each
other every day. The Duchess sees that an
easy tone is preserved, one of light familiarity,
that restrains itself before the Crown Prince, yet
gives a suggestion of the somewhat cavalier
roughness and *sans-gêne* that is the fashionable
tone at court. The Gothlandic officers are evidently not in the secret ; Von Fest, a giant of a
fellow, looks right and left and smiles. For the
rest the Duchess possesses in a very strong degree
this smart, informal manner, but moderates herself
now, although she does sometimes lean both her
comely elbows on the table. The Crown Prince
once more has that indescribable rigidity that
makes things freeze around him ; the naturalness
which he displayed at Altara has again made way
for something almost constrained, and at the same
time haughty ; his smiles for the Duchess are
forced, and the handsome hostess, in her private
heart, thinks her illustrious guest an unsufferable
prig.

Possibly Othomar behaves as he does because
of the conversations, which all focus themselves
about the Duchess, and concern the lesser gossip
of the Imperial; the inundations are hardly
referred to, hardly either the state of siege in
the capital; only a single word here and there
reminds one of them. But for the greater part
all this seems to be forgotten here in these delightful surroundings, at this excellent dinner,
under the froth of the soft gold lycilian from the
private Ducal vineyard. This lycilian is celebrated, and they celebrate it now too; even the
Crown Prince touches glasses with the Duchess
with a courteous word or two, which he utters
very ordinarily, but which they seem to think a
most witty compliment, for they all laugh with
flattering approbation, while they look at him
with the intelligence of comprehension, and the
Duchess herself no longer thinks him so unsufferable, but beams upon him with her full
laugh. But what has he said? He is astounded
at himself and at their laughter. He intended
nothing but a commonplace, and . . .

But he remembers: it is always like that, and
he now understands. And he thinks them feeble,
and turns to Ducardi and Von Fest; he forces
the conversation, and begins suddenly to talk

vehemently about the condition of the town of
Vaza, which has also had to suffer greatly. Then
about Altara. He gives the Duchess a long
description of the bursting of the Therezia Dyke.
The Duchess thinks him a queer boy; for an
instant she thinks he is posing; then she decides
that for some reason or other he is a little shy;
then she thinks that he has fine, soft eyes, looking
up like that under his eyelids, and that he has a
pleasant way of describing things. She turns
right round to him, forgets the officers around her,
asks questions, and, with her elbows on the table,
a goblet of lycilian in her hand, she listens attentively, hangs on the young Imperial lips, and
feels an emotion. This emotion comes because
he is so young and august, and has such eyes and
such a voice. She is attracted by his hands, in
that broad, delicate shape, as of an old strength
of race that is wearing out; she notices that he
looks now and then at his ring. And, becoming
serious, she talks of the dreadful times, of all
those thousands of poor people without roof, without anything. . . . This is, however, the second
moment that she has thought of those thousands;
the first was that short half-hour when the Duke's
almoner was asking her for money, and how she
wished it to be bestowed. . . . She remembers

that at the time of that conversation with the
almoner a cutter from Worth's was waiting for
her to try on the very dress that she is now wearing, and she thinks that the accidents of life are
really very interesting. She knows, in her inner
consciousness, that this philosophy is as the froth
of champagne, and she laughs at it herself. Then
she again listens attentively to Othomar, who is
still telling of the night-watching in the Church
of St. Therezia. The officers have become quiet,
and are listening too. His Imperial Highness
has made himself the centre of conversation and
dethroned the Duchess. She has noticed this
too, thinks it strange of him, but nice, above all
does not know what she wants of him, and is
charmed.

III

After dinner a comfortable reunion in two
small drawing-rooms ; in one of them is a
billiard-table, and the Duchess herself, gracefully pointing her cue and holding it between
her jewelled fingers, plays a game with Prince
Herman, Leoni, and young Thesbia. Sometimes,
in aiming, she hangs over the green table with an
incomprehensible suppleness in her heavy lines,

and the Venetian lace over the black velvet bodice flutters to and fro at her rapid movements. In the other room, under a lamp of draped lace, on an accurately detailed military map, Othomar and General Ducardi and the Gothlandic equerries are attentively engaged in studying the route which they are to follow to-morrow on horseback to the inundated villages. The major-domo and a lackey go round with coffee and liqueurs.

When the game of billiards is over, the Duchess comes into the next room with the gentlemen, laughing merrily. The Prince and his officers look up, smiling politely, from their map, but she, bewitchingly:

" Oh, do not let me disturb you, Highness. . . ."

She takes Dutri's arm for a stroll on the terrace outside. The doors are open, the weather is delicious: a little cool. The steward throws a fur mantle about her bare shoulders. On the long terrace outside she walks with Dutri to and fro, to and fro, always passing the open doors, and always throwing a glance to the group under the lamp: bent heads, and fingers pointing with a pencil. Her step is light on the arm of the elegant equerry; her train rustles joyously behind. She talks vivaciously, asks Dutri:

" How are you enjoying your tour ? "

" Awfully bored! Nothing and nobody was amusing, except the Primate's secretary! . . . Those Gothlanders are tedious, and so terribly provincial! And it's tiring too, all this toiling about! You see, I look upon it as war, and so I manage to carry on ; if I were to look upon it as times of peace, I should never manage to pull through. Fortunately our reception has been tolerably decent everywhere. Oh, there is no doubt the Crown Prince is making himself popular. . . ."

" A nice boy. . . ." she interrupts him. " I had not seen him for a long time; he was then studying at Altara, and after that I only remember seeing him once or twice at the Imperial, shot up from a child like an asparagus-stalk, and yet a mere lad. I still remember : he flushed when I courtesied to him. Then lately, at Myxila's. . . ."

Dutri is very familiar with the Duchess ; he calls her by her Christian name, he always flirts a little with her to amuse himself, from mere swagger, without receiving any further favours ; they know one another too well, they have been in one another's confidence too long, and she looks upon him more as a *cavaliere-servente* for trifling services and little court intrigues, than as one for whom it would ever be possible for her to feel any "emotion."

"My dear Alexa, take care . . . ! " says he, and shakes his finger at her.

" Why ? " she asks back, defiantly.

"As if I did not see. . . ."

She laughs aloud.

"See what you please! " she exclaims, indiffe-rently, with her voice of rough *sans-gêne*, which is in fashion. "No, my dear Dutri, you need not warn me. Why, my dear boy, I have two girls to bring out next year. In two years' time I may be a grandmamma. I have given up that sort of thing. I can't understand that there are women so mad as always to want that. And then it makes you grow old so quickly. . . ."

Dutri roars ; he can't restrain himself, he chokes with laughing. . . .

" What are you laughing at ? " she asks.

He looks at her ; he shakes his head, as though to say he knows.

"Really, there is no need for you to play hide-and-seek like that with me, Alexa. I know as well as you do. . . . that you yourself are one of those mad women . . . ! "

He bursts out laughing again, and this time she joins in.

" I ? "

" Get out ! You want that as much as you do food and sleep at their times. You would have been long dead if you had not chronically, at regular intervals, had your ' emotions.' And as to growing old, you know very well you hate the idea of it ! "

" Oh no. I do what I can to remain young, because that is a duty one owes one's self. But I don't fight against it. And you shall see later on how gracefully I shall carry my old age. . . ."

" As you carry everything."

" Thanks. Look here, when I begin to turn gray, I shall put something on my hair that will make me gray entirely, and I will powder it, do you see. That's all ! "

" A good idea. . . ."

" Dutri. . . ."

He looked at her, he understood that she wanted to ask him something. They walked on for an instant silently, in the dark ; in their constantly repeated walk they passed, each time, twice through the light that fell in two wide patches through the doors on to the terrace. The park was full of black shadow, and the great vases on the terrace shone faintly, vaguely white ; above, the sky hung full of stars.

"What did you want to ask me?" asked the equerry.

She waited till they had passed through the light, and were again walking in the darkness.

"Do you ever hear anything of him now?"

"Thesbia had a letter from him lately from Paris. Not much news. He is boring himself, I believe, and running through his money. It's the stupidest thing you can do: to run through your money in Paris. I think Paris a played-out hole. For that matter, it could not be anything else. A republic is a nothing-at-all. So primitive and uncivilized. There were republics before the monarchies: Paradise, with Adam and Eve, was a Republic of beasts and animals; Adam was President. . . ."

"Don't be an idiot. What did he write?"

"Nothing very particular. But what a mad notion of his to send in his papers as Captain of the Guards. How did he come by it? Tell me, what happened between you two?"

They were walking through the light again, she did not answer; then, in the darkness:

"Nothing," she said, and her voice no longer had that affected smartness of brutality and *sans-gêne*, but melted in a plaintive note of melancholy.

6

"Nothing?" said Dutri. "Then why . . . ?"

"I don't know. We had talked a great deal together, and so gradually begun to feel that we could no longer make one another happy. I really cannot remember the reason now, really not."

"A question of psychology therefore. That comes of all that sentiment. You are both very silly. To meddle with psychology when you are in love is very imprudent, because you then start psychologizing on yourselves, and cut up your love into little bits, like a tart of which you are afraid you won't be able to get enough to eat. Practise psychology on somebody else, that's better—as I do on you, Alexa."

"Come, don't talk nonsense, Dutri. Don't you know anything more about him?"

"Nothing more, except that he has made himself impossible for our set. And that perhaps through your fault, and through your psychology."

She walked on silently on his arm; her mouth quivered, her Egyptian eyes grew moist.

"Oh. . . ." she said, and she suddenly made the equerry stand still, grasped his arm tightly, and looked him straight in the face with her moist eyes. "I loved him, I loved him, as I have never loved any one! I. . . . I still love him! If he were to write me a single word, I should forget who I was, my husband, my position, I should go to him, go to him. . . . Oh, Dutri, do you know what it means, in our artificial existence, in which everything is so false around you, to, to. . . . to have really loved any one? And to know that you have that feeling as sheer truth in your heart? Oh, I tell you, I adore him, I still adore him, and one word from him, one single word . . ."

" Fortunate, that he is more sensible than you, Alexa, and will never say that word. Besides, he has no money: what would you do if you were with him? Go on the stage together? What a volcano you are, Alexa, what a volcano!"

He shook his foppish, curly head disapprovingly, adjusted the heavy tassels of his uniform. She took his hand, still serious, not yet relapsed into her tone of persiflage:

" Dutri, when you hear from him, will you promise to tell me about him? I hunger sometimes for news of him. . . ."

She looked at him with such intense, violent longing, with such hunger, that he was startled. He saw in her the woman prepared to do all things for her passion. Then he smiled, flippant as always:

" What silly creatures you all are! Very well,

I promise. But let us go in now, for the geo-
graphical studies seem to have finished, and I am
dying for a cup of tea. . . ."

They went indoors; busying herself at the tea-
table, letting her fingers move gracefully over the
antique Chinese cups, she immediately asked the
Crown Prince which road His Highness proposed
to take, very much concerned about the inundated
villages, the poor peasants . . . agreeing entirely
in everything with the Duke of Xara, bathing in
the sympathy which she gathered from his sweet,
black, melancholy eyes — eyes from which one
would like to kiss all the melancholy away!—
bathing in his youthful splendour of Empire. . . .

Dutri helped her to sugar the tea. He watched
her with interest: he knew her fairly well, she
retained very little enigma for him; yet she
always amused him, and she was never studied
out, he thought.

IV

It was one of the historic apartments of
Castel Vaza; an ancient, sombre room in which
the Emperors of Liparia who had been the
guests of the Dukes of Yemena had always
slept on an old gilt state-bed, five steps high,

above which the heavy curtains of dark-blue brocade and velvet hung down from an Imperial Crown borne by cherubs. There hung all the portraits of the emperors and empresses who had rested there; the Dukes of Yemena had always been very much beloved by their sovereigns, and the pride of the Ducal family was that every Liparian Emperor had been at least one night their guest. Historical souvenirs were attached to every piece of furniture, to every ornament, to the gilt basin and the gilt ewer, to everything, and the legends of his house rose one by one in Othomar's mind as he stretched himself out to rest.

He was very weary, and yet not sleepy. He felt a leaden stiffness in his joints, as though he had caught cold, and a continuous shivering went through his whole body, a mysterious quivering of the nerves, as if he were a strung string that is touched. The week spent at Altara, the subsequent five days at Vaza, the drives in the neighbourhood had tired him out. During the daytime he could not find a moment's time to give way to this fatigue, but at night, stretched out for rest, it broke him up, without being followed by a healthy sleep.

He was accustomed to his little camp-bed, on

which he slept in his severe bedroom in the
Imperial, the bed on which he had slept since
childhood. The state-beds, in the Episcopal, at
Vaza and here, made him feel strange, laid-out,
and uncomfortable. His eyes now too remained
open, and followed the folds of the tall curtains,
sought to penetrate the shadows which the faint
light of a silver lamp caused to creep back into
the corners. He began to hear a heavy humming
in his ears.

And he thought it singular to lie there on that
bed on which his ancestors had lain also. They
all peered at him from the eight panels in the
walls. What was he? An atom of life, a little
stuff of sovereignty, born of them all; one of the
last links of their long chain, which wound back
through the ages, and led to that mysterious,
mystical origin, half sacred, half legendary, to St.
Ladislas himself. . . . Would the same thing
come after him too? a second chain which would
wind forward into the future? Or . . . and
to what purpose was the ever returning, endless,
eternal renascence of life? What would be the
end, the great End. . . ?

Suddenly, like a vision, the night on the
Therezia Square returned to him, the thundering
salute from the fort, thrice repeated, and the

mighty roaring onslaught of an approaching blackness, that resembled a sea. Was it only humming in his ears, or. . . . or was it really roaring on? Did, in his reply to his question for the end, the great End, the black future come roaring on with the same sound of threatening waters, that would not be withheld by anything? It burst through dykes; it dragged with it all that was thrown up as a protection, inexorable, and—with its black frown of serious fatefulness and the sombre folds of its inundations, which resembled a shroud trailing over all that was doomed to end—it marched on to where they stood, his kin, on their high station of majesty by the grace of God and of St. Ladislas; his father, on their ages-old throne, crowned and sceptred, and bearing the orb of empire in his Imperial palm; and it did not seem to know that they were divine, and sacred, and inviolate; it seemed to care for nothing in its rough, sombre, indifferent, unbelieving, on-roaring profanation; for suddenly, fiercely, it dragged its black waves over them, dragged them with it, his father, his mother, all of them, and they were things that had been, they who were Imperial, they became a legend in the lustre of the new day that rose over the black sea. . . .

His ancestors stared at him, and they seemed
to him to be spectres, legends also, untruths
from which tradition would no longer be a protection. They seemed to him like ghosts, enemies
. . . . He opened wider his burning eyes upon
their stiff, trained and robed, or harnessed figures,
which seemed to step out towards him from the
eight panels of the walls, in order to stifle him
in their midst, to press him down in a narrow
circle of nightmare on his panting breast, with
iron knees squeezing the breath out of his lungs,
with iron hands crushing his head, from which
the sweat gushed down over his temples.

Then he felt afraid, like a little child that has
been told creepy stories. Afraid of those ghosts
of emperors, afraid of the glimpses of visions,
which again flashed pictures of the inundations
before him—the meadow with the corpses, the
men in the punt who fished up the woman. The
corpses began suddenly to come to life, to burst
out laughing, with slits of mouths and hollow
eyes, as though they had been making a fool of
him, as though there had been no inundations,
and the dusk of the bedchamber, which was filled
with the emperors, pressed down upon him as
with atmospheres of nitrogen.

" Andro ! Andro !" he cried, with smothered
utterance, and then, as though in deadly fear :

" Andro ! Andro. . . ! "

The door at the end of the room was thrown open ; the valet entered, alarmed, in his night-clothes. The reality of his presence broke through the enchantment of the night, and exorcised the ghosts back into portraits.

" Highness. . . ! "

" Andro, come here. . . ."

" Highness, what is the matter. . . ? How you frightened me, Highness ! What is it. . . ? I thought . . . ."

" What, Andro ? "

" Nothing, Highness, your voice sounded so terribly hoarse ! What is the matter. . . ? "

" I don't know, Andro ; I am ill, I think ; I can't sleep. . . ."

The man wiped Othomar's clammy forehead with a handkerchief.

" Will you drink anything, Highness ? Some water. . . ? "

" No, thank you, thank you. . . . Andro, can you come and sleep in here ? "

" If you wish it, Highness. . . ."

" Yes, here, at the foot of my bed. I believe I am rather unwell, Andro. . . . Bring your pillow in here."

The man looked at him. He was not much

older than his Prince. He had waited on him
from childhood, and worshipped him with the
worship of a subject for majesty; he felt wholly
bound to him, tied to him; he knew that the
Prince was not strong, but also that he never
complained. . . .

Growing suddenly angry, he turned to go to
his room and fetch his pillow.

"No wonder, when they tire you out like
that!" he cried, with a rage which he could no
longer restrain. "General Ducardi thinks, no
doubt, that you have just such another tough
hide as himself!"

Muttering in his mustachios, he returned with
his pillow, and laid it down on the step of the
state-bed.

"Are you feverish?" he asked.

"No . . . yes, possibly, a little. It will pass
off, Andro. I—I am. . . ."

He did not dare to say it.

"I am a little nervous," he continued, and his
eyes went anxiously round the room, where the
emperors were once more standing quiet.

"Would you like a doctor fetched from
Vaza?"

"No, no, Andro, by no means; what are you
thinking of, to make such a disturbance in the

middle of the night ? Go to sleep now, down
there. . . ."

" Will you try to sleep also then, my ' princeling ' ? " he asked, with the endearing diminutive
which in his language sounded like a caress.

Othomar nodded to him with a smile, and
suffered him to shake up the pillows with the
air of a nurse.

" What a bed," muttered Andro. " It might
be a monument in a cemetery. . . ."

Then he lay down again, but did not sleep ;
he stayed awake. And when Othomar asked,
after an interval :

" Are you asleep, Andro ? " he answered :

" Yes, Your Highness, nearly."

" Is there anything murmuring in the distance,
is it water, or. . . . or is it my fancy ? "

The man listened.

" I can hear nothing, Highness. . . . You are
probably a little feverish."

" Take a chair and come and sit here, by the
head of the bed. . . ."

The man did as he was told.

" And let me feel you near me, give me your
hand, so. . . ."

At last Othomar closed his eyes. In his ears
the murmuring continued, always continued. . . .

But under the very murmuring, while the lightness lifted like mist from his head, the Crown
Prince of Liparia fell asleep, his clammy hand
in the hard hands of his body-servant, who
watched his master's restless sleep in the quiver-
ings round the mouth, the shocks of the body,
until, in order to quiet him, he softly stroked his
throbbing forehead with his other hand, muttering
compassionately, with his strange, national voice
of caress, "My poor princeling. . . ."

Dawn rose outside; the light seemed to push
the window-curtains asunder.

V

The next day the Duchess was to preside at the
breakfast-table; she was already in the dining-
room with all the gentlemen when Othomar
entered, the last, with Dutri. His uniform, blue,
white and silver, fitted him tightly, and he saluted,
smilingly, but a little stiffly, while Herman shook
hands with him, and the others bowed, the
Duchess courtesying deeply.

"How pale the Prince looks!" said Leoni to
Ducardi.

It was true; the Prince looked very pale; his

eyes were dull, but he bore himself manfully, ate a little fish, trifled with a salmis of game. Yet the fatigue of the Prince was so evident, that Ducardi asked him softly, across the table :

" Is Your Highness not feeling well . . . . ? "

All eyes were raised to Othomar, and he determined to give the lie to their sympathy.

" There is nothing the matter with me," he replied.

" Has Your Highness not slept well ? " continued Ducardi.

" Not very well. . . ." Othomar was compelled to acknowledge, with a smile.

The conversation continued, the Duchess gave it a new turn ; but after breakfast, on the point of departure—the horses stood saddled in the court-yard—Ducardi said, bluntly :

" We should do better not to go, Highness."

Othomar was astonished, refused to understand.

" You look a little fatigued, Highness," resumed Ducardi, shortly, and more softly, excusing himself: " Nor is it anything to be surprised at, that the last few days have been too much for you. If Your Highness will permit me, I would recommend you to take some rest to-day."

A soft feeling of relaxation was already coming

over the Prince ; he felt himself too delighted at this idea of rest to continue his resistance, but yet his conscience pricked him at the thought of his father: a feeling of shame in case the latter should hear of his exhaustion, which seemed so clearly evident.

And he would absolutely not permit the whole expedition to be abandoned. He yielded in so far to Ducardi as not to go himself and to take repose, provided they thought he needed it ; but he urgently begged Prince Herman and the others to follow the route planned out for that day, and to go. And this he said with youthful haughtiness, feeling relieved already at the idea of the day of repose that was to come, a whole day, unexpectedly ! but before all afraid of allowing this delight to be perceived, and therefore sulking a little, as though he wished to go too, as though he thought General Ducardi foolish with his advice. . . .

The gentlemen went. The Duchess herself conducted Othomar to the West wing, pressed him to rest in her own boudoir. Through the windows of the gallery Othomar saw Herman and the others riding away ; he followed them for an instant with his eyes, then went on with the Duchess, and across the courtyard saw a groom lead back the horse that had been saddled for him to the stables, patting its neck. He was still disturbed by mingled emotions: joy in resting, a little anxiety lest he should betray himself, shame. . . .

In the boudoir the Duchess left him alone. It was quiet there: outside, the fallow deer grazed, peaceful, distinguished. The repose of the boudoir of a woman of the world, with the rich, silent drapery of silk stuffs, the inviting luxury of soft furniture, the calm brilliancy of the ornaments, each an object of art and costly, surrounded him with a hushed breathlessness, like a blush of tulle, fragrant with an indefinable, gentle emanation, the very perfume of that woman. The indolence of this present moment suddenly overcame Othomar, a little strangely, and dissolved his thoughts in gentle bewilderment. He felt like a galloping horse, that has suddenly been pulled up and stands still.

He sat down a moment, and looked out at the deer. Then he rose, reflected whether he should ring, and thought better to look round himself. On the Duchess's little writing-table—Japanese lacquer inlaid with mother-of-pearl landscapes and ivory storks—he found a piece of paper, a pencil.

And he wrote :

" To Her Most Gracious Majesty Elizabeth,
    " Empress of Liparia.
            " Castel Vaza,
                " —— *April,* 18—.
" Pray do not be alarmed if the newspapers
exaggerate and say that I am ill.   I was a little
fatigued, and General Ducardi advised me to rest
to-day.   Herman and the others have gone on ;
to-morrow I hope myself to lead our second expedition from here.   The day after to-morrow we go
to Lycilia.
                        " Othomar."

Then he rang, and when the lackey appeared.
" My valet, Andro."
The latter appeared after a few moments.
" Andro," said Othomar, " ask for a horse, ride
to Vaza, and dispatch this telegram as quickly as
possible to Her Majesty the Empress. . . ."
Andro went out, and the strange, indolent
vacancy overcame Othomar once more.   The
sun shone over the park, the deer gleamed with
coats like cigar-coloured satin.   The past fortnight came once more before Othomar's eyes.
And it was as though, in the perspective of that

very short past, he saw spreading out like one great whole, one picture of human calamity, the misery that he had seen and had endeavoured to soften. And the great affliction that filled the land made his heart beat, full of pity. A weak feeling of melancholy, that there was so much affliction, and that he was so impotent, rose up in him again, as it never failed to do when he was alone and able to reflect. Then he felt himself small, insignificant, fit for nothing, and something in his soul fell feebly, enervatedly from a factitious height, without energy and without will. Then that something lay there in despair, and upon it, heavy with all its affliction, the whole Empire, crushing it with its weight of quintals.

Serious strikes had broken out in the Eastern quicksilver mines, beyond the Gigants. He remembered once having made a journey there, and having suffered when he saw the strange, ashy-pale faces of the workmen, who stared at him with great, hollow eyes, and were destroyed through their own livelihood, in an atmosphere full of poison. And he knew besides that what he had seen then was a holiday sight, the most pros-perous sight that they could show him; that he would never see the black depth of their wretched-ness, because he was the Crown Prince. And he

7

could do nothing for them, and if they raised their heads still more fiercely than they were doing already, the troops, which had already started for the district, would shoot them down like dogs.

He panted loudly, as though to pant away the quintals on his chest, but they fell back again. His father's image came before his mind, high, certain, conscious of himself, without hesitation, always knowing what to do, confident that majesty was infallible, writing signatures with big, firm letters, curtly: "Oscar" . . . Everything that was signed like that: "Oscar," was immaculate in its righteousness as fate itself. How different was he, the son; and did then the old race of might and authority begin to pine with him, as with a sudden crack of the spine, an exhaustion of marrow?

Then he saw his mother, a Roumanian Princess, loving her near ones so dearly; womanliness, motherliness personified, in their small circle; to the people, haughty, inaccessible, tactless as he was, unpopular, as he was also, at least in Lipara and the Southern portion of the empire. He knew it; beneath that rigid inaccessibility she concealed her terror—terror when sitting in an open carriage, at the theatre, at ceremonial functions, and in church, even at visits to charitable

institutions; that terror had killed in her her
great love for humanity, and had morbidly con-
centrated her soul, which naturally looked wide
about her, upon love for that small circle. And
beneath this terror hid her acquiescence, her
expectation of the catastrophe, the outburst, in
which she, with hers, was to perish. . . !

He was their son, the heir to their throne:
whence did he derive his impotent hesitation,
which his father did not possess, and his love for
their people, which his mother no longer possessed? His ancestors he only knew of from
history; in the earlier Middle Ages, barbarian,
cruel; later on, refinedly sensual; one prince, a
weakling, ruled entirely by favourites, a *roi-
fainéant*, under whom the Empire had fallen a
prey to intestine division and foreign covetous-
ness; afterwards, more civilized, a resurrection of
strength, a reaction of rise after a fall, and the
fame and greatness of the Empire to the present
day . . . To the present day; to him came this
inheritance of greatness and fame; how would he
meet it, how should he in his turn hand it down
to his son?

Then he felt himself so small, so timid, that he
could have run away somewhere, away from the
gaping eyes of his future obligations. . . .

VI

The luncheon had all the intimacy of a most charming *tête-à-tête*, served in the small dining-room, only the steward behind the table. The Duchess inquired very sympathetically how Othomar was; the Prince already felt quite rested, had a good appetite, was vivacious, praised the cook and the famous lycilian. When the Duchess after luncheon proposed to him to make a small excursion in the neighbourhood, he thought it an excellent idea. He himself wished to ride—he knew that the Duchess was an excellent horse-woman—but Alexa dissuaded him, laughingly, said that she was afraid of General Ducardi, who had recommended the Prince to rest, and thought that a little drive in an open carriage would be less tiring. She had recollected betimes that a riding-habit made her look old and heavy, and she was very glad when the Prince gave way.

The weather had remained delightful; a soft sun in a blue sky. The landscape stretched out wide, the mountains stood up shrill and steep, pointing their ice-crests into the ether. The drive had all the charm of an incognito, free from etiquette; the Prince in his undress uniform

seated next to the Duchess, in a simple, dark gown
of mauve corduroy velvet, in the elegant, light
victoria, on which the coachman sat alone, without footman, setting the two slender bays briskly
about. The sun gleamed in patches over the
horses' sleek sides, cast reflections in the varnish
of the carriage, and in the facets of the cut
lanterns, on the coachman's hat, and on the
buttons of Othomar's uniform. All this sparkle
scintillated with short, bright flashes, and thus,
flickering lightly, the carriage rolled along the
road, through a couple of villages, whose inhabitants saluted their châtelaine, but did not know
who the simple young officer was that sat next to
her. A breeze had dried up the moistness of the
preceding days, and light clouds of dust blew up
from under the quick, revolving wheels.

The Duchess talked much of Lipara, the
Emperor, the Empress. She had the tact of
knowing intuitively what to say and what to talk
of, when she liked. Her voice was a charm. She
was sometimes capable of great simplicity and
naturalness, oftenest when she was not thinking
of appearances. Intuitively she assumed towards
the Prince, in order to make herself sympathetic
to him, that simplicity which came natural
to her. It made her seem years younger; the

smart brusqueness that was in fashion flattered
her much less, and made her seem older, and even
coarse.   When she was as at present, she refined
herself in the natural distinction of an ancient
race.   The little black veil on her hat hid the
ugly little wrinkles, and her eyes shone through
it like stars.

The Prince remembered stories told by his
equerries — Dutri not excepted — about the
Duchess ; he remembered names that had been
whispered.   He did not at this minute believe
in these slanders, as he considered them. Sensible
as he was to sympathy, he was won over by hers,
which he intuitively read in her, and it made him
think well and kindly of her, as he thought of all
who liked him.

The carriage had been going between terraces
of vineyards, when suddenly, as though by surprise, it drove past a castle, half-visible through
some very ancient chesnut-trees.

" What estate is that ? " asked the Prince.
" Who are your neighbours, madame ? "

" No one less than Zanti, Highness," replied
the Duchess; she shivered, but endeavoured to
jest.   " Balthazar Zanti lives here with his
daughter."

" Zanti ! Balthazar Zanti ! " cried Othomar,

astonished. He rose up and looked curiously at the castle, which lay hidden behind the chesnut-trees. "But how is it, madame, that last year, when I was hunting here with the Emperor, with the Duke, that I never heard of Prince Zanti, or that he lived here?"

The Duchess laughed.

"Presumably, Highness, because the Duke's covers lie in the other direction," she made a vague movement with her hand, "and you never drove past this way, and because His Majesty will never suffer the name of Balthazar Zanti to be spoken in his presence."

"But none of the equerries. . . ."

The Duchess laughed still more merrily, looked at the Prince, who was also laughing gaily, and said:

"It is certainly unpardonable of them not to have informed you more fully of the curiosities of the Government of Vaza. But . . . now that I think of it, it is quite natural, Highness. The castle was standing empty last year; Zanti was travelling about the country and making speeches. You remember, they were afterwards judicially forbidden. His name had, therefore, at that time no local significance yet. . . ."

The Prince continued to look at the castle,

which never came wholly into view, when the
carriage, in a turn of the road, almost touched a
little group as it drove past them against the
slope of a vineyard: an old man, a young
girl, a dog; the young girl, frail, slender, pale,
fair-haired, dressed in furs in spite of the sun, and
retaining beneath them a certain morbid elegance;
she sat on the grass, wearing a dark fur toque on
her silvery fair hair; her long, white hand, un-
gloved, patted soothingly and insistingly on the
curly head of a retriever, who barked at the carriage; and next to her stood, erect, a tall old man,
looking queer in a wide, gray smock-frock; a gray
giant, with a heavy beard and sombre eyes, which
shone with a dull light from under the brim of a
soft felt hat. The dog barked; the girl bowed—
she recognised the Duchess as a neighbour—
without knowing the Prince; the old man, however, looked straight before him, frowning, and
made no sign. The carriage rattled past.

" That was Zanti. . . ." whispered the
Duchess.

"Zanti. . . !" repeated the Prince. " And
since when has he been living here?"

"Since a very short time; I believe the doctors
think the air of Vaza healthy for his daughter."

" Was that young girl his daughter?"

"Yes, Highness, I have seen her once before; she appears to be delicate."

"Prince Zanti, is he not?"

"Certainly, Highness, but by his own wish, Zanti quite plain. . . . Titles are all nonsense in the nineteenth century, Highness."

She jested, and yet she felt a silent shudder, she knew not why. She thought it ominous that Zanti had come to live so near to Castel Vaza. Shivering, she gave a quick side-glance at the Prince. She perceived a strange pensiveness drawing over his face like a shadow. Then, in order to change the conversation, and to think no longer of that horrid man:

"You are looking much better, Highness, than you did this morning. The air has done you good. . . ."

She suppressed her tremor. The Prince, on the other hand, remained strange: a sudden emotion seemed to be stirring within him. When they were back at the castle, in the boudoir, the Duchess proposed herself to make the Prince a cup of tea. He stood looking out of the window at the deer, but, while busying herself with the crested, gilt array of her tea-table, she saw him turn pale, white as chalk—as he was that morning—his eyes dilating strangely. . . .

" What is the matter, Highness. . . ? " she cried, alarmed, and approached him.

He turned towards her, endeavoured to laugh.

" I beg pardon, madame, I am very discourteous . . . . to behave like this, but . . . . but that man took me by surprise. . . ." He laughed. . . . " I did not know he was here, and then the air. . . . that clear air. . . ."

He put his hand to his forehead ; she saw him grow paler, his blood seemed to be running out of him, and he staggered. . . .

" Highness ! " she cried.

But Othomar, feeling vaguely for a support with his hand, fell up against her ; she caught him in her arm, against her bosom, mortally frightened, and she saw that he had swooned. A thin sweat stood on his forehead ; his eyes closed beneath their weary lids, as though they were dying ; his mouth was open without breathing.

The Duchess was violently alarmed ; she was terribly frightened lest anything serious should happen to the Duke of Xara, alone with her in the castle ; she felt suddenly that the future of Lipara was entrusted to the support of her arms ; she already beheld the Prince lying dead, herself disgraced at the Imperial. . . . All this flashed across her brain at the first moment. But she looked at him long, and a soft expression came over her face. Pride that the Duke of Xara lay there half-fainting on her shoulder, and sudden passion in which much motherliness and pity resolved into a strange feeling in her soul. She softly smoothed back his hair, wiped his perspiring forehead with her pocket-handkerchief. . . . And the strange sensation became still stranger within her, intenser in its two constituent parts : intenser in pride, intenser in compassionate love—that of a mistress and a mother in one. Then, with a smile, she pressed the handkerchief, lightly moistened with the Imperial sweat, to her trembling lips. The soft aroma of the moisture seemed to make her giddy with a fragrance of virile youth. . . . She thought of the letters and photographs in the silver casket with the turquoises. A deep melancholy, because of life, smarted through her soul; yet more of her memories seemed to fly away like dust. Then, refusing to give way any longer to this melancholy, she bent her head, and serious now, giving herself to the present, which revived her with new happiness, she pressed her lips, still trembling, on Othomar's mouth. For a moment she lingered there, her eyes closed ; then she gave her kiss.

They opened their eyes together, looked at one another. Earnestly sombre, tragically almost, she flashed her glance into his. He said nothing, remained gazing at her, still half in her arms. The colour came mantling back to his cheeks. Their eyes imbibed one another. He felt the unknown opening up before him, he felt himself being initiated into the world of knowledge, which he suspected in her and did not know of himself. But he felt no joy because of it: her eyes remained sombre. Then he merely took her hand, just pressed it in a solitary caress, and said, his eyes still gazing into her intense, quiet, deep glances of passion, his features still rigid with surprise:

"I was a little giddy, I fear, just now. . . ? I beg you to forgive me, madame. . . ."

She too continued to look at him, at first sombrely, then smilingly humble. Her pride soared to its climax with one beat of the pinion: the mouth of her future Emperor was still sealed with her kiss! Her love touched her intimate life as a wafting breeze skims over a lake, rippling it into entire silveriness with a single fresh gust, and stirring it to its very depths; she worshipped him because of his youthful highness, which so graciously accepted her kiss without further acknowledging it, because of his Imperial candour, his boyish voice, his boyish eyes, the pressure of his hand: the only thing he had given her; and she experienced all this as a very strange, proud pleasure: the delight of assimilating that candid youth, as a potion that should restore her her youth.

VII

They dined late that evening, as they had waited for Herman and the others. The conversation at table turned on the condition of the lowlands, on the peasants, who had lost everything. The Duchess was silent; the conversation had no interest for her, but her silence was smiling and tranquil.

That evening Othomar again studied the map with Ducardi, under the lace lamp. The evening had turned cold, the doors of the terrace were closed. The Duchess did not feel inclined for billiards, but sat talking softly with Dutri in the second drawing-room. She looked superb, serene as a statue, in her dress of antique lace stained pale-yellow, her white bosom rising evenly with her regular breathing; in front, a single star of brilliants in her hair.

Othomar pointed with the pencil on the map.

"Then we can go like this, along this road. . . . Look, General Ducardi, look here, Colonel Von Fest, this is where I drove this afternoon with the Duchess, and here, I believe, is where Zanti lives. Did you know that?"

The gentlemen looked up, looked down at the spot to which the Crown Prince pointed, expressed astonishment.

"I thought that he lived in the South, in Thracyna," said the young Count of Thesbia.

Othomar related what the Duchess had told him.

"Zanti!" cried Herman. "Balthazar Zanti? Why, but then it is he! . . . I was walking this afternoon with a party of peasants; they were telling me of the refuges which a new landlord was fitting up in the neighbourhood, but they spoke in dialect, and I could not understand them well; I thought they said Xanti, and so I never thought that it could be Balthazar Zanti. So he's the man!"

"Refuges?" asked Othomar.

"Yes, a village of refuges, it seems; they said he was so rich and so generous, and harboured I don't know how many farmers, who had lost all they had."

"I seem now to remember having read in the papers that Zanti had gone to live in Vaza," said Leoni.

"I should like to see those refuges, we can go there to-morrow," said Othomar. General Ducardi compressed his bushy eyebrows.

"You know, Highness, that His Majesty is anything but enamoured of Zanti, and is even thinking of exiling him. It would perhaps be more in His Majesty's spirit at present to ignore anything that Zanti is doing here."

Othomar, however, did not feel disposed to give way to the General; a youthful love of contradiction bubbled up in him.

"But, General, to ignore anybody's good work in these times is neither gracious nor politic."

"I am convinced that if His Majesty knew that Zanti was staying at his castle here, he would have specially requested Your Highness not to hold any communication with that man," said Ducardi, with emphasis.

"I am not so sure of that, General," said Othomar drily, "and I believe, on the contrary, that if His Majesty knew that Zanti did so much for the victims of the inundations, His Majesty would look over a good deal of his amateur communism."

Ducardi gnawed his moustache with a wry smile.

"Your Highness speaks rather light-heartedly of that amateur communism. Zanti's theories and practice are more than mere dilettantism. . . ."

"But, General," rejoined Othomar gently, "I really do not understand why Zanti's socialism need prevent us at this moment—I repeat, at this moment—from appreciating what he is doing, nor why it need interfere with our visiting his refuges, when we have come to Vaza in order to inform ourselves of everything that concerns the inundations. . . ."

Ducardi looked at him angrily. He was not accustomed to being contradicted like that by His Highness. The others listened. The Duchess herself, attracted by the discussion, in which she heard Othomar's voice dominating with young authority, had approached with Dutri, curiously.

"To say the least of it, it could do no harm just to have a look at those refuges, I must grant my cousin that, General," said Herman of Gothland, who began to like Othomar.

Von Fest also supported this view, convincingly, roundly, honestly, considered that they could do no less, having regard to the victims whom Zanti had housed. Every one now gave his opinion: Leoni thought it impossible that the Crown Prince should visit Vaza and not those refuges; it would look as though I is Highness were afraid of a bugbear like Zanti. The fact that Othomar was contradicting Ducardi gave them all grounds for opposing the old General, who had hitherto conducted the expedition with a sort of military despotism that had frequently annoyed them. Even Dutri, generally pretty indifferent, joined himself to them, cynically, his eyes gleaming, because Ducardi was being put in his place for once. He winked at the Duchess.

And only Siridsen and Thesbia took Ducardi's side, hesitating, because the General declared with such conviction that the Emperor's will would be different from his son's wish; especially Thesbia.

"I can't understand why the Prince insists so," he whispered in alarm to the Duchess. "Ducardi is right: you yourself know how the Emperor detests Zanti. . . ."

The Duchess shrugged her handsome shoulders with a smile, listening to Othomar, whom she heard defending himself, supported by exclamations and nods of the head from the others.

8

"Well," she heard Ducardi answer drily, "if Your Highness absolutely insists that we should go there, we will go; I only hope that Your Highness will always remember that I did not agree with you in this matter. . . ."

The Duke of Xara now answered laughingly, was the first to make peace after this victory, and during the rest of the route that was worked out on the map all the way to Lycilia, he agreed with the General in everything, with little flattering intonations of approval and appreciation of his penetrating and practical way of looking at things. . . .

"He may not have the makings of a great commander," whispered Dutri to the Duchess, "but he will turn out a first-rate little diplomat. . . ."

But Ducardi was inwardly very angry. For a moment he thought of ascertaining the Emperor's wishes by a secret telegram, but he rejected this idea, as it would make a bad impression at the Imperial if the Duke of Xara were not left free in such an apparent trifle. He therefore only attempted the next morning once more to dissuade Othomar from this visit, but the Prince held firm.

"You seem very much opposed to this expedition, General," said Von Fest. "Isn't it really quite reasonable?"

"You don't know the prejudice His Majesty has against that man, Colonel," replied the General. "As I have told you before, His Majesty is thinking of exiling him, and is sure to do so when he hears that he has now turned up at his castle, doubtless with the object of stirring up the peasantry, as he has already stirred up the working-men in the towns. That man is a dangerous fanatic, Colonel—dangerous especially because he has money with which to carry his visions into practice. He instigates the lower orders not to fulfil their military duties because it is written: 'Thou shalt not kill.' He looks upon marriage as a useless sacrament, and I have heard that his followers simply come to him and that he marries them himself, with a sort of blessing, which also in its turn is based upon a text—I forget which. He is always writing socialistic pamphlets, which are promptly seized, and he makes seditious speeches. And the man is even proposed as a candidate for the House of Representatives!"

"One who abjures his title a member of the House of Representatives!" smiled Von Fest.

"Oh, those inconsistencies swarm in his

doctrine," growled Ducardi. "He will tell you of course that so long as there is nothing better than the House of Representatives he wishes to be a member of the House of Representatives. And the Crown Prince wants to take notice of what a man like that does!"

Von Fest shrugged his shoulders.

"Let him be, General. The Prince is young. He wants to know and see things. That is a point in his favour."

"But . . . the Emperor will never approve of it, Colonel!" thundered the General, with a curse.

Again Von Fest shrugged his shoulders.

"Nevertheless I should not dissuade him any longer, General. If the Prince wants a thing, let him have it, it will do him good. . . . And if afterwards he gets blown up by his father, that will also do him good, by way of reaction."

Ducardi looked him straight in the face.

"What do you think of our Prince?" he asked, directly.

Von Fest looked back at the General, smilingly, full into his searching eyes. He was honest by nature, and upright, but sufficiently a courtier to be able to dissimulate when he considered it necessary.

"A most charming boy," he replied. "But

life—or rather he himself—will have to change him very much if he is to hold his own . . . later on."

The officers understood one another. Ducardi heaved a deep sigh.

" Yes, there are difficult times coming," he said, with an oath.

" Yes," answered the Gothlandic Colonel, simply.

The Princes mounted in the courtyard ; they rode along the same road over which Othomar had driven the preceding afternoon with the Duchess, and past Zanti's castle. Leoni had discovered where the refuges lay ; the mountains began to retreat, the road wound curve after curve beneath the trampling hoofs of the horses. Suddenly the Zanthos spread itsef out on the horizon : the broad expanse of overflown water, one great lake under the broad, gleaming, vernal sky.

" That is where we are bound for," said Leoni.

His finger pointed to a hamlet of long wooden buildings, evidently newly built, smelling of new wood in the morning breeze that met them. When they rode nearer, they saw carpenters, masons ; a whole work-yard showed itself, full of industry, heaps of red bricks, piles of long

planks.   Singing was heard, with a pious intona-
tion, as of psalms.

Ducardi, whose custom was always to ride in
front, on the left of the Crown Prince, purposely
reined in his horse, allowed the others to come
up with him ; Othomar perceived that he did
not wish to act here.   He thought the General
petty, and said to Thesbia :

"Ask if Zanti is here. . . ."

The aide-de-camp turned with the question to
a sort of foreman.   None of the workpeople had
saluted ; the equerries doubted whether they had
recognized the Crown Prince.   Yes, Zanti was
there.   Plain "Zanti."   Very well, let him call
him.

The man went.   It took a long time.   Othomar,
waiting with the others on horseback, already
began to find his position a difficult one, lost
his tact, assumed his stiff rigidity, talked in a
forced way with Herman.   He found it was
difficult to wait when one had never done so
hitherto.   It made him nervous, and he made
his horse, pulling at the reins with coquettish
movements of the head, nervous too, and was
already thinking whether it would not be better
to go on. . . .

But Zanti, with the foreman who had called

him, was just approaching, slowly, in no way
hurrying himself. He looked from the distance
under his hand at the group of officers on horseback, flashing in the sunlight; stood still; asked
something further of the foreman; looked again.

"The unmannerly fellow!" muttered Thesbia.

The aide-de-camp rode up to him angrily, spoke
in a loud voice of His Imperial Highness the
Duke of Xara; the Duke wished to see the
refuges.

"They are not refuges," said Zanti, peevishly
contradicting him.

"What then?" asked the aide, haughtily.

"Dwellings," answered Zanti, curtly.

Thesbia shrugged his shoulders indignantly.
But the Crown Prince himself had ridden up,
and saluted Zanti, before the latter had given
him any greeting.

"Will Your Excellency give us leave to look
over what you are doing for the victims of the
inundations?" he asked, gently, graciously.

"I am no Excellency," muttered the gray-
beard; "but if you like to look, it's all one
to me."

"Very willingly," replied Othomar, a little
haughtily; "but not unless we have your entire
approbation. You are the master on your own

property, and if our visit is unwelcome, we will not force our presence on you."

Zanti looked at him.

"I repeat, if you like to look round, you can. But there is not much to look at. Everything is so simple. We make no secret of what we do. And the property is not mine, it belongs to all of them."

Othomar dismounted, the others followed; with difficulty Leoni and Thesbia found a couple of lads to look after the horses for a gratuity.

Othomar and Herman had already walked on with the old man.

"I hear that you are doing much good work, to mitigate the misery of the inundations," said Othomar.

"The inundation is no misery."

"No misery?" asked Herman, surprised. "What then?"

"A just punishment of Heaven. And there will be more punishments. The times are sinful."

The Princes looked at one another with a quick glance; they saw that the conversation would not proceed very easily.

"But the sinners whom Heaven punishes are helped by you nevertheless, Mr. Zanti," said Herman. "For all these refuges . . ."

"Are not refuges. Sheds, workshops, or temporary dwellings. There is to be a settlement here, if God will. In order to live simply, by work. Life is so simple, but man has made it so strange and complicated."

"But you take in the farmers who have lost everything in the inundations?" Herman persisted.

"I don't take them in. When they feel their sins, they come to me, and I save them from destruction."

"And do they not come to you also, without feeling their sin, because they feel that they will get food and lodging for nothing?"

"They get no food and lodging for nothing, they have to work here, sir," said the old man. "And perhaps more than you do, who walk round in a uniform. . . . They get rewarded according to the work they do, out of the common treasury. They are building here, and I build with them. Do you see that tree there, and this axe? I was employed in hewing down that tree when you came and interrupted me."

"A capital exercise," said Herman. "You look a vigorous man."

"So you say you are forming a settlement here?" asked Othomar.

"Yes, sir. The cities are destruction, life in the country purifies. Here they can live; further on lies building-land, which I give them, and meadow-land; I shall buy cattle for them."

"So you simply try to recruit farmers here," said Herman.

"No, sir!" answered the gray-beard sternly. "I recruit no farmers; they are not my farmers. They are their own farmers. They work for themselves, and I am a simple farmer like themselves. We are all equal. . . ."

"You are a simple farmer," repeated Prince Herman, "yet you live in a castle."

"No, young man," replied Zanti; "I do not live in a castle; I live here; my daughter lives there by herself. She is ill. . . . She would not be able to bear an alteration in her mode of life, or any deprivation. But my child will not live long. , . ."

He glanced up, looked at the Princes alternately, askance, almost anxiously.

"She is my only weakness, I think," he excused himself, in a faint voice. "She is my sin; I have taken doctors for her, and believe in what they say and prescribe. You see, she would not be able to do it. . . . to follow me in all things, for she has too much of the past in her poor blood. For her, a castle, comfort, are necessities, vital necessities. Therefore I leave her there. . . . But she will not live long. . . . And then I shall sell it, and I will divide the money entirely among them all. . . . You see, that is my weakness, my sin; I am only human. . . ."

The Princes saw him becoming moved; his hands trembled. Then he felt convinced that he had already spoken to them too much, too long of what lay nearest to his heart—his sin. And he pointed to the buildings, explained them to them. . . .

"I have read some of your pamphlets, Mr. Zanti," said the Crown Prince. "Do you apply your ideas on matrimony here?"

"I apply nothing," the gray-beard growled once more in contradiction. "I leave them all free. If they wish to get married by law they can do so, but if they come to me I bless them, and let them go in peace, for it is written, 'Again I say to you, that if two of you shall agree upon earth, concerning anything whatsoever they shall ask, it shall be done for them by My Father who is in heaven. . . . For where there are two or three gathered together in My name, there am I in the midst of them.'"

"And how do you rule so many followers?"
asked Herman.

"I don't rule them, sir!" roared the old man,
clenching his fists, his face red with fury. "I
am no more than any of them. The father has
authority in his own household, and the old men
give advice because they have experience, that
is all. Life is so simple. . . ."

"As you picture it to yourself, but not as it is
in reality," objected Herman.

Zanti looked at him angrily, stopped still, in
order to be able to talk more easily, and passionately, violently, he exclaimed:

"And do you in reality find it better than I
picture it to myself? I do not, sir, and I hope
to turn my picture into reality. You and yours
once, ages ago, made your picture reality; now
it is the turn of us others, your reality has
lasted long enough. . . ."

Othomar, haughtily, tried to say something in
contradiction; the old man, however, suddenly
turned to him, and gently though roughly, with
his penetrating, fanatical voice, which made
Othomar shudder:

"For you sir, I feel compassion. I do not
hate you, although you may think I do. I hate
nobody. The older I have grown, the less I have

learned to hate, the more softness has entered into me. See here, I hear something in your voice, and I see something in your eyes that. . . . attracts me, sir. I tell you this straight out; it is very foolish of me, perhaps, to talk like that to my future Emperor. But it is so; something in you attracts me. And I feel compassion for you. Do you know why? Because the time is at hand!"

He suddenly pointed upwards with his finger on high, with a strange impressiveness, continuing:

"The hour is at hand. Perhaps very near. If it does not come while your father is reigning, it will come during your reign or your son's. But it will come! And therefore I feel pity for you. For you will not have sufficient love for your people. Not sufficient love to say to them, 'I am as all of you, and nothing more. I will possess no more than any of you, for I do not want superfluity while you suffer need. I will not rule over you, for I am only a human being like yourselves, and no more human than you.' Are you more human? If you were more human, then you would be entitled to govern, yes, then, then. . . . See here, young man, you will never have so much love for your people as to do all

this, oh, and more still, and more. You will
govern, and have superfluity, and wage war. But
the time is at hand! Therefore I have compassion for you . . . although I ought not to
have it."

Othomar had turned pale; even Herman gave
a little shudder. It was more because of the
oracular voice of the man who was prophesying
the doom of their sovereignty, than because of
his words. But Herman shook off his shuddering,
and angrily, haughtily :

" I cannot say that you are courteous towards
your guests, Mr. Zanti; I will not even refer to
His Imperial Highness. . . ."

Zanti looked at Othomar.

" Pardon me," he said. " I spoke like that for
your sake. Your eyes are like my daughter's.
That is why I spoke as I did."

Herman burst out laughing.

" That is a valid reason, no doubt, Mr. Zanti."

Othomar, however, signed to him not to continue his tone of persiflage, and also with a look
restrained his equerries, who had listened to
Zanti's oracular utterances in speechless indignation : the old man had spoken to Othomar almost
in a whisper. His last words, however, that
resounded with emotion, changed this indignation

into bewilderment, quieted their anger, made them look upon the prophet as a semi-maniac, whose treason the Crown Prince was gracious enough to excuse. And the officers looked at one another, rasied their eyebrows, shrugged their shoulders. Dutri grinned. Othomar asked Zanti calmly whether they had not better proceed.

The settlement was very much in its first stage, yet a few peasant's-dwellings began to rise up, chesnut-trees were felled, hundreds of peasants were at work.

The group of officers excited great curiosity; the Princes had been recognised. On almost every side the people stopped work, followed the uniforms with their eyes.

The Princes and their suite felt instinctively that a hostile feeling was passing through Zanti's peasants. When they put a question here and there concerning the misery undergone, the answer sounded curt, rough, with a reference to the will of God, and was always like an echo of Zanti's own words. Pecuniary assistance was not to be offered here. And Zanti had really nothing to show. The settlement made a poor impression on Othomar, perhaps because of a sort of mortified sovereignty. Accustomed always to be approached with respect, as a future majesty,

his sensitiveness was more deeply wounded with
Zanti's roughness, with the surliness of his
peasants, than he was willing to acknowledge to
himself. He felt that in this place they did not
see in him the Crown Prince who loved his people
and wanted to learn how to succour them, but the
son of a tyrant, who would tyrannize in his turn.
He felt that, although Zanti called himself the
apostle of peace, that peace was not in his dis-
ciples; and when he looked into their rough,
sullen faces, he saw hatred gleam luridly from
deep, hollow eyes, as with sudden lightning-
flashes. . . .

The quintals fell heavy upon his chest, his
impotence pressed with a world of inconsolable
misery and unappeasable grief upon his shoulders,
as though to bear him to the ground. The misery
and grief not of one, but of thousands, millions.
Vindictive eyes multiplied themselves around him
in a ferment of hatred; each one of his people
who asked happiness from him, demanded it, and
did not receive it, seemed to be there, staring at
him with those wide eyes. . . .

He felt himself turning giddy with a wide,
immense feeling of helplessness. He looked for
nothing more, this was the end. And he was not
surprised at what happened. The man with the

distorted, hairy, brown face, who rushed down
upon him like a nightmare, seized hold of him,
full of hatred. A foul, tobacco-laden breath swept
over his face, a coarse knife flashed in a coarse
fist towards his throat. . . .

A cry went up. The report of a shot was
heard, sharp, determined, with no suspicion of
hesitation. The man cursed out a hoarse cry,
gnashing his teeth in revolt, and struggled against
it, dying. His brains splashed out, over Othomar,
soiling the Prince's uniform. And the man had
already plumped down at his feet on the ground,
grown limp at once, with relaxed muscles, still
clutching the knife in his hairy fingers; all this
had happened in one instant.

It was Von Fest who had sent the shot from a
revolver. The colonel drew up his broad figure,
looked around him, still held the revolver slant-
ingly, threateningly, in his fist. The people
stared, motionless, perplexed by the sudden reality
before their eyes.

Zanti, stupefied, stared at the corpse; then he
said—the officers, dismayed, standing in fussy
confusion around the Prince:

" Now go, and if you can, go in peace. . . ! "

Full of bitterness, he pointed to the corpse.
He shook his head, with the gray locks under the

9

felt hat; tears sprang to the corners of his
eyes.

"Thou shalt not kill. . . !" they heard him
mutter. "They seem not to know that yet;
nobody knows it yet. . . !"

A strange look, full of insanity, troubled his
otherwise clear, gray eyes; he seemed for a
moment not to know what he should do. Then
he went to a tree, took up the axe, and without
taking further notice of the Princes, began to hew,
like a madman, blow upon blow. . . .

The officers hurried to their horses. Dutri
turned to look back; near the corpse, which the
peasants were now surrounding, he saw a woman
standing; she sobbed, threw out her arms full of
despair towards heaven, howled, shook her fist at
the equerry's turned face, screaming.

Othomar had said nothing. He heard the
woman howling behind him. He quivered in
every nerve. On the road, preparing to mount,
Ducardi asked him, agitatedly:

"Shall we return to Castel Vaza, Highness?"

The Prince looked at the General haughtily.
Quickly the thought flashed through him that the
General had very strongly opposed his coming
here. He shook his head. Then his eyes sought

Von Fest; they looked up at the Colonel under their eyelids, deep black, moist, almost reproachfully.

But he held out his hand.

"I thank you, Colonel," he said, in a husky voice.

The Colonel pressed the Prince's hand.

"Glad to be of service, Highness!" he replied, with soldierly brusqueness.

"And now let us go on to the Zanthos," said Othomar, and went up to his horse.

But the old General could no longer master himself. In these last moments he had felt all his passionate love—rooted hereditarily, firmly, in his blood, of a piece with him, his very soul, and all that soul—for the reigning house. His fathers had died for it in battle without hesitation. And with the mad, wide embrace of his long, powerful old arms, he ran up to Othomar, grateful that he was alive, pressed him as if he would crush him against his breast, until the buttons of his uniform scratched Othomar's cheek, and cried, sobbing, under his trembling moustache:

"My Prince, my Prince, my Prince. . . !"

VIII

The attempt on Othomar's life was already known at Castel Vaza before the Princes returned, from peasants of the Duke's, who had told the servants of the castle long stories of how the Prince had been severely wounded. The Duchess had first refused to believe it; then, in rising anxiety, in the greatest tension and uncertainty she had walked round the galleries. She had first tried to persuade herself that the people were sure to exaggerate. When she reflected that, in the event of Othomar's being wounded, the Princes and the equerries would have at once returned, she became more tranquil, and waited patiently.

But the under-steward, who had been to Vaza, returned in dismay: people were very uneasy in the town, pressed round the doors of the news-paper-offices to read the bulletins, which mentioned the attempt shortly, with the provoking comment that further particulars were not yet to hand. The Duchess understood that by this time the bulletin had also been telegraphed to Lipara, and she not only feared that Othomar had met with harm, but that she would lose favour with the Empress. . . .

When the Duchess at last, after long watching from a window in the West corridor, saw the Princes and their suite come trotting, very small, along a distant road, she could not restrain herself, she went to meet them in the courtyard. But she saw that Othomar was unhurt. The Duke of Xara dismounted, smiled, gave her his hand; she kissed it, courtesying, passionately; her tears fell down upon it. The steward approached, assured Othomar, in the name of all the Duke's servants, of their heartfelt gratitude that the Duke of Xara had been spared, by the grace of God and the succour of St. Ladislas. Ducardi had not been able to telegraph anywhere before, but he now sent in all haste to Vaza with a despatch for the Emperor, mentioning at the same time that the Prince had, immediately after the attempt, calmly resumed the expedition. The dinner was partaken of in a babel of conversation; the Duchess was very much excited, asked for the smallest details, and almost embraced Von Fest. The Crown Prince drank to his preserver, and every one paid him tribute.

Afterwards Ducardi advised the Crown Prince, aside, to retire early to rest. The General spoke in a gentle voice; it seemed as though the thought that he might have lost his Crown Prince had made him fonder of him. Herman too pressed Othomar to go to bed.

He himself had grown calm, but a vague feeling of weariness had come over all his being: he had even drunk Von Fest's health in a strange voice of lassitude. He now took their advice, withdrew, undressed; his soiled uniform, which he had changed before dinner, still hung over a chair; he shuddered to think that he had worn it a whole afternoon.

"That thing!" he said to Andro, who was still quite confused, and, weeping with nervousness, was tidying up; "Burn it, or throw it away, throw it away. . . ."

Othomar threw himself down in his dressing-gown on a couch in the room that adjoined his bedroom. Also an historical apartment: tapestry on the walls with scenes from the history of Lipara: the Emperor Berengar I. triumphantly riding into Jerusalem, with his crusaders, holding aloft their white banners ; the Empress Xaveria, seated on horseback in her golden armour before the walls of Altara, falling backwards, struck dead by a Turkish arrow. . . .

The Prince lay staring at them. A deadly calm seemed to make him feel nothing, care about nothing. In his own mind he reviewed the

whole history from Berengar to Xaveria. He
knew the dates; the scenes clouded before him
as though tapestries were unrolling themselves,
kaleidoscopic, with the faded colours of old art-
work. He saw himself again, a small boy, in the
Imperial, in an austere room, diligently learning
his lessons ; he saw his masters, who relieved one
another : languages, history, political economy,
the law of nations, stratagem ; it had all heaped
itself up in his young brain, piled itself up, built
itself up like a tower. By way of change his
military education—drilling, riding, fencing—conducted by General Ducardi, who praised him or
grumbled at him, or growled at the sergeants
who instructed him. He had never been able to
learn mathematics, had never understood a word
of algebra; in many subjects he had always
remained weak : natural philosophy and chemistry,
for instance. For a time he had taken great
pleasure in the study of mineralogy and zoology
and botany, and afterwards he had grown enthu-
siastic about astronomy. And then came the
university and his legal studies. . . .

He remembered his little vanities as child and
boy, when in his ninth year he had become a
Lieutenant in the Throneguards ; when later
he had received the Order of the Garter from

the Queen of England, and the Black Eagle
from the German Emperor, and the Golden
Fleece from the Regent of Spain. With such
little vanities there had always been mingled a
certain dread of possible obligations which the
Garter or the Eagle might imply: obligations
which hovered vaguely before his eyes, which
he dared not define, and still less inquire into of
Ducardi, of his father. Gradually those threatening obligations had become so heavy, and now,
now they were the quintals. . . .

The quintals. But he did not stir, strangely
calm. Then he thought of Von Fest, of the
Duchess. . . . Yesterday, her kiss . . . He had
lain swooning on her shoulder, and she had
kissed him, and watched him long with passionate looks. And all those stories of the
equerries. . . .

Then it came over him as with a fierce wave,
foaming over his deathly calm. . . .

Why did that man hate him, try to murder
him, propose to slay him like a beast . . .?
Pride quivered up in him, pride and despair.
That man had touched him, soiled him with his
breath—him, the Crown Prince, the Duke of
Xara! He gnashed his teeth with rage. . . .
That was a thing Berengar I. would never have

suffered to be done to him! Off with his head!
off with his head! . . . Oh, that proletariat
which did not. know, which did not feel, which
pressed up against him, seething like sea-foam
against the throne, which terrified his mother,
however haughtily she might look over it, im-
perially calm, into the distance. . . .

How he hated it, hated it, with all the hatred,
oh! of his race for those who were now free, and
were yet once its slaves! How he would have
them shot down, would later on have them shot
down. . . .

He looked at Xaveria; she was shot down
herself, the haughty amazon; backwards she
fell, wounded by the arrow of a Turkish soldier.
And he, that morning, if Von Fest had not . . .

He threw himself wildly back, buried his face
in his hands, and sobbed. No, no, oh no! Not
shoot them down, not kill them, not hate them!
He was not like that; he might be like that for
one moment, but he was not like that! He was
fond of his people; he was so grateful when they
rejoiced, when he was able to help them. Surely
he would never have them shot on! He was
only growing excited now. What was there in his
soul for all of them, for those millions, of whom
he had perhaps only seen some thousands, and

knew some hundreds, but one great love, that
threw out arms towards them in every direction,
to embrace them ? Had he not felt this, there in
that black night on the Therezia Square ? Were
hatred and violence his ? No, oh no ! He was
soft, perhaps too soft, too irresolute, but he
would grow older, he would grow stronger; he
would wish to, and he would make all of them
happy. Oh, if they only loved him, loved him
with their great mass of surging, black, swarming, crowding humanity; inken milky-way of
swarming souls, each soul a spark, like his own ;
oh, if they only loved him ! But they must not
hate him, not look at him with such bloodshot
eyes of hatred, not aim at his throat with such
coarse, hairy fingers, not try to murder him,
O God, try to slay him like a bullock, with a
common knife, him, their future sovereign . . .!

And he felt that they did not belong to him,
and did not know him, and did not understand
him, and did not love him, all of them, and that
they hated him, only out of instinct, because he
was born upon the throne !

And his despair for this reason spanned out,
immense, a desert of black night, which he felt
eternally wide all around him, and he sobbed,
sobbed, like an inconsolable child because this

was so, and would become more desperate with every day that brought him nearer to his future as Emperor, and their future: the mournful day which would rise upon the old world's desolation. . . .

Then there came a knock at a little door, and the door was softly opened. . . .

"Who is there?" he asked, startled, feeling the breach of etiquette, not understanding why Andro did not come to announce through the anteroom whomever it might be.

"If Your Highness permits me. . . ."

He recognized the soft voice of the Duchess, rose, went to the door.

"Come in, madame. . . ."

She entered, hesitatingly; to go through the chilly passages of the castle she had thrown a long cloak over her bare shoulders. . . .

"Forgive me, Highness, if I intrude . . . if I disturb you. . . ."

He smiled, declared no, apologized for his costume, surprised, pleased. . . .

She saw that his eyes were swimming with moisture.

"I am indiscreet," she said, "but I could not resist it; I felt I must ascertain for myself how you were, Highness. . . . Perhaps I did wish to surprise you, I don't know myself. Something impelled me. . . . I could not but come to you. You are my guest and my Crown Prince; I longed to see for myself how you were. . . . Your Highness bore up well at dinner, but I felt . . ."

Her voice flowed on, soft and monotonous, as though with drops of balsam. He asked her to sit down; she did so; he sat down by her side; the dark cloak glided off, and she was magnificent, with her white neck, siren-like in her opalescent pale-green moiré. He noticed that she had put aside the jewels which she had worn at dinner.

" I wanted to come to you quietly, through that door," she resumed, " in order to tell you once more, to you alone, how utterly thankful I am that Your Highness's life has been preserved. . . ."

Her voice trembled; her ebony glances became moist; the light of the great candles in the silver candelabra shimmered over the silk of her dress, played with soft light and slumbering shadow in the modelling of her face, in the curve of her bosom.

He pressed her hand, she retained his.

" Was Your Highness crying when I came in?" she asked.

His tears were still flowing, a last sob heaved through his body.

"Why?" she asked again. "Or am I indiscreet . . . ?"

He looked at her; at this moment he could have told her everything. And if he contained himself, he nevertheless gave her the essence of his grief.

"I was melancholy," he said, "because they seem to hate me. Nothing makes me so sad as their hatred."

She looked at him long, felt his sorrow, understood him with her feminine tact, with her courtier-like swiftness of comprehension, which had ripened in the immediate contact with her sovereigns. She understood him; he was the Crown Prince, he must suffer his special Crown Princely suffering; he must drink to the dregs an Imperial cup of bitterness. She remembered that she herself had suffered, so often and so violently, for love, passionate woman that she was; she understood that his suffering was different from hers, but doubtless more terrible, as it seized him at already so young an age, and as it was not about his own single soul, but about the millions of souls of his empire. She too had suffered because she had not been loved; he also suffered like that. And so she understood him in one instant quite entirely, with all her strange woman's heart.

A thrill of compassion welled up in her breast
as a yet unknown delight, and like a fervent, gentle oracle, she uttered the words:

" They do not all hate you. . . ."

He recognized her passionate glances of the
day before. He remembered her kiss. He looked
at her long, still hesitating a little in the presence
of the unknown. Then he extended his arms,
and with a dull cry of despair, hoarse with
hunger for consolation, he called to her in his
helplessness.

IX

To his Most Gracious Imperial Highness Othomar, Duke of Xara, Lycilia.

The Imperial, Lipara,
—— *April*, 18—.

My dear Brother,—Before you learn it from those tedious papers, I want to tell you that our respected father and Emperor this morning, on my tenth birthday, dubbed me a Knight of St. Ladislas in the Knights' Hall of the Palace. You can understand how proud I feel. I shall not tell you about the ceremony, because you will remember that yourself. I was very much impressed as I walked up to our father between all those tall knights in their blue mantles, and knelt before his throne. I wore my new uniform of a Lieutenant in the Guards. The King-at-Arms, the Marquis of Ezzera, held up the rule of the Order on a cushion, on which I took the oath. I must have looked rather small with my little mantle—the Cross of St. Ladislas was as large on it, however, as on all the others. I felt that they were all looking over my head, and that is not a pleasant feeling when you are the hero

of the day. But of course I am the youngest of
the knights, so there is no harm in my being a
little shorter. The sword our father gave me is
also a little smaller than that of the other knights,
but the hilt is rather pretty, and blazes with precious stones. I think, however, that I prefer the
chasing on the sheath of yours, but when I am
eighteen years old—so in eight years!—I am to
have another sword, and of course another mantle
too.

Mamma was terribly alarmed and nervous when
she heard of that man who attacked you, and she
wanted to have you recalled at once, because it
did not seem safe there ; and she simply could
not understand that that could not be done. But
safe, what is safe after all ? You're not safe in
war either, and not even here in the Imperial.
You shouldn't think so much of all that safety, I
think; but of course Mamma is a woman, and
therefore she thinks differently to what we do.
The riots and the state of siege upset her also,
but I think it rather jolly : everything is military
now, you know. That Von Fest is a fine fellow ;
I should like to shake hands with him, and to
thank him myself; but as I can't do so, I beg
you *particularly* to do it for me, and *on no account*
to forget it. You know, no doubt, through General

Ducardi, that papa is going to make him a Commander of the Imperial Orb; what a pity that we can't create him a Knight of St. Ladislas, but for that of course he would have to be a Liparian and not a Gothlander.

Now, dear brother, I must finish, because Colonel Fasti is expecting me for my fencing lesson. Give my *kindest* regards to Herman and to General Ducardi, and remember me to the others; and accept the tender embrace of your affectionate brother,

BERENGAR,
Marquis of Thracyna
(Knight of St. Ladislas).

CHAPTER III

I

IT was after the opening of the new Parliament.
The sun streamed as though with square patches
of molten gold along the white palaces of the
town, and only just touched with blue what was
shadow in the corners.

Two regiments of infantry, Grenadiers, red and
blue, stood in two double lines, drawn up along
the pavements of the principal streets which led
from the Parliament House to the Imperial.
Behind them pressed and tossed and revelled the
multitude; all the windows, open wide, swarmed
with heads; people looked on from every balcony.
A shot thundered from Fort Wenceslas on the
sea; the Emperor returned; the infantry presented arms in company after company. . . .

The Lancers in front, blue and white, with
streaming pennants at the points of their lances,

six squadrons of them. The whole strength of the
Throneguards, white, with breastplates of glistening gold flashing in the sunlight above the black
satin skins of the stallions, halberd on thigh, surrounding the gently oscillating state - carriages,
heavily gilt and bright crystal, scintillating, and
two of them crowned with the Imperial crown, with
teams of six and eight plumed grays. The horses
foam over their bits, impatient, nervously pawing
the ground, prancing because of the slow ceremonious pace over the dazzling, flagged roadway.
In the first coach, the Master of Ceremonies, the
Count of Threma ; in the second, with the crown
and the team of eight—and the roar of the cheers
ascends from behind the hedge of soldiers—the
Emperor, his uniform all gold, his robes of scarlet
and ermine, his crown upon his head. It is the
only time that the people have seen their Emperor wearing his crown.

And they cheer. But the Emperor makes no
acknowledgment; through the crystal of the
coach he looks out, to left and right in turns, at
the crowd, with a proud smile of self-consciousness
and triumph, and his face, full of race, full of
force, cold with will, proud with authority, is
inaccessible in its smile as that of a Roman
emperor on his triumphal entry.

It is a triumphal entry, this return from the
Parliament House to his Imperial; triumph over
what they denied him, on which he has now laid
his heavy hand, showing them all that his will
alone can bend them to his word and purpose.
And the cheers rise louder and louder from that
capricious crowd, restrained like a woman by a
ruler whom it now adores for his strength, admires
for his Imperial might, upon which he leans, as he
passes from the Parliament right up to his own
palace, as though it were a whole army that lived
upon his nod; and louder and louder, louder and
louder the vivats ring out that sunny afternoon
over the marble houses, and the Emperor smiles
continually, as though his smile means, " Cheer,
what else can you do but cheer . . . ? "

In the next coach rides the Duke of Xara,
robed, crowned; he stares rigidly over the vocife-
rating crowd with the same look that his mother
reserves for the populace. In the next one to
that, the new Governor-General of the capital,
the head of the Emperor's military household, the
Duke of Mena-Doni, a rougher soldier and less
practised courtier than the Marquis of Dazzara,
under whose military fist the white capital, like
a beaten slave, crouched low during the state of
siege, proclaimed after a single hour of disturbance

that ventured to follow upon the resolution of the Emperor to dissolve the House of Representatives. His coarse, sensual mouth smiles with the same smile as the Emperor's, whose rude force he seems to impersonate, and he too seems to say, " Cheer away, shout your vivats ! "

Then the succeeding carriages: the Imperial Chancellor, Count Myxila ; the ministers: seven of them forming part of the twelve who wished to resign, the others chosen from among the most Authoritative of the old nobility in the House of Nobles itself !

Cheer away, shout your vivats . . . !

Behind the coaches of the higher court-officials, the Cuirassiers of Xara, the Crown Prince's own regiment ; behind them a regiment of Colonials : Africans, black as polished ebony, with eyes like beads, their thick mouths protruding, clad in the muslin-like snow of the burnooses ; behind them, two regiments of hussars on heavy horses, in their long green coats with gold frogs and tall plumes.

Has ever Parliament been opened thus, with such a display of military force ? And outside the town, on the high Champ de Mars, do not the people know that there are troops summoned together from all the governments, camping there for the manœuvres, the date of which has been accelerated? And the increased garrisons of the forts, the fleet in the harbour? Do the people themselves feel that they can do nothing else than cheer, and is that why they just cheer away now, happy once more in their cheering, with Roman docility and Southern submission, enamoured of the Emperor because of the weight of his crushing fist, loving the Crown Prince by reason of the sympathetic charm of his conduct in the North— or perhaps because they think him interesting after an unsuccessful attempt on his life?

And they seem not to feel that, through the presented arms of the Grenadiers, they see neither the Emperor nor the Crown Prince salute; they cheer, loving them in spite, perhaps because, of their indifference; they cheer like madmen. . . .

Slowly the state procession wends along the interminable main streets. The whole city, despite its marble, trembles with the clatter of the horses' hoofs upon the flagged pavement. Between the front escort and the endless escort in the rear, the state-carriages, with their glittering Throne-guards, shimmer like a kind of jewel, small, rare, carefully guarded. The cavalry are at this moment the soul of Lipara; their resounding step its heart-beat, and between the Grenadiers and

the tall houses the massed, cheering populace
seems to have hardly room to breathe.

The procession approaches the Imperial. Along
the colossal marble fore-court the Lancers and
Cuirassiers range themselves on three sides,
before the wings and along the façade. Outside
them the Guards are drawn up. The Africans
close off the court. . . .

The carriages pull up; the Emperor steps out.
With the Crown Prince by his side, he goes
through the vestibule, up the stairs. The corridors of the palace swarm with golden uniforms,
a packed suite crowds up behind Oscar and
Othomar. The Grand Master of the Robes, with
twelve grooms of the bedchamber, comes towards
the Emperor, who takes off his crown, as does
the Crown Prince; their robes are undone for
them.

They go to the great White Hall, white with
the Corinthian columns, with gilt capitals. The
Empress, the Princess Thera are there, surrounded
by their ladies-in-waiting. It is a great day; the
monarchy is triumphing, in this sun-apotheosis
of the opening of Parliament, over the threats of
the future, and defers this future itself. The
Empress, in her trailing pale-mauve velvet, steps
towards her spouse, and courtesies before him cere-

moniously.   The Princess, the Grand Mistress of
the Robes, the ladies-in-waiting courtesey . . .

Outside, in front, the square is now filled with
the people; an excited popular clamour now
surges up against the immovable palace, as it
were the sea against a rock.   The doors of the
centre balcony are opened.   The Emperor and
the Prince will show themselves. . . .

"Only just salute once," whispers the Emperor
to his son, sternly.

The sun outside rains down gold upon the
swarming mass, tinges it with many-changing,
chameleon, Southern tints between the white,
motionless front-wings of the Imperial, whose
caryatides placidly look down.   The Imperial
pair step out on to the balcony.   Hats are
thrown up towards them; the yelling bellows up
with a shout as from one noisy, vulgar throat,
and echoes through the open doors against the
gilt ceiling and columns of the White Hall.   The
Empress is frightened by it, turns pale; her
breath catches. . . .

On the balcony the Emperor of Liparia with
one solitary wave of the hand salutes his excited
people; the Duke of Xara bows his head slightly.

II

There was no more talk of a revision of the Constitution and reform of the hereditary House of Nobles. The Constitutional majority of three-fourths which is required in the House of Representatives before such a proposal can be taken into consideration, though there at first, no longer existed after the new elections. Oscar, immediately after his return from Altara, had shown them his strength of daring. Lipara was surrounded with troops; they came at a good time, for the manœuvres, for the King of Syria, who was expected. The forts were strengthened, the fleet lay in the harbour; then came the Imperial decree that the House of Representatives should simply . . . be dissolved. How they had cried out, after the promulgation of that decree, in the newspapers and in the streets! For one moment, at night, there was an abortive riot. But the Emperor, furious with the Marquis of Dazzara for his delay in taking prompt energetic measures, had the next day affirmed his high dissatisfaction. The Marquis was shown that there were moments when the Emperor was not to be trifled with; the Emperor announced his dismissal to him then and there, and told him he could go. Crushed, his eyes full of despair, the Marquis left the Imperial; in the fore-court his carriage crossed that of the Duke of Mena-Doni, Lieutenant-General of the Hussars; he saw the Duke's sensual Nero-head, covetous with ambition, staring up at the façade of the palace. The Marquis threw himself back in his carriage and wrung his hands, wept like a child. . . .

That same morning Lipara was proclaimed in state of siege; the Duke of Mena-Doni appointed Governor of the Capital. With great military display and three words of address the Emperor dissolved the House of Representatives. The people trembled, beaten off, thrashed down, reduced to crouching at the Imperial feet. The new elections were decreed. Need the people be chastised to make them attached to their Emperor? Was it because of the innumerable articles in the newspapers of the Northern governments—Altara, Vaza, and Lycilia—which bestowed all their sympathy upon their most charming, charitable Crown Prince, indefatigable, omnipresent, mitigating what suffering he could? Was it because of the colossal, fabulous presents of millions given from the Imperial privy purse for the victims of the disaster? The result of the elections became known; the new House of Representatives contained an impotent bare majority of Constitutionals. What did it profit that the Liberal papers shrieked of intrigue and compulsion? Without and within the city lay the army; each day the Emperor showed himself, and by his side the Duke of Mena-Doni. . . .

The Emperor invited the old ministry to remain in office, but dismissed those of the ministers who were not absolutely Authoritative.

The crisis was at an end. The great spring manœuvres were to take place on the Champ de Mars so soon as the King and Queen of Syria arrived at Lipara.

In Othomar there sprang up a vast admiration for his father. He did not love him with the fondness, the intimacy, the still almost childish dependence with which he loved the Empress; he had always looked up to him, as a child he had been afraid of him. Now, after the personal courage which he had seen the Emperor display, the sovereign power which he had exercised, his majesty soared up higher before Othomar's eyes, as it were the statue of a demi-god. He himself felt a lowly mortal beside him, when he

thought: " What should *I* have done, if I had
had to act in this case? Should I have dared to
come to a prompt decision to dissolve the House
of Representatives, and should I not have feared
an immediate revolution in every corner of the
country? Should I, immediately upon the disturbances, have been able to dismiss the Marquis
of Dazzara, have dared to send him away like a
lackey, attached as he was to our House, a
descendant of our most glorious nobility?
Should I have dared to summon to my presence
that Duke, that swashbuckler, with his cruel
head, even before I had dismissed the Marquis,
so that the one arrived as the other departed?"

And he saw himself already hesitating in
imagination, not knowing what would be best,
above all not knowing what would be most just;
he pictured himself advised by old Count
Myxila, at last determined to dissolve the Representatives, but not dismissing the Marquis, not
declaring Lipara in state of siege, and assembling
the troops too late, and seeing the revolution
burst out at all points simultaneously with bomb
upon bomb. . . .

To do what was most just, this seemed to
him the most difficult of all for a sovereign.

But the Emperor's monarchic triumph had

this result, that, however clearly he saw his own weakness, a reflex of strength and determination was cast down upon him from his father himself, by whose side he stood. With that, he had not much time for brooding. Each day brought with it its special duties. Scarcely was he able to arrange for himself one hour of solitary repose. He was accustomed to this life of constant movement, of constant personal appearance, now here, now there, so accustomed to it that he did not perceive the fatigue which was already exhausting him before his tour in the North, which had now eaten into his marrow and nerves. He gave this fatigue no thought, looked upon it, perhaps, as an organic heaviness, something transitory, which would doubtless pass away. And each day brought its own fatigue. Thus he had grown accustomed to rise early, at seven every morning; Lipara then still lay in its rosy slumber of dawn, peacefully white; he rode out on his thoroughbred Arab, black Emiro, with his favourite collie just behind him, galloping with him, its pointed nose poked out, its hairy collar sticking up; unaccompanied by equerries, he rode through the park of the Imperial to the Elizabeth Parks, in the afternoon the resort of elegant carriages and horsemen, in the morning quiet and wide and deserted, with barely a solitary early rider, who respectfully made way for the Prince and took his hat off low. Then he rode along the white quays with their villas and palm-trees, their terraces and aloes; and the incomparable harbour lay before him, always growing an intenser blue beneath the pink dawn that became cruder. Further on, the docks, the ships; the hum of energy was there. Slowly he walked his horse along the harbour; in the porticoes of the villas he sometimes caught a glimpse of a woman's figure, saw her eyes following him through roses and clematis. He loved this ride because of the fresh air, because of his horse, his dog, because of his solitude with those two, because of the long, silent quays, the wide, silent sky, the distant horizon still just enveloped in latest morning mist. The morning breeze blew against his forehead under the cap of his uniform; thoughts wandered at random through his brain. Then he shook himself free from this voluptuousness, rode back to the town, and went to the Xaverius Barracks, those of the Lancers; to the Wenceslas Barracks, of the Grenadiers; or to the Berengar Barracks, those of the Hussars. Here he inquired, he investigated, he inspected,

and here he found his equerries, Dutri and
Leoni; he rode back with them to the palace,
and repaired to his father's study. This was
the time at which Count Myxila came to
the Emperor, and affairs of State were discussed with the Imperial Chancellor; lately the
Crown Prince had assisted at these meetings.
Then he visited the Empress, who expected
him; it was generally a most delightful moment,
this that they spent confidentially together before
lunch; full of charm and intimacy. He sat
close by her on a low chair, he took her hand,
poured out to her the burdens of his heart, com-
municated to her his anxiety about the future,
about himself when later on he would have to
wear the Imperial crown. His eyes then peered
up from under his eyelids, with their dark
melancholy; his voice was querulous, and he
begged for comfort. And she encouraged him;
she told him that nothing happened but what
must happen, that everything was necessary in
the great system of the world, joined together
link by link; that he must wait for what might
come, but that he must at the same time do his
duty, and that he must not unnerve himself with
such endless pondering, which led to nothing.
He told her how much afraid he was of his

own hesitations, and how he suspected that his decisions would always come too late; and she answered him, laughing gently, that if he knew his own failings so well, he should train himself in making up his mind; he questioned her about justice—the one thing on earth insoluble to him—and she referred him to his own feeling as a human soul. But yet, entirely sweet as were these hours, he felt that he remained the same under their interchange of words, and that yet, though words had been interchanged, nothing had been changed in him. Wherefore he thought himself wicked, and was afraid that he did not love his mother sufficiently, with sufficient conviction. Then he looked at her, saw her smiling, divined beneath her smile that nervous dread which would never again relinquish its grasp of her, and felt that she spoke like that only for his sake, to cheer him, and not out of conviction. And his thoughts no longer wandered loosely through him, as on his morning ride along the quays: they fell like fine mists upon one another in his imagination, and formed his melancholy.

Lunch was taken privately. After lunch he sat for an hour to Thera, who was painting his portrait. In the afternoon there were always different things to do : exhibitions, charitable institutions, establishments of all kinds to be visited, a foundation-stone to be laid, a man-of-war to be launched. Every minute was filled up, and each day filled up his minutes differently from the preceding one. The dinner was always partaken of with great etiquette and splendour ; every day there were numerous guests, diplomats, high officials, officers. It lasted long ; it was the daily ceremonial banquet of the Emperor. Then in the evening the parties at Court, or at the houses of the ambassadors or dignitaries; the theatres and concerts. The Prince, however, never stayed late. He then read for a couple of hours in his own study, or worked ; he went to bed at twelve o'clock.

He was used to this life of monotonous variety, had grown up in it. So soon as he returned from Lycilia to Lipara—the city then still in state of siege—he found it waiting for him busier than ever ; the opening of Parliament had followed close upon his return. The Emperor was pleased with the Crown Prince's conduct in the North, perhaps because of the praise which the Northern newspapers, full of sympathy, bestowed upon the Duke of Xara, because of his moment of popularity. He wanted to let his

son take more and more part in affairs of State,
and spoke more with him about them, either
alone or together with the Imperial Chancellor.
But the stern measures of rough violence which
the Duke of Mena-Doni had taken—he himself
at Lipara, his officers at Thracyna: furious
charges of Hussars upon the threatening crowds
—revolted Othomar; he had learnt them with
despair and anguish, although he knew that
there was nothing to be achieved by gentleness.
And with his veneration of the Emperor, as of
a demi-god of will and force, there was mingled a
something of antipathy and disinclination, which
divided him from his father, and made any interchange of thought between them difficult.

Now, after the opening of Parliament, the
town, the whole country, had quieted down;
the troops, however, remained on the Champ de
Mars, for the approaching manœuvres. The
arrival of the King and Queen of Syria was fixed.
Othomar's days followed on one another as
before. He was entertained at banquets by
the officers of the Throneguards, and of the
other regiments to which he belonged. Yes,
this was his hour of popularity. It was already
said that his surname later would be Othomar
the Benevolent. In these days he laid the

foundation-stone of a great almshouse, to whose establishment the will of an immensely wealthy, childless duke—one of the oldest families in Liparia, which had become extinct—had contributed millions.

Othomar's gentleness was in amiable contrast with Oscar's justly exerted but rough force. But he himself was inwardly very much astonished at this talk of benevolence ; he liked to do good, but did not feel a love of doing good as a principal trait of his character.

After the dinner given him by the officers of the staff, Othomar was to go in the evening with Ducardi, Dutri, and Leoni, to the Duke of Yemena, to thank the Court Marshal officially for the hospitality shown him at Castel Vaza. The Duke occupied at Lipara a large, new mansion ; his old family mansion was at Altara.

It was nine o'clock ; the Crown Prince was not yet expected. The Duke and Duchess, however, were already receiving their guests ; the Duchess had sent out numerous invitations when Othomar had announced his visit. The spacious reception-rooms filled up ; almost the whole of the diplomatic corps was present ; some of the ministers and great court officials with their wives, old Countess Myxila and her daughters, a number of officers. They were the intimate circle of the Imperial. A jaunty familiarity prevailed among them, with the *sans-gêne* which was in vogue.

Near the Duchess stood Lady Danbury, the wife of the English First Secretary, and the Marquis of Xardi, the Duke's son. They were talking busily about the Dazzaras.

"I have seen them," said Lady Danbury. "It is shocking, shocking. They are now living at Castel Dazzara, that old ruin in Thracyna, with their five daughters, poor things! The ceilings are falling in; three crooked old men in livery, and the liveries even older than the servants. And debts, I hear—debts! I was astonished to see how old the Marchioness had grown; she has taken it terribly to heart, it seems."

"Grown old?" asked the Duchess. "I thought she looked quite young still, last time I saw her. . . ."

She detested Lady Danbury, who was tall, thin, and sharp-featured, and had the air of a graceful adder. And she continued:

"She still looked so well; she is slender, but she has a splendid figure. . . . I really cannot understand how she can have grown so old. . . ."

And as though brooding over this puzzle, the

Duchess stares at the lean shoulders of Lady Danbury.

Xardi's eyes glitter; he expects a skirmish.

"They say that the Marquis was one of your intimates, formerly, do they not?" insinuates the Englishwoman. But the hateful "formerly" displeases Xardi.

"I am very fond of the Dazzaras," says the Duchess; "but. . . ." and she laughs mysteriously, with intention; "he has always been an unlucky bird. . . ."

"His Excellency the Duke of Mena-Doni," the major-domo announces.

"The rising sun!" Xardi whispers to Lady Danbury.

Mena-Doni bows before the Duchess, who smiles to him. Lady Danbury, standing by Xardi's side, continues:

"And the lucky bird, do you think?"

"Oh no!" says Xardi, with conviction. "At least, not altogether. . . ."

They look at one another, and laugh.

"Imperial eagles are the finest birds, after all, are they not?" says Lady Danbury, jestingly.

"What do you know about it?"

"Alas, I am too insignificant to know anything. Before I get so far in my zoological studies . . . !"

" But what have you heard ? "

" What everybody hears when Dutri can't hold his tongue."

" What about ? "

" About a certain tender parting at Castel Vaza. . . ."

The Marquis of Xardi bursts out laughing. Lady Danbury suddenly clutches his arm.

" I say, Xardi, I know less slender people than the Marchioness of Dazzara who would fall into a decline if they lost the Imperial favour. *Et toi ?* "

The Marquis laughs loudly, and :

" Even the Crown-Princely favour. . . ." he whispers, behind Lady Danbury's Watteau fan. They choke with laughter together.

" His Imperial Highness the Duke of Xara ; Their Excellencies Count Ducardi, Prince Dutri, the Marquis of Leoni ! " are slowly, impressively announced.

There is a slight movement in the groups. The room divides into two rows ; a couple of ladies get entangled in their trains, and laugh. Thus they wait.

Othomar appears at the open door ; Ducardi, Dutri, and Leoni are behind him. The old Duke hastens towards the Prince ; the Marquis of

Xardi hurriedly thrusts Lady Danbury's fan into her hand, and joins his father.

The old Duke is a thin, elegant man, full of the refinement of race, with a clean-shaven face; he is dressed simply in evening clothes, with the broad green riband of a Commander of the Imperial Orb slanting across his breast, and the Grand Cross of St. Ladislas round his neck.

Othomar wears his full uniform as commanding officer of the regiment of the Cuirassiers of Xara—silver, red and white; he holds his helmet, with its plume, under his arm; he presses the Duke's hand, speaks cordially to him, but in the naïveté of his young soul he feels bitter remorse gnawing at his conscience, now that he is speaking of Castel Vaza, now that he listens to the cordial protestations of the Duke. Othomar also shakes hands with the Marquis of Xardi.

Then the Duchess approaches and salutes the Crown Prince with her famous courtesy. Lady Danbury envies her her grace, and asks herself how it is possible with those statuesque forms; she cannot deny that the Duchess of Yemena is a splendid woman. . . . Between the Duke and the Duchess, the Prince walks down the row of guests, who bow; the Marquis of Xardi follows with the equerries.

Othomar has seen the Duchess once or twice at the Imperial since his return to Lipara, but never alone. They now exchange courteous words, with official voices and intonations. The groups form once more, as at an intimate rout.

The Duchess walks on with Othomar, till they reach the long conservatory, dimly lighted, duskily green, with the stately palm-foliage of the tall plants, with the delicate fasces of the bamboos, which exude pearls of dew against the square panes. They are silent for a moment, look at one another; and Othomar feels that his emotions for this woman are nothing more than fleeting moments, cloudlets in his soul. The unknown has been revealed to him, but has turned to disillusion. Nevertheless he is thankful to her for what she has given him: the consolation of her passion, when his eyes were still moist with tears. She strengthened him by this consolation and made a man of him. But everything in life is twofold, and his gratitude has a reverse of sin. He sees the Duke in the distance holding an animated conversation, underlined with elegant, precise gestures, with Ducardi; and remorse softly punctures his boyish soul.

And next to his gratitude he feels his dis-illusion. Love! is this love? . . . He feels nothing; nothing new has come into his heart. He sees how deliciously beautiful the Duchess is in her ivory broché, her train edged with dark fur, her bodice cut square, a string of pearls round her neck. The half-light comes past her through the plants with a faery green, with a gentle, slumbering effect and shadows full of mystery; her face, with its delicate smile, stands out against the background of blurred darkness. He recalls her kiss, and the mad embrace of her arms. Yes, it was a divine enervation, an intoxication of the flesh, an unknown giddiness, a physical comfort. But love! was it love? . . . And he must make up his mind. Maybe it is love; and though he feels what is lacking in his soul, he makes up his mind nevertheless. Yes, perhaps that is what it is . . . love.

"And when shall I see Your Highness again?" she whispers.

The question is put crudely and takes him by surprise. But this single second of momentary solitude is so precious to the Duchess that she cannot do otherwise. She observes his surprise, and adores him for his innocence; and her eyes look at him so fixedly, that he replies:

" To-morrow I am dining with the French Ambassador; after that I am going to the opera. . . . Can I find you here at eleven o'clock ? "

He is surprised at the logical sequence of his thoughts, at his question, which sounds so strangely in his ears. But she answers, laughing disconcertedly :

" For God's sake, Highness, not here, at eleven o'clock ! How could we ! . . . But . , . come to . . . Dutri's."

She stammers; she remembers the equerry's luxurious rooms and sees herself there again . . . with others. And in her confusion she does not perceive that she has wounded him deeply, and torn his sensitiveness as though with sharp finger-nails; she fails the more to perceive this, as he answers, confusedly :

" Very well. . . ."

They return, laughing, with their official, colourless voices ; they walk back ; he, so young in his silver uniform, with the helmet, with its drooping plume, under the natural gracefulness of his rounded arm ; she, with her expansive brilliancy, trailing her ivory train, waving her fan of feathers and diamonds up and down against her bosom of white marble. Every eye is turned towards them and observes the Duchess's triumph. : . .

And Othomar now knows that his "love" will become what is called a *liaison*, such as he has heard of in connection with this one and with that one, and has read of in novels. He had not yet imagined such an arrangement. He does not know how he is to tell Dutri that he has made an assignation with the Duchess in his rooms, and when he thinks of the equerry, something of his innate sovereignty is chipped off as little pieces of marble or alabaster might be from a frail column. . . . .

Going up to the Duke and the General, he talks of the approaching manœuvres. He now sees the Duchess standing at a distance, and Mena-Doni bending his Nero-head close to her face. His great antipathy for this man is mingled with jealousy. And while listening smilingly to the Duke of Yemena, he thinks he now knows for certain that his love is love after all, because jealousy is added to it.

III

The next morning, when Othomar was riding alone, he thought the whole time of Dutri. The

difficulty attending his conversation with his
equerry seemed to him unsurmountable. His
heart beat when he met Dutri waiting for him
in the Xaverius Barracks. But the young officer
had the tact to whisper to him, very calmly and
courteously, as though this were the simplest
matter in the world:

" I was talking with the Duchess of Yemena,
Highness. . . . Her Excellency told me that
Your Highness wished to speak to her in private,
and did me the honour . . . Will Your Highness
take this key. . . ? "

Othomar mechanically accepted the key. His
face remained rigid, serious, but inwardly he felt
very much annoyed with the Duchess, and did
not understand how and why she could drag
Dutri into their secret. The ease and simplicity
with which evidently she had done this flashed
across him as something alarming. A confusion
seemed to whirl through his head, as though the
Duchess and Dutri had there blasted, with one
breath, all sorts of firmly established convictions
of his youth. He thought of the old Duke. He
thought all this wrong. He knew that Dutri
was a young profligate; he heard through him
the whole gazette of court scandal, but he had
never believed one-half of what Dutri told him,

and had often told the equerry roughly that he did not like to hear ill spoken like that of people whom they saw every day, people attached to his House. Now it seemed to him that everything Dutri related might be true, and that yet worse things could take place. This key, which had been offered with such courtly directness, with such libertine ease, appeared to him as an object of searing dishonour. He was already ashamed of having put the thing in his pocket. . . .

He went on, however. The key burned him while he spoke with General Ducardi, and, on his return to the Imperial, with his father and Myxila. Before he went to visit the Empress, who was already expecting him, he locked up the key in his writing-table; after which, slowly, his forehead overshadowed, step by step, he went through the long galleries to the Empress's apartments. In the anteroom the lady-in-waiting rose, courtesied, knocked at the door, and opened it.

" His Highness the Duke of Xara. . . ."

Othomar silently made the sign of the Cross, as though he were entering a church.

" May God and His Mother forgive me ! " he murmured between his lips. Then he entered the Empress's room.

She was sitting alone in the large room, at one of the big windows which overlooked the park. She wore a very simple, smooth, dark dress. It struck him how young she looked, and he reflected that she was younger than the Duchess. An aureole of dainty purity seemed to quiver around her tall, slender form like an atmosphere of light, and gave her a distinction that other women did not possess. She smiled to him, and he approached slowly and kissed her hand.

She had not yet seen him that day; she took his head between her cool, slim hands and kissed him.

He sat down on a low chair by her side. Then she passed her hand over his forehead.

" What is it ? " she asked.

He looked at her, and said there was nothing particular. She suspected nothing further; this was not the first time he brought her a clouded forehead. She stroked it once more.

" I promised Papa to have a serious talk with you," she said.

He looked up at her.

" He thought it better that I should talk to you, because it was his idea that I could talk to you more easily. He is, for the rest, very pleased with you, my boy, and rejoices to find that you have such a clear judgment, sometimes, upon various political questions."

This opinion of his father's surprised him.

"And about what did you promise to talk to me?"

"About something very, very important," she said, with a gentle smile. "About your marriage, Othomar."

"My marriage. . . ?"

"Yes, my boy. . . . You will be twenty-two soon. Papa married much later, but he had many brothers. They are dead. Uncle Xaverius is in his priory. And we—Papa and I—are not likely to have any more children, Othomar."

She put her arms about him, and drew him to her. She whispered:

"We have no one but you, my boy, and our little Berengar. And . . . Papa thinks, therefore, that you ought to marry. We want an Heir-Presumptive, a Count of Lycilia. . . ."

His eyes became moist; he laid his head against her.

"Two to become Emperor? Berengar, if I should no longer be there; is not that enough, Mamma?"

She smilingly shook her head in denial. No,

that was not sufficient certainty for the house of Czyrkiski-Xanantria.

"Mamma," he said, gently, "when sociologists speak of the social questions, they deplore that so many children are born among the proletariat, and they even hold the poor parents, who have nothing else but their love, responsible for the greater social misery which they cause through those children. Does not this reproach really affect us also? Or do you think an Emperor so happy?"

Her forehead become overcast.

"You are in one of your gloomy moods, Othomar. For God's sake, my boy, do not give way to them. Do not philosophize so much; accept life as it has been given to you. That is the only way in which to bear it. Do not reflect whether you will be happy later on, when you are Emperor, but accept the fact that you must become Emperor."

"Very well, for myself: but why children, Mamma?"

"What sovereign lets his house die out, Othomar? Do not be foolish. Cling to tradition, that is all in all to us. Do not have such strange ideas on this question. They are not those of a future—I had almost said—autocrat; they are not those of a monarch. You understand, Othomar, do you not . . . ? you must, you must marry. . . ."

Her voice sounded more decided than was its wont—almost hard.

"And, dearest boy," she continued, "bless the circumstances, and marry now, as speedily as possible. Our relations with foreign countries are at this moment such that there are no particular indications as to whom you should marry. You can choose, as it were. For you are the Crown Prince of a great empire, my boy, of one of the greatest empires of Europe. . . ."

He tried to speak; she continued, hurriedly:

"I repeat, you can . . . . very nearly. . . . choose. You don't know how much that means. Appreciate this, appreciate the circumstances. Travel to all the courts of Europe that are worth considering. See with your eyes, make your choice. There are pretty princesses in England, in Austria. . . ."

Othomar closed his eyes an instant, as though exhausted with weariness.

"Later on, Mamma. . . ." he whispered.

"No, my boy," said the Empress; "do not speak of later on, do not put off. Think it over. Think how you will order your journey, and whom you will take with you, and then talk it over with Papa and Myxila. Will you promise ? "

He just pressed his head against her, and promised, with a smile full of fatigue.

"But what is the matter with you, my boy ? " she asked. " What is it ? "

His eyes grew moist.

" I don't know, Mamma. I am so tired sometimes. . . ."

"Are you not well ? "

" Yes, I am well, but I am so tired. . . ."

" But why, my child ? "

He began to sob softly.

"Tired . . . of everything . . . Mamma."

She looked at him long, shook her head slowly, disapprovingly.

" Forgive me, Mamma," he stammered, and he wiped his eyes. " I will not give way to it again. . . ."

" You promised me that once before, Othomar."

He leant his head against her again, like a child.

" No, really," he declared, caressingly. " I shall really resist it. It is not right of me, Mamma. I will employ myself more, I shall grow stronger. I swear to you I shall grow stronger for your sake. . . ."

She again looked long in his eyes, with her pure smile. Utter tenderness went out from her to him; he felt that he would never love any one so much as that mother. Then she took him in both arms, and pressed him close against her.

"I accept your promise, and I thank you . . . my poor boy!" she whispered through her kiss.

At this moment there came a buzz of young voices, as though from birds set free, out of the Park, through the open windows. The tripping of many little feet grated on the gravel. A high, shrill child-voice suddenly resounded with furious words from amongst the others; the others were silent. . . .

The Empress started up with a shock that was electric. She drew herself up hastily, deadly pale.

"Berengar!" she cried, and her voice died away.

"And I shall tell His Majesty what a rascal you are, and then we shall see! Then we shall see, then we shall see. . . !"

The Empress trembled and leant out of the window. She saw ten or eleven little boys; they looked perplexed.

"Where is His Highness?" she asked.

"His Highness is over there, Madam!"

shyly answered a small count, and pointed with
his little finger to the back-court, which the
Empress could not see.

"But what is happening? What a noise to
make! Let His Highness come here at once!
Berengar! Berengar!"

His Highness Berengar was called, and came.
He passed through the little Dukes and Counts,
and looked up at the window through which his
mother was leaning. He was a small, sturdily
built, vigorous little chap; his face was crimson
with indignation, his two small, furious eyes were
like two black sparks.

"Berengar, come here!" cried the Empress.
"What is all this? Why cannot you play without quarrelling?"

"I am not quarrelling, Mamma, but. . . . but I
shall tell Papa. . . . and—and then we shall see!
Then we shall . . ."

"Berengar, come in here at once, through the
palace, at once!" commanded the Empress.

Othomar looked out at the group of boys from
behind the Empress. He saw Berengar excusing
himself with a single word to the biggest little
Duke, and disappearing along the back-court.
After a minute the child entered the room.

"Berengar," said the Empress, "it is very bad

manners to make such a noise in the Park, and just behind the palace too."

The child looked at her with his serious little crimson face.

" Yes, Mamma," he assented gently.

" What happened ? "

Berengar's lips began to tremble.

" It was that wretched sentry. . . ." he began.

" What about the sentry ? "

" He. . . . he did not present arms ! "

" Did not the sentry not present arms ? Why not ? "

" I don't know ! " cried Berengar indignantly.

" But surely he always does ? "

" Yes, but this time he did not. He did the first time when we passed, but not the second time. . . . We were playing ' touch,' and when we ran past him the second time he didn't present ! "

Othomar began to scream with laughter.

" You need not laugh ! " cried Berengar angrily ; " and I shall tell Papa, and then you shall see."

" But Berengar," said the Empress, " did you expect that man to present arms to you every time you ran past him while you were playing ' touch ' ? "

Berengar reflected.

"He might at least have done it the second time. If it had been three, four, or five times. But only the second time! . . . What will the boys have thought of me?"

"Listen, Berengar," said the Empress; "whatever happens, it is not at all proper for you to call people names, whoever it is, nor to make such a noise in the Park, right behind the palace. An Emperor's son never calls names, not even to a sentry. So now you must go straight to that sentry, and tell him you are sorry you lost your temper so."

"Mamma!" cried the child in consternation.

The Empress's face was immovable.

"I insist, Berengar."

The boy looked at her with the greatest astonishment.

"But am I to say that . . . to the sentry, Mamma?"

"Yes."

Clearly Berengar at this moment failed to understand the order of the universe; he suspected for one instant that the revolution had broken out.

"But, Mamma, I can't do that!"

"You must, Berengar, and at once."

"But, Mamma, will Papa approve of it?'

"Certainly, Berengar," said Othomar; "whatever Mamma tells you to do Papa of course approves of."

The boy looked up at Othomar helplessly; his little face grew long, his sturdy little fists quivered. Then he burst into a fit of desperate sobbing.

"Come, Berengar, go," said the Empress again.

The child was still more dismayed by her severity; that was how he always saw her stare at the crowd, but not at her children. And he threw himself with the small width of his helpless little arms into her skirts, embraced her, and sobbed with great, gulping sobs.

" I can't do it, Mamma ! "

" You must, Berengar. . . ."

"And. . . . and. . . . and I sha'n't, I sha'n't !" the boy suddenly screamed, furiously stamping his feet.

The Empress did nothing but look at him, very long, very long. Her reproachful glance crushed the child. He sobbed aloud, and seemed to forget that his little friends outside would be certain to hear His Highness sobbing. He saw there was nothing to be done, that he must do it. He must ! His Imperial Highness Berengar, Marquis of Thracyna, Knight of St. Ladislas, must say he was sorry to a sentry, and one moreover who had wronged him.

His mediæval child's soul was all upset by it.
He understood nothing more. He only saw that
he must, because his mother looked at him with
such a sad look.

"Othomar!" he sobbed out in his despair.
"Othomar! Will . . . . you . . . . go with me
. . . . then? But how am I to do it, how am
I to do it?"

Othomar smiled to him compassionately, and
held out his hand to him. The Empress nodded
to the Princes to go.

"How am I to do it? O God, how am I to do
it?" she still heard Berengar's voice sobbing out
in the anteroom in despair.

Elizabeth had turned deadly pale. As soon as
she was alone, she sank into a chair, her head
falling back. Hélène of Thesbia just then came
in.

"Madam!" cried the young Countess. "What
is it?"

The Empress gave her her hand; Hélène felt
that it was icy cold.

"Nothing, Hélène," she replied; "but Berengar frightened me so terribly. I thought. . . . I
thought they were murdering him!"

And in an hysterical fit of spasmodic sobbing
she threw herself into the Countess's arms.

IV

That night, before Othomar left with his equerries to dine at the French Ambassador's, he detained Dutri.

"I see that Her Excellency the Duchess confides in you very much, Prince," he said curtly. "I will not question as to whether her confidence is well placed. But I assure you of this: that if it should ever appear that it was misplaced, I shall never—now nor at any later period—forget it. . . ."

Dutri looked up strangely; he heard his future Emperor address him. Then he pouted like a sulky child, and said:

"I cannot say that Your Highness is very grateful for the hospitality which I have offered you."

Othomar smiled painfully, and gave him his hand. . . .

"Or that it is kind of Your Highness to threaten me to-day with your displeasure," Dutri continued.

"I know you, Dutri," the Prince said in his ear. "I know your tongue. For that reason alone I warn you. . . . And now, for God's sake,

say no more about this, for all—all of this gives
me pain. . ."

Dutri was silent, thought him child and Prince
in one.   He shrugged his shoulders quietly at
Othomar's incomparable innocence, but he shuddered when he thought of a possible disgrace.   He
had no fortune; his position with the Crown
Prince was his life, his ambition, his all, for now
and for later: when the Prince should be Emperor! . . . How pleased he had been at first
that Alexa had told him everything, that he knew
a secret of his Prince, who never seemed to have
secrets!   A vague pleasure that this secret would
give him a power over his future Emperor had
already flitted through his head, full of light-
hearted calculations.   And now the Prince threat-
ened him, and that power was already frustrated at
its inception!   And Dutri was now almost sorry
that he had learned this secret; he even feared
that the Emperor might come to hear of it, that
he would be visited with the father's displeasure
even before that of the son. . . .

"If only Alexa had not dragged me into it!"
he now complained to himself, with his superficial
fickleness of thought.

But although Dutri was silent, and even contradicted, the Crown Prince's *liaison* was dis-

cussed, possibly only on account of Alexa's triumphant glances whenever Othomar spoke to her for a moment at a reception, at a ball. Nevertheless Dutri's contradiction, while he was known as a tell-tale, brought confusion, and people did not know what to think, nor what to believe.

But Othomar did not feel happy because of this love; the fierce passion of this woman with her fiery glances, who overpowered him one moment with her kisses, and crept before him the next like a slave, and crouched at his feet in humility before her future sovereign, at first astonished him, and in one or two of his fits of despair carried him away, but in the long run aroused in him a feeling of disinclination and op-position. In the young equerry's perfumed room where they met—it was coquettish as a young girl's boudoir, and padded like a jewel-case—he sometimes felt a wish to repulse this woman, for all that she loved him with her strange soul and did not feign her love—to kick her, to beat her. His temperament was not fit for so animal a passion. It was as though she harried his nerves. She revolted him at times. And yet, one single word from him, and she restrained her fierceness, sank down humbly by his side, softly stroked his hand, his head, and he could not doubt that she adored him, perhaps just a little because he was the Crown Prince, but yet also much for himself.

And so April came, and it was almost summer; the King and Queen of Syria were expected. They had been to the Sultan first, and afterwards to the Court of Athens. From Liparia they were to go on to the Northern states of Europe. On the day of their arrival, Lipara fluttered with flags; the Southern sun, already potent, rained down gold upon the white city; the harbour rippled a brilliant blue. A hum of people—tanned faces, many peasants still wearing their multicoloured national dress from Thracyna—swarmed and crowded upon the quays. On the azure of the water, as on liquid metal, the ironclads, which were to welcome the King and Queen and escort them in, steamed out to the mouth of the harbour. There, on the *Xaveria*, with their suite of admirals and rear-admirals, were the two Princes, Othomar and Berengar, and their brother-in-law, the Archduke of Carinthia. Innumerable small boats glided rapidly over the sea, like water-spiders.

A shot from Fort Wenceslas, tearing the vivid ether, announced the moment at which the little fleet met the Syrian yacht and the Eastern potentates left the latter for the *Xaveria*. From the

villas on the quays, from the little boats full of
sight-seers, every glass was directed towards the
blue horizon tremulous with light, on which the
ships were still visibly shimmering. Half an
hour later there rose, as though coming from the
Imperial, the cheers of the multitude, surging
louder and louder towards the harbour. Through
the rows of the Grenadiers, who lined the streets
from the palace to the pavilion where the august
visitors were to land, came the landaus, driven by
postillions, in which sat Their Majesties. These
were followed by the carriages of the two sisters,
the Archduchess of Carinthia and Thera, and of
the suite.

The fleet, with the Syrian yacht in its centre,
had steamed back into the harbour. Across
the body-guard formed by the Throneguards,
through the purple draperies and the flags, the
crowd were able to see something of the meeting
of the sovereigns in the pavilion. They shouted
out vivats ! and then the procession drove to the
Imperial, the Emperor with the King of Syria in
the first carriage, the Empress with the Queen
in the next ; after those, the landaus with the
Princes and Princesses and the suite.

A succession of festivals and displays ensued.
After the tragedies of the inundations and of the

parliamentary crisis, a mood of merriment blew over the capital, as it glittered in the sun, and lasted till late in the lighted rooms and parks of the Imperial. This merriment was because of the Eastern Queen. The King of Syria had possibly a few drops of the blood of Solomon still flowing through his veins. But the Queen was not of Royal descent. She was the daughter of one of the Syrian magnates, and her mother's name was not mentioned in the Almanach de Gotha. That mother was doubtless a favourite of dubious noble descent, but who she had been exactly, nobody knew. A light-o'-love from Paris or Vienna, who had stranded in the East and made her fortune in the harem of some great Syrian ? A half-European, half-Egyptian dancer from a Cairene or Alexandrian dancing-house ? Whoever she was, her fortunate daughter, the Queen of Syria, showed an unmistakable mixture of blood, something Eastern and European at once. Next to the genuine Semitic type of the King, who had a certain nervous dignity in his half-European, half-Oriental uniform, which glittered with diamonds, the Queen, small, fat, plump, pale-brown, had the exuberant smiles, the restless movement of the limbs, the turning head and rolling eyes of a woman of colour. Already her first appearance, as she sat in the carriage, next to the delicate figure of the Empress Elizabeth, in a gaudy travelling dress and a hat with huge feathers, bowing and laughing on every side with profuse amiability, had affected the Liparians, accustomed to the calm haughtiness of their own rulers, with a merriment that seemed inextinguishable. The Queen of Syria became the universal topic, and in reference to her all conversations were accented with a smile of wickedness. Withal she seemed so entirely good-natured that it was impossible to say any harm of her, and people only amused themselves about her. They remembered that the Syrians had made fabulous donations at the time of the inundations. And the merriment that blew over Lipara was a Southern merriment, without malice and with sheer good laughter and bursts of delight, because the Liparians had never seen so funny a queen.

The great manœuvres took place on the Champ de Mars. The King accompanied the Emperor and the Princes on horseback, with a swarm of European and Oriental aides-de-camp. Their consorts with their suite watched the march-past from landaus. Berengar marched bravely with his company of Grenadiers, in which he was a

lieutenant, as well as he could march with his
short little legs, and stiffened his small features,
so as not to betray the difficulty it cost him to
keep pace with the long marching step. The
Hussars astonished the Syrian monarch by the
understanding they had with their horses, when
in wild career they threw themselves half off, and
in still more rapid rushes picked up a flag from
the ground, swung themselves up again with a
yell, and waved the bunting. The Africans exe-
cuted their showy fantasias, brandished their
spears, which flashed like loosened sheaves of
sunbeams, and came fluttering on in clouds of
white burnooses and dust, in which their negro
heads clustered darkly with endless black patches,
and their eyes glistened.

Moreover a tournament, garden parties, races,
regattas, athletic sports and fireworks. Lipara
was one city of pleasure. Every day it was
traversed by royal processions, the array of
uniforms glittered like live gold, the Imperial
landaus rattled in the sun with the spokes of
their wheels flashing through the light dust which
flew up from the flagged pavement of the town.
Gleamed most of all, like drops of white flame,
the diamonds which the Syrian pair wore even
in the streets. At night, when the sun ceased

shining, there gleamed over the white town, vague with evening, over its violet harbour, festoons of salamanders and gaudy bridges of fire, factitiously bright beneath the silent silver glances of the stars; fireworks fell hissing into the water, upon which the boats became black; they left behind them a slight, oppressive savour of gunpowder in the night.

In the great Hall of Columns the ceremonial banquets followed upon one another, with a display of gold plate of fabulous value. The Queen of Syria wore her curious, theatrical dresses, her broad bosom always crossed by the blue riband of an order covered with badges, and with tall plumes, hung with small diamonds, in her hair. She talked animatedly, thankful for the kindness of her Liparian friends, for the enjoyment and for the cheering. Her profuse gestures enlivened everybody, brought fun into the Liparian stateliness, full of etiquette. Elizabeth herself could not but laugh at them. The Queen played her Royal part with the self-possession of a bad but good-natured actress. She spoke to everybody, spread in little atoms over everybody the amiability of her small, soft, brown majesty. Next her sat the King, looking dignified, as wise as Solomon. The Emperor praised him for a sensible monarch with broad views; the King had already paid many visits to Europe. The Syrian equerries were distinguished also, calm, rather stiff, forming themselves upon Western manners; the Queen's ladies-in-waiting wore the trains of their Paris or London dresses a little strangely, but still were slender in them, brown and attractive, with little curly heads, and long almond-shaped eyes: they would have looked better nevertheless in draped gold-gauze.

The Syrians remained twelve days before going on to Italy. It was the last evening but one: in the Imperial a suite of fourteen rooms had been lighted up around the great ballroom for a ball. Three thousand invitations had been sent out. In the fore-court and in the neighbouring main-streets stood the Grenadiers.

The ballroom was at the back of the palace; the tall, balconied windows were opened and looked across their balustrades upon the shadows of the park of plane-trees. The band resounded from out of the groups of palms in the gallery. The Imperial quadrille had been formed in the centre of the room: the Emperor with the Queen, the King and the Empress, the Archduke of Carinthia and Thera, and Othomar with the Archduchess. The other official quadrilles

formed their figures around them. Hundreds
of guests looked on.

From the coruscating rock-crystal of the
chandeliers, the electric light flowed in white
patches from the high dome, gilded along the
inlaid marble walls and porphyry pillars of the
ballroom, and poured in millions of scintillations
upon the smooth facets of the jewels, on the gold
of the uniforms and court-dresses, on the shimmering white brocades of the trains : for white
was prescribed : all the ladies were in white, and
the snow of the velvets, the lily glow of the satins
were bright with light. One blinding whirl of
lustre went through the immense room with its
changing glamours. For the light never stood
still, continually changed its brightest spot, turned
the ball into one kaleidoscope of brilliancy. The
light gilded each bit of gold-lace, let itself be
caught in each brilliant, remained hanging in
every pearl. The music seemed to be one with
that light : the brass resounded like gold.

The Duchess of Yemena stood amongst a
group of diplomats and equerries ; she rose up
tall in her beauty, which was statuesquely
splendid in this changing illumination. She
seemed supernaturally large through the heavy
Watteau plait which trailed off from her back in

white broché. She wore her tiara of emeralds
and brilliants, and the same green stones sparkled
in a great spray of jewels that blossomed over her
bodice.

The Emperor approached her; she drooped
down with her famous courtesy, and Oscar spoke
jestingly to her for a moment. When the Emperor had passed on, she saw the Crown Prince
approaching. She courtesied again, he bowed
smilingly and offered his arm. Slowly they went
through the ballroom.

"I have something important to communicate
to you," he whispered, in a conversational voice.

He could not withdraw with her; they would
be missed. So they continued to walk through
the rooms.

"I have not seen you for so long . . . alone!"
she whispered, reproachfully, in the same voice.
"And what did . . . Your Highness desire to say
to me?"

They spoke cautiously, with the smile of cold
conversation on their lips, deadening the sound of
their voices between them, casting indifferent
glances around, to see whether they could not be
overheard.

"Something . . . that I have long wanted to
tell you. . . . A decision that I have to take." . . .

The words came crumbling in fragments from his lips, and not sounding with their true accent, from caution. She perceived that he was about to communicate some great piece of news to her. She trembled without knowing why. . . . He himself did not know whether what he was doing was cruel or not : he did not know this woman well enough for that. But he did not know that he had purposely chosen this difficult moment for his interview, because he was uncertain as to how she would bear it. How she would bear it in a *tête-à-tête*, when she would be able to give way to her passion. Here he knew how she would bear it : smilingly, as a woman of the world, although it turned to anguish for her. Possibly nevertheless he was cruel. . . . But it was now too late : he must go through with it.

She looked up at him, moving the feathers of her fan. He continued :

" A decision. . . . When our Syrian guests are gone . . . I . . . am going on a journey. . . ."

" Where to, Highness ? "

" To . . . the different courts . . . of Europe . . . ."

She asked nothing more ; her smile died away ; then she smiled again, like an automaton. She asked nothing more, because she well knew what

it meant when a Crown Prince went on a journey
to the different courts of Europe. That meant
a bridal progress. And she only said, and her
voice could not but sound plaintively:

" So soon. . . ."

So soon ! . . . Was her Imperial romance to
last so short a time ? She had indeed known
that this might be the end of it, for she knew
him to be too pure to retain her by the side of
a young consort. Also she had pictured an end
like this after a year, two years perhaps, she
withdrawing herself, and she had pictured to herself
that she would do so without any feeling of spite
against her young Empress to be. But now !
So soon ! Barely a few weeks ! So short a
time as that no romance of her life had yet
endured ! She felt an aching melancholy; a
moisture came over her eyes like a mist, and
the lights of the ballroom shimmered before her
like water. She constantly forgot to smile,
but so soon as she thought of it, she smiled
again.

" So soon . . .? "

" It must be. . . ."

Yes, it must be, it could not be otherwise. For
her, this was the end of her life. She felt no
despair because of this end; only a smarting

melancholy. It was the end. After this Imperial
romance, no other. Oh no, never more. She
would sacrifice her youth to it ; she would bring
her stepdaughters into society. She would be
grateful that she had lived, and would now grow
old. But old. . . . She was still so young, she
still felt herself so young. She now first perceived
how she loved her Crown Prince. And she would
have liked to be away, out of the brilliancy of
that entertainment, to embrace him once more,
alone, for the last time. . . . Oh, this melancholy
because everything must end, as though nothing
were any more than a perfume that evaporates
. . . .

"I trust you, madame . . ." he now said ;
"I hope you will say nothing of this journey.
You understand, it is all still a secret ; no choice
has been made yet . . . it has only been talked
of with Their Majesties and Myxila. I can trust
you, can I not ? "

She smilingly nodded yes.

"But I wished nevertheless to tell you at
once," he continued.

She smiled again. At this moment a strange
storm seemed to burst out behind the palace,
under the palace, where . . .? Right through
the resonance of the music and the shimmering

of the light, a crash of thunder shook and rolled on. It was as though the lightning had struck the palace, for immediately afterwards, through the open windows, one heard from one of the back wings of the palace a rattling clatter of stones, which seemed tossed into the air, of great rafters, which came down noisily and roughly, of sherds of glass, which seemed to be springing to pieces shrilly on every side. . . .

The music was suddenly silenced. The uniforms, the court trains rushed on to the open balconies, which looked out upon the park, but the night was dark, the park was hushed. A couple of last rafters seemed to be still falling, with a last downcrash of stones. . . .

In the bright glare of the electric light the faces turned deathly pale, as the faces of corpses. The eyes stared at one another affrightedly. The Duchess half sank against Othomar, when she saw Elizabeth rushing past her with wild, vacant eyes, and out at a door; her long, white velvet train trailing helplessly after her, round the corner. The Grand Mistress followed her, and Hélène of Thesbia. The Emperor appeared to be giving the chamberlains hurried instructions, and then he also left the ballroom, with a few officers.

Shortly afterwards the music again burst out from the loggia of the gallery. Many equerries and aides-de-camp were seen bowing to their partners; the ladies rising tremblingly. The ball was continued; the uniforms and trains glittered as before in the windings of the waltz. But the smiles seemed to have been wiped away from the features, and the deadly pale faces of the dancers turned the ball into a Dance of Death.

Leoni bowed shivering before Othomar.

" A dynamite explosion, down in the cellars of the West back wing. The ante-rooms of His Majesty's private apartments are destroyed. His Majesty requests Your Highness to make every effort to carry on the ball. All officers and ladies of the Court are commanded to dance."

The Duchess clutched Othomar's arm, almost swooning. The rumour spread around them. The equerries dragged their partners along half swooning. Two could be seen carried fainting away. The Queen of Syria stood vacantly beside the Archduke of Carinthia, who put his arm round her heavy waist to dance. She seemed not yet able to make up her mind.

Othomar passed his arm round the Duchess.

" My God, I cannot . . ." she stammered. " For God's sake, Highness, I cannot . . . ! "

" We must," he said. " His Majesty wishes
it. . . ."

" His Majesty wishes, . . ." she repeated.

Her legs quivered under her as though with
electric thrills. Then she let him take her, and
they danced. Every one danced.

The Empress had rushed up the stairs and
along the galleries to the bedroom floor. She did
not see that two ladies were following her: she
tore open a door.

" Berengar! " she screamed.

The young Prince's bedroom was lighted. The
child had half risen, in his little shirt, from his
camp-bed. His valet and a tire-woman stood in
dismay in the middle of the room.

" Berengar! " the Empress gasped out, re-
joicingly, when she saw him unharmed.

She threw her arms around him, pressed him
to her bosom.

" Oh, Mamma, you hurt me! " cried the child,
indignantly.

Her jewels had scratched a drop of blood from
his little bare chest. She now embraced him
more gently, with nervous sobs that choked in
her throat. A diamond tuft of ostrich feathers
fell to the ground; the tire-woman picked them
up with nerveless fingers.

" Mamma, are they blowing up the palace ? "

" No, Berengar, no, it is nothing. . . ."

" Mamma, I want to go to it! I must see what is the matter."

" Berengar. . . ."

The door stood open; the Emperor entered, calmly. The ladies stood in the corridor, waiting for the Empress. . . .

" Papa, may I go with you and look ? "

" No, Berengar, there is nothing to see. Go to sleep. . . ."

Then he offered his arm to Elizabeth.

" Madam . . . ." he said, tranquilly.

She threw him an imploring glance. He continued to hold out his arm to her. Then she kissed the boy once more, soothed him down to sleep.

" Wait a moment . . . ." she stammered to Oscar.

She went to the glass; the tire-woman with awkward fingers fastened the jewelled tuft to the edge of the low-cut bodice, folded out the square train.

" I am ready," said the Empress to Oscar, in a dead voice.

She took his arm, the Emperor just pressed her hand, and they nodded once more to Berengar, and went.

Arm-in-arm the Imperial pair appeared for the second time at the ball. The Empress was pale, but smiled. She was magnificent, delicate with dainty majesty in the trailing white velvet, upon which, on the bodice and over the front of the skirt, flickered diamond ostrich feathers in the shape of fleur-de-lys. An Empress's coronet of brilliants crowned her small round head.

It was two o'clock. Generally the sovereigns were accustomed to stay till one o'clock at the Court balls. The Queen of Syria, however, in her exuberant love of life, had begged them to stay longer. They had consented. Had they left at one o'clock, the explosion would have taken place at the moment that Oscar would probably just have entered his own rooms. They had first talked of the ante-rooms only: but it would appear now that great damage had been done also to the Emperor's study itself.

Supper commenced. They supped in a large hall; from each table rose a palm-tree, and the hall was thus turned into a forest of palms. The floor was strewn with gold sand, that powdered the trains as their wearers walked upon it. Electric light shone through the long leaves like moonshine. In this moonshine the faces remained deadly white, like patches of chalk, above the glittering crystal and all the gold plate. The music clattered with great cymbal-strokes of brass.

V

TO HER MAJESTY OLGA, QUEEN OF GOTHLAND.

IMPERIAL, LIPARA,
—— *May*, 18——.

MY DEAREST SISTER,—At last I can write you the letter which I have already long written you in my thoughts. The agitation of our good Syrians is over, and Lipara has calmed down. But my reflections are nothing but sadness. And this is why, Olga.

I fear that Othomar is more ill than the doctors believe. He has become thinner, and looks very ill. He never complains much, but yet he told me lately that he often felt tired. The doctors are of opinion that he needs rest for a time, and recommend a long sea-voyage. His journey through Europe, of which I wrote you recently, will thus have to be postponed. And now I want to ask you this favour.

I know that Herman is soon going to make a long voyage on the *Viking* to India, Japan, and

America, and it would at this moment be my
dearest wish if Othomar might accompany him.
When the doctors advised a sea-voyage, I spoke
about it with Oscar, but we came to no decision.
My child, you must know, has no friend of his
own age, Olga, and that made me so sad, and we
did not know how, nor with whom, we would
send him on this voyage in a way that would be
pleasant for him, and that would not be a solitary
banishment from our circle.   He is on very good
terms with his equerries, but yet that is not what
I should desire : a cordial, mutual, confidential
friendship with some one of his own age with
whom he would be some time together, solely
with a view to enjoyment and relaxation.

I know very well that it is a little my own
child's fault, and due to a certain incapacity
for spontaneity and attraction.   But yet he has
qualities for which he could be very much loved,
if they were known, if he let them come out.   Is
it not so, you are fond of him too, Olga, and it is
not only my own blind mother's love which finds
my child lovable and sympathetic ?   And that is
why I should be so very glad if Herman would
take him with him, and learn to know him better ;
who knows whether they would not then get to
love one another.   Othomar has already told

me that on their tour through the North of
Liparia they came much nearer together than
they had thought they would, but it was a busy
time : every moment was filled with duties and
occupations, and they had no time to talk
together and get to know one another. But
yet, in such a difficult period of joint labour, you
can learn to know one another even without
talking; however this may be, they have already
become more friendly; formerly it used to be
antipathy between them, Olga, to my utter
sorrow; they would even not meet one another,
even outwardly there was nothing but coolness
between them ; oh, how unhappy all this used to
make me, when I saw our boys so opposed to one
another, and remembered how *we* used to be,
Olga, when we were young girls together in our
beautiful old castle near Bucharest ! How we
lived bound up in each other ! Olga, Olga, how
terribly long ago that all is ! Our parents are
now dead, our brothers dispersed, the castle is
deserted, and we are separated : when do we see
one another ? Scarcely a couple of days now and
then, when we meet somewhere for a wedding of
relations : and then always restless days, when
we can see nothing of one another. Then, sometimes, not even every year, a fortnight either in

Gothland or here. You sometimes reproach me that I, who am so fond of Gothland, come so seldom to you, but it is always for the same reason. Othomar does not care to leave Liparia, and I cannot leave my husband. I can be strong when I am by his side, but alone I am so weak, Olga. That anything might happen to him in which I should not share increases my dread unbearably. I felt that again recently, when I was with Thera at Altara; our visit was announced and binding upon us, was it not, and however unwilling I was to leave Oscar, I was compelled to go. It was just at that trying period; Lipara was in state of siege! But Oscar wished me to go, and I went. Oh, how I suffered at that time!

But I am becoming used to my fears, I do not complain, and I accept life as it is given to us ; and I only hope that my boy will also learn to accept it thus. Perhaps he will learn. It is indeed difficult for him, for he will have to do more than his mother, who, as a woman, can be much more passive, and it is easier to learn to acquiesce passively than actively. But the Saints will surely give him strength later to bear his lot and his crown ; this I rely upon. And yet, O Olga, immeasurable is my melancholy that we are rulers! But let me not continue in this strain; it enfeebles one, it is not right, it is not right. . . .

There is besides a secret reason why I should like to get Othomar away from Lipara, although it always costs me so much to part from my darling. There seems after all to be some truth in those rumours about the Duchess of Yemena: Oscar asked Myxila about it, and he could not deny it, and even said that it was generally known. I do my best not to take it too much too heart, Olga, but I think it a terrible thing. O God, let me not think or write about it any more; otherwise it will go whirling so in my poor head. What can my child see in a woman who is older than his mother? How terrible that sort of thing is in the world, Olga, and how can there be such women, whom we can never understand, for, after all, temperament is not everything : for every woman has her heart, and in that we ought all to find one another again, but it would seem not to be so. In my sadness about this, I prefer to assume that that woman loves my boy, and therefore deceives her husband. Oh, it is so wicked also of my child; why need he be like that, he who is otherwise so good! I just assume now that she loves him ; lately it was

14

my last Drawing-room, the function with which, as you know, our winter season ends, and when she came up to me, and bowed before me, and pressed her lips to my hand, she must have felt my disapproval and my sorrow radiating from my fingers, for she drew herself up from her courtesy, with a despairing anguish in her eyes, and a sort of sob in her throat! I continued to look at her coldly, but all the same I pitied her, Olga, for when a woman of our world is able to control herself so little in the presence of her Empress at a ceremonial moment, her soul must have sustained a severe shock: do you not agree with me in this?

We are now quiet. In a week we are going to our summer quarters in Xara, at Castel Xaveria; it is already becoming very warm here. I should so like to have your answer before we leave, and know how Herman takes my request. I know that he is very fond of me, and will doubtless gladly grant it, and that he will try for my sake to like Othomar; and let me hasten to add, that it is also *Othomar's* dearest wish that he should go with Herman. The sea-voyage did not at first attract him in the least, because he knew of no one to take with him, and he said he preferred to go with us to Castel Xaveria, but when I mentioned Herman, he joined entirely in my plan.

Olga, what will the summer bring us? Peace or not? I dare not hope. The winter has been horrible; our Northern governments have not yet recovered from the disasters. The misery there is not to be mitigated. There are dangerous typhoid fevers prevalent, and there have been many cases of cholera. The strikes in the East are now over, but I am so afraid of that repression with rough violence. Oh, if everything could only be done with gentleness! That attempt upon Othomar and the explosion at the last ball have also made me so ill. How I should love to see you, and take you in my arms: can you not come to Castel Xaveria this summer? You would give me such intense, intense pleasure!

Kiss Siegfried and all yours for me. Answer me soon, will you not? I embrace you with both my arms.

ELIZABETH.

CHAPTER IV

I

AUGUST, on the Baltic. The gray billows curl up against the rocks with high, round crests of foam. The sky above is one round dome, through which drive great mountain-ranges of clouds, a whitish gray. They come on slowly, fill the firmament with their changing shadowy masses, like chains of rocks and Alps floating through the air, and driving slowly on again, and away. The sea has a narrow beach, with many crumbling rocks; quite close at hand there looms a sombre green pine-wood. With the gloom of the pine-wood for a background, as it were straight out of the rocks rises old Altseeborgen. It is a weather-beaten castle, at which the writhing waves seem to gnaw; its three tall, uneven towers soar round and massive into the sky. The road to the castle runs up out of the wood terrace-wise, broad and slanting, leads to the back square, where the main entrance is. Round the castle the wide granite terraces are cut in stairs, with their rugged balustrades, whose freestone is eaten into by the salt air. These terraces have a wider view over the sea in proportion as they rise higher; seen from the topmost terrace, the sea lies up against the beach, to right and left, in one great expanse, strangely mobile, a living element. Across the sea the South winds blow upon the castle; the pine-wood shelters it to a great extent from the Northern gusts.

From the tallest tower flaps an imposing standard: two stripes of yellow and between them one of white with the dark blazon of the castel-lated fortress which forms the arms of Gothland. It floats there on the sunless morning like a smile in the sky; it swells out, and falls limply down again, and again lets itself be blown high up by the wind, which comes swinging lustily over the water.

A young man and a young girl are walking on the beach; they talk, smile, look at one another. She is taller than he, very fair; under her little sailor-hat a few of her brown hairs, tinged with ruddy gold, entangled by the wind, blow across

her face; she keeps on smoothing them away.
She wears a simple blue serge skirt and a white
serge blouse; a broad leather belt around her waist.
Her dainty little feet are constantly being un-
covered by the wind, in their black silk stockings
and yellow leather shoes.   In one hand she care-
lessly swings a pair of gloves.

The young man wears a light, check summer
suit and a straw hat.   He is short, slender; his
black eyes have a look of gentle melancholy.   He
appears to be telling the girl by his side a tale of
travel; she listens to him with her smile.

Round about them, in spite of the wind, the
atmosphere is full of peace.   Walking along the
beach, they come past the castle, pass round
behind it, and look up.   From one of the windows
somebody gaily waves a hand, and calls out something.   They try to hear, with their hands to their
ears, but they shrug their shoulders: the wind has
blown the words away.   They wave their hands
once more, and go on.

They do not go far, however, always along the
beach.   Yonder lies the fishing village, lie a
couple of small villas, lodging-houses.   One of
them seems just to have been taken by a large
family, for the holiday month no doubt; a hum of
voices issues from it, children chase one another

along the beach; a tiny girl bumps up in her course against the young man.

"Hullo there," he says, pleasantly, and laughs; laughing they go on.

The children run further on. A fisherman comes along with his nets, grins good-naturedly, and mutters a greeting. A fat lady in the verandah has been watching the young people inquisitively; she sees the fisherman touch his cap, she detains him.

"Who are that lady and gentleman?"

The fisherman points good-naturedly to Altseeborgen.

"From the castle."

"But who are they?" asks the lady, alarmed.

"Well, the gentleman is the Prince of Liparia, and the young lady is an Austrian Princess," says the fisherman, as if it could be nobody else.

The lady looks in dismay after the Princely pair, and then in despair at her running children. The young people are just turning back in their walk to and fro; they are now laughing still more merrily, and are hastening a little more quickly towards the castle, as though they had delayed too long. The lady, still pale, does not dare to make any excuses, but makes a low bow; she receives a pleasant salute in return.

II

The Royal Family of Gothland were accustomed to spend the whole of the summer at
Altseeborgen. The beach was particularly suited
for the establishment of a seaside resort round
about the fishing village, but King Siegfrid had
never been willing to hear of this: the beach and
the village were Royal domains; only a couple of
humble lodging-houses had been permitted to rise
up. Generally in the summer these were visited
by one or two middle-class families with their
children. Altseeborgen should never become a
modern bathing-place, however excellent the
elegant world might think it for summer display, lying in the immediate neighbourhood of
the Royal castle.

But the Gothlandic family made a point of
carefully guarding the freedom of their summer
lives. They lived there for four months, without
the etiquette of palaces, in the greatest simplicity.
They formed a numerous family, and there were
always many visitors. The King attended to
affairs of State at the castle in homely fashion.
His grandchildren sometimes ran into his study
while he was discussing important matters with

the Prime Minister who on certain days came down to Altseeborgen. He just patted them on their light, curly heads, and sent them away to play, with a caress. There were there the Crown Prince Gunther, and the Crown Princess Sofie, a German Princess, Duke and Duchess of Wendeholm; they had four children, a girl and three boys. After the Duke came Prince Herman, after him Princess Wanda, twenty years old; after her, the younger Princes, Olaf and Christofel. Furthermore there were always there two old Princesses, sisters of the King, widows of German Princes. From all the courts of Europe, which are like one great family, different members came from time to time to stay, and brought with them the *nuance* of a different nationality, something exotic in sound of voice and in state of morals, so far as this was not merged in their cosmopolitanism.

Othomar had been three months at sea with Herman; they had touched at India, China, Japan, and America. The voyage had been incognito, so that they might avoid any official reception, and Othomar had borne no other title than that of Prince Czykirski. The voyage had done Othomar much good ; he even felt so well, that he had written to the Empress Elizabeth to say that he would like to stay some time longer in the family circle at Altseeborgen, but that he would afterwards undertake his already long-proposed journey to the European courts.

Their easy life together had done much to bring the cousins nearer to one another. Herman had learnt to see in Othomar, beneath his stiffness and lack of ease, a young Crown Prince who looked askance upon his future, but who possessed much reasonableness, was willing to learn to acquiesce in life and to fortify himself for his future heavy yoke of empire. He understood Othomar and sympathized with him. He himself took a vital pleasure in life; merely to breathe was an enjoyment; his existence as a second son, with only his naval duties, which he loved, as a descendant of the old sea-kings can hereditarily love them, opened up to him a perspective of nothing but one long freedom from care; that he was a king's son gave him nothing but satisfaction, but delight, and he appreciated his high estate with jovial pleasure; he skimmed off the cream from a chalice out of which Othomar would afterwards drink wormwood. If at first he used to compare Othomar with his brother, the Duke of Wendeholm, and a Crown Prince too, of Gothland he, Herman now compared them no longer; his judgment had become more reasonable:

he understood that no comparison was possible. Liparia was a redoubtable, almost despotic Empire ; the people in the South always very changeable, always kept in check by force, on account of their childish uncertainty as to what, in their capriciousness, they should do next ; the Gothlanders, calmly Liberal in temperament, without undue vehemence, ranged themselves peacefully, with their already long-established, ample Constitution, round King Siegfried, whom they called the Father of his Country. That Gunther was not displeased at one day having to wear the crown, was this a reason why Othomar should be without his fear ? Did Othomar not possess the gentler qualities which are valued in the narrow circle of intimate surroundings and arouse esteem among a few sympathetic natures rather than that fiercer brilliancy of character, which makes its possessor stand out in clear relief in high places, and awakes admiration in the multitude ? Was this boy, with his soul full of scruples, his nostalgia after justice, his yearning for love, his easily wounded sensitiveness, was he the son of his ancestors, the descendant of Berengar the Strong, Wenceslas the Cruel, of the Valiant Xaveria, or was he not rather the child of his gentle mother alone ?

It was not in Herman's way to reflect much
and long on this, but it came to him suddenly,
brusquely, like a new view that is opened out in
a brighter light. And what had been antipathy
in him became compassion, friendship, and astonishment at the disposition of the system of the
universe, which knew not what else to do with a
soul like Othomar's but crush it beneath a crown.

The simple family life at Altseeborgen worked
on Othomar like a cure. He felt himself reviving
amidst natural surroundings, his humanity deve-
loping wide and free. Accustomed to the ceremonial life of the Imperial, whose etiquette the
Emperor Oscar kept strictly in hand, the almost
homely simplicity of his Gothlandic relations
surprised him at first, and delighted him later.
In former years, it is true, he had now and then
spent a short time at Altseeborgen, but never
long enough to be able to count himself, as now,
entirely one of themselves.

Besides Othomar there were at this moment no
other visitors except the Archduchess Valérie, a
niece of the Emperor of Austria. Did the young
people suspect anything, or not? Were their
names coupled together by the younger Princes
and Princesses? Apparently it would seem not;
on a solitary occasion the Princess Sofie or

Wanda had found it necessary to quiet her young brothers with a glance. And yet it was with a serious intention that the Queen of Gothland, in concert with the Emperor of Liparia and Valérie's parents—the Archduke Albrecht and the Archduchess Eudoxie, who lived at the castle of Sigismundingen—had brought the young people together. The Emperor Oscar would doubtless have preferred one of the young Russian Grand Duchesses, a niece of the Czar, for his daughter-in-law, but the difference in religion was always an insurmountable obstacle; and meantime the Emperor, in spite of his preference, had no objections to the Austrian alliance.

Perhaps Othomar and Valérie guessed these intentions, but the secret of them caused no constraint between them; they were on both sides so accustomed to hearing the names of well-known princes or princesses in connection with theirs, and even to see them mentioned in the papers: announcements of betrothals that were immediately contradicted; they had even jested together about the number of times that public opinion had married them out, each time with somebody else; sometimes even there were surprises for themselves, which they found in the newspapers and made much fun of. They paid no heed therefore to one of the rare mischievous remarks of Prince Olaf or Prince Christofel, sturdy lads of seventeen and fifteen, who thought it sociable to tease. And withal Queen Olga, sensibly and reasonably, did not bring the least influence to bear upon them. She had invited them at the same time, but she did nothing more. Perhaps she observed silently how they behaved towards one another, and wrote just once about it to her sister, but she kept quite outside the meshes which were to be weaved between their two crowned lives. Yet it was difficult for her to do so. She was fond of Valérie, and thought that this marriage would be in every way good. But added to that there came urgent letters from Sigismundingen, and even from Vienna, where nothing better was wished for than to see the young Archduchess Duchess of Xara. For this, in addition to the Austrian court attaching value to a renewed alliance with Liparia, there were still other reasons, of a more intimate nature.

III

The sun had broken out in the afternoon, and made the gray of the sky and the water turn blue with the misty blueness of a Northern summer. The sea glowed and put on scales of gold; the weatherbeaten castle stood roasting its broad granite pile in the sun, as an old man does his back. On the top terrace, which gave into the great hall through three glass doors, the striped canvas awning was let down. Rugs lay on the ground. Princess Sofie and the Archduchess Valérie sat in great wicker-work chairs, painting in water-colours. From the hall sounded, monotonously, the soft exercises of Princess Elizabeth, the Crown Princess's eldest daughter, who was practising. The Princess Wanda sat on the ground, and romped a trifle boisterously with her two youngest nephews, Erik and Karl. On a long wicker chair lay Prince Herman, with both legs up; next to him, a little table heaped up with newspapers and periodicals, some of which had fallen to the ground; a great tumbler of sherry-cobbler on the wicker ledge of his chair; the blue smoke rose from a cigarette between his fingers.

Sofie and Valérie compared their sketches, and laughed. They looked at the sky, which was cut right in two by the awning; the clouds, woolly white, surged one above the other; the sea was dazzling with its golden scales, like a giant cuirass.

"What are you painting there?" asked Herman, who was turning over the leaves of an illustrated paper.

"Clouds," replied Valérie, "nothing but clouds. I have persuaded Sofie to make studies of clouds with me. Presently, if your're not too lazy, you must come and look at my album"—she gave a little laugh—"it contains nothing but clouds!"

"Ha!" said Herman, drawlingly. "How strange. . . ."

"Yes," said Sofie, dreamily; "clouds are very nice, but you never know how to catch them, they change every instant."

"Erik, just ask Aunt Valérie for her album for me," asked Herman.

"No, no," cried Wanda, "go and fetch it yourself, lazybones. . . ."

But Erik wanted to go all the same: there came a struggle. Wanda held the little boy tight in her arms, Karl joined in; they romped, and Wanda, laughing, fell over sideways on the ground.

"But Wanda!" said Sofie, reprovingly.

Valérie stood up and went to Herman.

"All the same you don't see my clouds, you lazy boy. I suppose I must take pity on you. Look here. . . ."

Herman now suddenly pulled himself up, took the album.

" How funny ! " he said. " Yellow, and white, and violet, and pink. All sunsets ! "

"And sunrises. I dare say I see more of them than you do ! "

" The things you see in clouds, Valérie ! It's astonishing. How one person differs from another. I should never take it into my head to go and sketch clouds. You ought to come and travel with me one day ; then you could make whole collections of clouds."

" Why did you not propose that earlier ? " said Valérie, jestingly. " Then I might have gone with Xara."

" But where is Othomar ? " said Herman.

Valérie replied that she did not know. . . .

Herman sipped his sherry-cobbler. Wanda wanted a taste, but Herman told her that she could ring for a glass for herself, and refused. Wanda insisted ; he took hold of her wrists.

" But Wanda ! " Sofie said again reprovingly, heavily ; she drew her hand over her forehead, and laid down her brush.

Wanda laughed merrily.

" But Wanda ! " she imitated Sofie, and they all laughed at Sofie ; Sofie laughed too.

"Did I talk like that?" she asked, with her drowsy voice. "I don't know, I get so sleepy here, so lazy. . . ."

They were now all making merry at Sofie, when voices sounded from the hall, shrill old voices. It was the two dowagers with Othomar; the old ladies talked in a courtly, mincing way to the young Prince, who brought them chairs. The aunts had had a siesta after lunch; they now made their reappearance, with tapestry-work in large reticules. All greeted them with much respect, beneath which lurked a spark of mischief.

"*Pardon, lieber Herzog*," murmured the old Princess Elsa, the elder; "I would rather have that little chair. . . ."

The Princess Marianne also wanted a small, straight chair; the old ladies thanked Othomar with an obeisance for his gallantry, sat stiffly down, and began their embroidery: great coats-of-arms for chair-backs. They were very stately, with clear-cut but wrinkled faces, gray *tours*, and a head-dress of black lace; they wore crackling watered-silk gowns, of old-fashioned cut. Now and then they exchanged a quick, sharp word, with a sudden cackling movement of their sharp cockatoo-profiles; they looked thoughtfully for a moment out to sea, as though they were bound to see something important arriving from out of the distance ; then they went on working again. . . . Their old-fashioned, stately, tightly-laced, shrivelled figures made a strange effect in conjunction with the easiness of the young people in their simple serge summer suits : they made the tangled hair and dishevelled blouse of the Princess Wanda seem quite disreputable.

A third old lady came sailing up ; she bore a certain resemblance to the dowagers ; but she was the Countess von Altenburg, formerly Grand Mistress to the Princess Elsa ; behind her came two lackeys with trays, on which were coffee and pastry, the old Princesses' *gouter*. The Countess made a ceremonious courtesy before the young Princes.

"The territory is occupied ;" whispered Herman to Valérie. They had all sat down again, and among themselves they were teasing Othomar . with his three Fates, as they nicknamed them, without the aunts or the Countess, who was rather deaf, being able to hear. A noisy babel of tongues went on : the aunts spoke German, and screamed, in order to make themselves understood, something about the calmness of the sea into the poor ears of the Countess, as she poured out the coffee and nodded that she understood.

The younger Princes for the most part spoke English; Herman sometimes a word or two of Liparian with Othomar; and the children, who had gone to play on a lower terrace, babbled noisily in Gothlandic and French impartially.

The lackeys brought out afternoon-tea, and placed it before Princess Sofie, when a lady-in-waiting appeared. She bowed to the young Crown Princess, and, in Gothlandic:

" Her Majesty begs Your Highness to come to her in the small drawing-room."

" Mamma has sent for me," said the Princess Sofie, in English, rising from her chair. "Wanda, will you pour out the tea? Children, will you go upstairs and get dressed? Wanda, tell them again, won't you?"

The Crown Princess went through the hall, a great, round, dome-shaped apartment, full of stags' antlers, elks' heads, hunting-trophies; and then up a staircase. In the Queen's ante-room the lackey opened the door for her. Queen Olga sat alone; she was some years older than her sister, the Empress of Liparia, taller and more heavily built; her features, however, had much in common with Elizabeth's, but were more filled out.

" Sofie," she began at once, in German, " I have had a letter from Sigismundingen. . . ."

The Duchess of Wendeholm had sat down.

"Anything concerning Valérie ? " she asked, in alarm.

" Yes. . . ." began the Queen, with a reflective look. " Poor child. . . ."

" But what is it, Mamma ? "

" There, read for yourself. . . ."

The Queen handed the letter to her daughter-in-law. She read it hurriedly. The letter was from the Archduchess Eudoxie, Valérie's mother, written with a feverish, excited hand, and told, in phrases that tried to seem indifferent but that betrayed a great satisfaction, that Prince Leopold of Lohe-Obkowitz was at Nice with the celebrated actress, Estelle Desvaux, that he was about to resign his seigniorial rights in favour of his younger brother, and that he would then marry his mistress. The letter requested the Queen or the Crown Princess to communicate this to Valérie, in the hope that it would not prove too great a shock to her. Further, the letter ended with violent attacks upon Prince Leopold, who had caused such a scandal, but at the same time with manifest expressions of delight that now perhaps Valérie would dream no more of becoming the lady of a territory six yards square ! The Archduke added a postscript to say that this was not a vague report but a certainty; and that Prince Leopold himself had told it to their relations at Nice, who had written about it to Sigismundingen.

"Has Valérie ever spoken to you about Prince Lohe?" asked the Queen.

"Only once, Mamma," answered the Duchess of Wendeholm, giving back the letter; "but we all know well enough that this news will be a great blow to her. Is she not in the least prepared for it?"

"Most likely not; you see, we had none of us heard or read anything about it yet. Shall I tell her? Poor child. . . ."

"Shall I tell her, Mamma? As I told you, Valérie did once speak to me. . . ."

"Very well, you do it. . . ."

The Duchess reflected, looked at the clock.

"It is so late now, I shall tell her after dinner; we are none of us dressed yet. . . . What do you think?"

"Very well then, after dinner. . . ."

The Crown Princess went out, she must hurry and dress. At seven o'clock a loud bell sounded, protractedly. They assembled in the hall; the dining-room looked out with its large bow-windows upon the pine-wood. It was a long table : King Siegfried, a hale old sovereign with a full, gray beard ; Queen Olga ; the Crown Prince Gunther, tall, fair, two-and-thirty ; Princess Sofie and her children ; Othomar, between his aunt and Valérie ; Herman and Wanda ; Olaf and Christofel ; the two Dowagers with the Countess von Altenburg ; equerries, ladies-in-waiting, chamberlains, Princess Elizabeth's governess, the little Princes' tutors. . . .

There was the unconstraint of cheerful conversation. The ladies were in simple visiting-dresses ; the King was in dress-clothes, the younger Princes and equerries in dinner-jackets. The young Princesses wore light summer dresses of white serge or pink muslin ; they had stuck a flower or two out of the conservatory into their waist-bands.

Valérie talked merrily, Herman teased her again about her cloud-sketches, but Othomar said that he admired them very much. Queen Olga and Princess Sofie exchanged a glance, and were quieter than the others. The King also looked very thoughtfully at the young people. After dinner the family dispersed ; the Crown Prince and Herman went for a row with the younger Princes and the children on the sea, in two boats. Wanda and Valérie, their arms wound round

each other's waists, strolled up and down along
the long front terrace; the awning was already
pulled up for the night. The sea was still blue;
the sky pearl-coloured, and no longer so bright;
above the horizon the sun still burnt ragged rents
in the widely scattered clouds.

The young girls strolled, laughed, looked at the
two little boats on the sea, and waved to them.
Very far away went a steamer, finely outlined,
with a dirty little stripe of smoke. The young
Princes shouted: "Hurrah! hurrah!" and hoisted
their little flag.

"Do look at those papers of Herman's," said
Valérie. "Aunt Olga dislikes that rubbish. . . ."

She pointed to all the periodicals and newspapers which the lackeys had apparently neglected
to clear away. They lay over the long wicker
chair, on the table, and on the ground.

"Shall I ring for them to clear them up?"
asked Wanda.

"Oh, never mind," said Valérie.

She herself picked up one or two papers, folded
them, put them together; Wanda waved again
to the boats with her pocket-handkerchief.

"My God!" she suddenly heard Valérie
murmur faintly.

She looked round; the young Archduchess had

turned pale and sunk into a chair. She had
dropped the papers again; one of them she held
tight, convulsively, crushing it; she looked down
at it with eyes vacant with terror.

"It is not true . . ." she stammered. "They
always lie. . . . They lie!"

"What is it, Valérie?" cried Wanda, frightened.

At this moment the Duchess of Wendeholm
came out from the hall.

"Valérie!" she cried.

The young girl did not hear. The Duchess
approached.

"Valérie!" she repeated. "Could I talk to
you a moment, alone?"

The Archduchess raised her pale little face.
She seemed not to hear, not to understand.

"My God!" whispered the Duchess to Wanda;
"does she know?"

"What?" asked Wanda.

But a lackey appeared through the hall; he
carried a silver tray with letters. There were a
couple of letters for the Duchess; he offered
them to her first; then one to Valérie. In spite
of her blurred eyes, the Archduchess seemed to
see that letter; she snatched at it greedily. The
lackey went.

"O . . . God . . . !" she stammered at last.

She pulled the letter from the envelope, half
tore it in her eagerness, and read with crazy eyes.
Sofie and Wanda looked at her in dismay.

"O . . . God . . . !" screamed the Archduchess
in agony. "It is true . . . it is true . . . it is
true . . . ! Oh. . . ."

She rose trembling, looked about her with wild
eyes, threw herself madly into the Duchess's
arms. A loud sob burst from her throat, as
though a pistol shot had gone through her
heart.

"He writes it to me himself!" she cried out.
"Himself! It is true what the paper says. . . .
Oh!"

And she broke down with her head upon Sofie's
shoulder. Sofie led her back into the hall;
Valérie let herself be dragged back like a child.
Wanda followed, crying, wringing her hands,
without knowing why. From the boats, which
were now very far away, the young Princes waved
once more; little Princess Elizabeth even tried
to call out something; she did not understand
why Wanda and Valérie were such muffs as not
to wave back.

On the horizon the sun went down; the glowing
clouds were all masked in little foaming gold-rose
mists with radiant edges; but it became evening;

the sky grew dark; one by one the little pink clouds melted away; still one last cloud, as though with two wings formed of the last rays of the setting sun, softly flickered up, as though it wanted to fly, and then suddenly sank down, with broken wings, away into the violet darkness. The first stars twinkled up, brightly visible.

IV

The next morning, still very early, at half-past five, the Archduchess Valérie climbed down the terraces of Altseeborgen. She merely told her tire-woman that she would be back in time for breakfast, which they all took together. Determinedly, as if moved by impulse, she went down from one terrace to the other. She met nobody but a couple of servants and sentries. She walked along the bottom terrace to the sea; there there was a little square harbour cut out of the granite, where, in a boat-house, the rowing and sailing-boats lay moored. She chose a long, narrow dinghy, and loosened it from its iron chain. She took her seat adroitly, and grasped the sculls : a few short strokes took her out of the harbour and out to sea.

A South-Westerly wind was blowing over the
sea. The water was strangely gray, as though it
were mirroring in its oval the uncertain sky
above: a dull white sky in which hung dirty
shreds of clouds blown asunder. The horizon
was not visible; light mists floated over it,
which blotted out the division between sea and
sky with blurred tints. The wind blew up
strongly.

Valérie took off her little sailor hat, and her
hair blew across her face. She had intended to
row to the fishing village, but she felt at once
that it was beyond her strength to work up
against the wind. So she let herself go with
it. For a moment she thought of the weather,
the sky, the wind; then she threw off that
thought. She pulled sturdily at the sculls.

Though the sea was comparatively calm, the
dinghy was constantly balanced on the smooth
back of a wave, and then sank down again, as
into a lap. Spray flew up. When Valérie, after
a little while, looked round, she was a trifle
startled to see Altseeborgen receding so far from
her. She hesitated once more, but soon let herself go again. . . .

On leaving the castle, she had had no thought;
only an impulse to act. Now, with her very

action, thought rose up within her, as though roused from its lethargy by the wind. Valérie's eyes stared out before her, burning and large, without tears.

It was true, real. This was the wheel that continually revolved in her thoughts. It was true, real. It stood in the papers which Herman had skimmed through for hours ; Sofie had told her; his own letter informed her of it.

She no longer had that letter, it was torn up. But every word was still branded on her imagination.

It was his letter ; they were his own words, his style. How she had worshipped his words once ! But these, were they indeed his ? Did he write like that ? Could she realize to herself that he would ever talk to her thus ?

He could not bring himself to make her unhappy by loving her against the wish of her parents, her Imperial relations. It was true, after all, that he was not her equal in birth. His house was of old nobility, but no more. She was of the blood Royal and Imperial. He was grateful to her for stooping to him and wishing to raise him up to her. But it was not right to do this. The traditions of mankind should be inviolate : it was not right, especially for them, the great ones of the earth, to act in opposition to tradition. They should be grateful for the love which had brought happiness to their souls, but they must not expect more. It was not desired at Vienna that they should love one another. Would he ever be able to make her entirely happy—would she, if they were married, and retired with their love to a foreign country, never look back with yearning, and feel homesick for the splendour from which he had dragged her down? For, if they married, he would be still less her equal than he was before, thanks to his Emperor's disfavour. No, no, it could not be. They must part. They were not born for one another. For a short moment they had shared the divine illusion that they were indeed born for one another; that was all. He would remain grateful to her for that memory all his life long.

With a breaking heart he took leave of her, farewell, farewell. It was all over, his high career, his life, his all. He asked her forgiveness. He knew that he was too weak to love her in opposition to the will of his Sovereign. And for that he asked her forgiveness. She would hear mentioned in connection with his the name of a woman; for this also he asked for forgiveness. He did not love that woman, but she was willing to comfort him in his anguish. . . .

The wind had suddenly increased in violence, with heavy, regular blasts. The sky was dark overhead. The waves rolled more wildly against the boat, and swung it up on their backs as it were backs of sleek amphibians. The spray had wetted Valérie. She looked round. Altseeborgen lay very far away, scarcely within sight ; she still saw the flag defined against the sky like a little riband.

" I must be mad," she thought. " Where am I going to . . . ? I must go back. . . ."

But it was difficult to turn the boat round. Each time the wind beat it off again, and drove it further. Despair came upon Valérie, body and soul, moral and physical despair.

" Well, let it be," she thought.

She let the sculls drop, drifted further away, away. And why not ? Why should she not let herself drift away ? Without him, without him . . . . she could not live ! Her happiness was ruined ; what was life without happiness ? For she wanted happiness, it was essential to her. . . .

She had half sunk down into the boat. The sculls flapped against the sides. A wave broke over her. Her eyes stared burning before her, into the distance.

A second wave broke, her feet were wet through. She slowly drew herself up, looked at the angry sea, at the lowering sky. Then she seized the sculls again, with a sigh of anguish.

"Come on!" thought she.

She rose higher and sank lower. But with a frantic effort she made the boat turn.

"It *shall!*" she bit out between her teeth.

She kept the boat's head to the wind, and began to row. It *shall.* Her forehead was drawn up, she gnashed her jaws, her teeth grated together. She felt her muscles straining. And she rowed on, up against the wind. With her whole body she struggled up against the stiff breeze. It *shall.* It *must.* And she grew accustomed to her exertion of strength; mechanically she rowed on. So much accustomed did she become to it, that she began to sob while she rowed. . . .

O God, how she had loved him, with all her soul! Why? could she tell? Oh, if he had only been a little stronger, *she* would have been so too! What mattered to them the disfavour of her uncle, the Emperor, so long as they loved each other? What the fury of their parents, so long as they loved each other? What did they

care for all Europe, so long as they cared for each
other! Nothing, nothing at all. . . . If he had
only dared to grasp happiness for them, when
it fluttered before them, as it only flutters once
before mortal men! But he had not dared, he felt
himself too weak to risk that grasp, he acknow-
ledged it himself. . . . And now . . . . it was
over, over, over. . . .

Still sobbing, she rowed on. Her arms seemed
to swell, to burst asunder. Some solitary fat
drops of rain fell. Why was she really rowing
on? The sea was death, release from life, obli-
vion, extinction of scorching pain. Then why
did she row on?

"O God! I don't know!" she answered herself aloud: "but I must! I must . . .!"

And with the spring of her robust Imperial
body she worked herself back, towards life. . . .

But at Altseeborgen they were in great alarm.
It was three hours since Valérie had departed.
The tire-woman was unable to say more than
that Her Highness had assured her she would be
back to breakfast. The sentries had seen her
descend the terraces, but had paid no further heed
as to the direction Her Highness had taken.
They thought it was towards the wood, but they
were not sure. . . .

Every minute the alarm increased; no suspicions were uttered, but they read them in each other's eyes. King Siegfried ordered that they should themselves set out and search quietly, so as to cause no fuss among the household and the people of the village. There could be no talk of her having lost her way; the pine-wood was not large, and Valérie knew Altseeborgen well. And for that matter, there was nothing else but the wood and the beach and the village.

The King and the Crown Prince themselves went into the wood with an equerry. Herman and his younger brother Olaf went into the village, to the left; Othomar and Christofel along the sea, to the right. The Queen remained behind with the Princesses, in palpitating uncertainty. For all their efforts to bear up and to eat their breakfasts, a sort of rumour had already spread through the castle.

Othomar had gone with Christofel along the rocky shore; the rain began to come down, in hard, thick drops.

"What is it we are really looking for here?" asked Othomar, helplessly.

"Perhaps she has thrown herself into the sea!" answered the young Prince, and, for the first time of his life, he felt afraid of those depths, which were death. Without knowing it, they went on, on. . . .

" Let us go back," said Othomar.

They still went on some time, however; they could not give up. . . .

Then a scream sounded over the water; they started up, but saw nothing at first.

" Did you hear?" asked Christofel, and turned pale, thinking of the ghostly legends of the sea.

"A seamew, no doubt!" said Othomar, but listened nevertheless. The scream was heard again.

"There, don't you see something?" asked Christofel, pointing.

He pointed to a long streak that came surging over the water.

Othomar shook his head.

" No, that is impossible!" he said; "that is a fisher-lad."

" No, no, it's a dinghy!" cried Christofel.

They said nothing more, they ran along. The streak became plainer: a dinghy; the scream was heard; piercingly.

" My God: Valérie!" shouted Othomar.

She called back a few words; he only partly understood them. She was rowing not far from the shore towards the castle. Othomar took off his coat, his shoes, turned up his trousers, his shirt-sleeves.

"Take those with you," he cried to Christofel, "and go back to the castle, tell them. . . ."

He ran with his bare feet over the rocks and into the sea, flung himself into the water, swam out to the dinghy. It was very difficult for him to get into the little boat without capsizing it. It lurched madly to right and left; with a single movement, quick and light, however, Othomar succeeded in springing into it.

"I give up. . . ." said Valérie, faintly.

She let go the sculls; he seized them and rowed on. For an instant she fell up against him, but then held herself straight, so as not to impede him.

V

The young Archduchess did not appear at lunch-time; she was asleep. Just before dinner —it was raining, and the Queen was taking tea in the hall with the Princesses, the aunts, the children—she appeared. She looked a little pale; her face was rather drawn, her eyes strange, wide, burning. She wore a simple summer costume of pale-lilac supple material, with a couple of white ribbons tied round her waist; the colour matched well with her strange hair, which now looked brown, and then again seemed auburn. The Queen put out her hand to Valérie; she shook her head and said :

" You wicked child ! How you frightened us ! "

Valérie kissed the Queen on the forehead.

" Forgive me, aunt. The wind was so strong, I could hardly make way against it. I ought not to have started. But I felt a need . . . . for movement."

The Queen looked at her anxiously.

" How do you feel ? "

" Oh, very well, aunt. Rather stiff; and a little headache. It is nothing. Only my hands are terribly blistered, just look. . . ."

And she laughed.

The old aunts asked copious details of what had occurred: it was difficult to make them understand. Wanda sat down between the two of them, told them the story; the sharp cockatoo-profiles wagged continually up and down, in astonishment, to Wanda. The aunts laid their hands upon their hearts, and looked at Valérie with terror in their eyes; she smiled at them pleasantly. When the Countess Von Altenburg appeared, the aunts took the old Grand Mistress between them, and in their turn told them the story, screeching into the Countess's poor ears. King Siegfried entered; he went up to Valérie, who rose, took her head in his hands, looked at her, and shook his gray head; nevertheless he smiled. Then he looked at his sisters; he was always amused at them : they were still in the middle of their story to the Countess, kept on taking the words out of one another's mouths :

"Come, it was not so dreadful as all that!" said the King, interrupting them. "It is very pleasant to have a row like that once in a way, and an excellent remedy for a sick-headache. You ought to try it, Elsa, when you have a sick-headache."

The old Princess looked at him with an insipid smile; she never knew whether her brother meant a thing of this kind or not. She shook her stately head slowly from side to side.

"No, *lieber Siegfried,* that is more than *we* can do. *Unsere liebe Erzherzogin* is still a young thing. . . ."

Othomar, Gunther, and Herman entered; they had been playing billiards; the young Princes followed them. Valérie gave a little shiver, rose and went up to Othomar.

"I thank you, Xara," she said. "A thousand, thousand times!"

"But what for?" replied Othomar, simply. "I have done no more than row you a bit of the way back. There was no danger. For if you had been too tired to row any longer, you could always have sprung into the sea and swum ashore. You are a strong swimmer. You would only have lost the boat."

She looked at him.

"That is true," she said. "But I never thought of it. I was .... bewildered perhaps. I should not have done that; I had the fixed idea that I ought to row back. If I had not been able to go on rowing, I should certainly .... Don't refuse my thanks, I beg you: accept them."

She put out her hand, he pressed it. He looked up at her with quiet surprise, and failed to understand her. He did not doubt but that she had that morning left the castle with the idea of committing suicide. Had she felt remorse on the water, or not dared; did she want to live on, and did she therefore turn back? Was she so superficial that she had already recovered from the great grief which last night had crushed her? Did she realise that life rolls with its indifferent chariot-wheels over everything that is part of

ourselves, joy or anguish, and that it is best to
care for nothing, and also to feel nothing? What
was it with her of all this? He was unable to
get to the bottom of it. And once more he saw
himself standing perplexed before this question of
love! What was this feeling worth, if it weighed
so little in a woman's heart? What did it
weigh in his own for Alexa? What was it then
. . . . or was it then still something . . . . different?

At dinner Valérie talked as usual, and he continued not to understand her. It irritated him,
his want of penetration of the human heart: how
could he develop it? A future ruler ought to be
able to see with a single glance. . . . And suddenly, perhaps merely because of his desire for
human knowledge, the idea rose within him that
she was concealing her emotions, that she was perhaps still suffering intensely, but that she pretended,
bore up; was she not a princess of the blood:
they all learnt that, they of the blood, to pretend,
to bear up! It was bred in their bones. He
looked at her askance, as he sat next to her; she
was quietly talking across him with the Queen.
He did not know whether he had guessed right,
and he still hesitated between these two thoughts:
is she bearing herself up, or is she superficial?

But yet he was happy in being able to doubt
about her, and to refute that first suspicion of
superficiality by his second thought. He was
happy in this, not solely because of Valérie, that
she should be better than he had at first thought ;
he was especially happy in it for the general conclusion he drew from it : that a person is mostly
better, thinks more deeply, feels more nobly than
he allows to appear in the every-day common-
places of life, which compel him to busy himself
with trifles and with words, at every moment. A
gentle feeling of joy took possession of him that
he had thought this out so. A contentment that
he had discovered something fine in life: a fine
secret. Everybody knew it perhaps, but nobody
let it be perceived. Oh yes, people were good ;
the world was good, in the essence of it. Only a
strange mystery compelled it to seem different, a
strange tyranny of the world's system. He looked
around him across the long table. Every face
wore a look of pleasantness and sympathy. He
was attached to his uncle; so calm, gentle,
strong, with the seeming stubborn silence of his
Norse character, with his tranquil smile, and now
and then a little spark of fun, especially directed
against the old aunts, but also against the children, and even against the equerries, the ladies-

in-waiting. He knew that his uncle was a thinker, a philosopher; he would have liked to have a long discussion with him on points of philosophy. He was fond also of his aunt: a goodly Queen; what a lot she did for her country, what a number of charitable institutions she called into existence, how sensibly she performed her difficult task: the bringing up of Royal children. She was more beloved in her country than was his mother, whom yet he adored, in hers; she had more tact, less fear, less haughtiness too towards the crowd. It should perhaps have been the other way about: his mother Queen here, her sister Empress yonder. . . .

And the Crown Prince with his simple manliness; Herman with his joviality; the younger brothers with their sturdy boyish chaff: how fond he was of them! Sophie, Wanda, the children: how he liked them all! He even thought the aunts sympathetic, and the devoted old Grand Mistress. Oh, the world was good, people were good! And Valérie was not indifferent, but suffered in quiet silence, as a princess of the blood must suffer, with unclouded eyes and a smile!

After dinner Queen Olga took Othomar's arm.

" Come with me a moment," she said.

The rain had ceased, a lackey opened the folding-doors. Behind the dining-room lay the long back-terrace; it looked out upon the wood. The Queen put her arm in Othomar's, and began to walk up and down with him.

"And so you are going to leave us?" she asked.

He looked at her with a smile.

"You know I am, aunt: with much regret. I shall often feel homesick for Altseeborgen, for all of you. I feel so much at home in your circle. But yet I am longing to see Mamma again; it is now nearly four months since I saw her."

"And are you feeling better?"

"How could I but feel better, aunt? The voyage with Herman made me ever so much stronger, and then living here with you has been a delightful after-cure. A delightful holiday."

"But now this holiday will soon be over: will you be able to attend to things again?"

He smiled with calm confidence in his melancholy eyes.

"Certainly, aunt, it can't always be holidays. I should think I had had my fill of them: doing nothing for six weeks except lie on the sand, or in the wood, or in that very comfortable wicker chair of Herman's!"

" Have you done nothing besides ? " she asked, slyly.

" How do you mean ? "

" Saved Valérie's life, for instance ? "

He gave a slight movement of gentle impatience.

" But, aunt, I really didn't. I suppose the papers will go and say that now, but there was really no saving in the matter. Valérie knows how to swim, and she was close to the shore."

" I have had a letter from Papa, Othomar."

" From Papa ? "

" Yes . . . . have you never thought of . . . . Valérie ? "

He reflected a moment.

" Perhaps," he laughed.

" Do you feel no affection for her ? "

" Certainly, aunt. . . . I thought Papa preferred the Grand Duchess Xenia ? "

The Queen shrugged her shoulders.

" There is the religious question, is there not ? And Papa would be very pleased with an alliance with Austria. How do you propose to make the journey ? And when do you start ? "

" Ducardi and the others will reach here this week. Towards the end of the week. First to

Copenhagen, London, Brussels, Berlin, and then
to Vienna."

"And to Sigismundingen."

"Yes, to Sigismundingen, if Papa wishes it."

"But what do you wish, Othomar?"

He looked at her gently, smiling, shrugging his
shoulders.

"But, aunt, what have I to wish in the
matter?"

"Could you grow fond of Valérie?"

"I think so, aunt; I think she is very sweet
and very noble."

"Yes, that she certainly is, Othomar! Would
you not speak to her before you go?"

"Aunt. . . ."

"Why not?"

"Aunt, I could not do that. I am only staying
here a few days longer, and . . . ."

"Well?"

"Valérie has had a great sorrow. She cannot
but still be suffering under it. Think, aunt, it
was yesterday. Good God, yesterday . . .! And
to-day she was so calm, so simple. . . . But it
cannot be otherwise, can it? She must still be
suffering very severely. She went on the sea this
morning, in this weather . . . we do not know, do
we, aunt, but we all think the same thing! Per-

haps we are quite mistaken. Things are often different from what they seem. But however that may be, she is certainly in sorrow. And so I cannot ask her, now. . . ."

" It is a pity, now that you are here together. A thing of this sort is often decided at a distance. If it was arranged here, you would perhaps not have to make that journey."

" But, aunt, Papa was so bent upon this journey."

" That is true; but then nothing was yet decided."

" No, aunt, let me make the journey. For to arrange it here is impossible in any case. If Papa asked me himself, I should tell him . . . . that it was impossible."

" Papa does ask you, Othomar, in his letter to me."

He seized her hands.

" Aunt, in that case, write back to Papa that it is impossible, at this moment. Oh, impossible, impossible. Let us spare her, aunt. If she becomes my wife, she will become so, neverthe- less, while she loves another. Will that not be terrible enough for her, when it is decided, months later on? Therefore let us spare her now. You feel that also, as a woman, do you not ? There is no political question which makes it necessary for my marriage to be so hurriedly arranged."

" Yet Papa wishes you to marry as soon as possible. He wants a grandson. . . ."

He made no reply: a look of suffering passed over his face. The Queen perceived it.

" But you are right," she replied, giving way. " It would be too cruel. Valérie, for the rest, bears up well. That is how a future Empress of Liparia should be. . . ."

He still made no reply, walked silently beside her ; her arm still lay in his : she felt the latter quivering.

" Come," she said, gently ; " let us go in ; to walk up and down like that is fatiguing. . . ."

VI

DUCARDI, Dutri, Leoni and Thesbia arrived at Altseeborgen ; they were to accompany Othomar on his official journey through Europe. It was one of the last days, when Othomar was walking with Herman, in the morning, towards the wood.

The sun was shining, the wood was fragrant, the foot slid over the smooth needles. The

Princes sank down to the ground, near a great
pool of water; around them rose the straight
pine-trunks, with their knotty pikes of side-
branches; the sky stretched feebly with blue
chinks between the projecting pine-foliage, away
into the distance.

Herman leant up against a tree-trunk; Othomar
stretched himself out upon his back, with his
hands beneath his head.

" It will soon be over now," he said, softly.

Herman made no reply, but mechanically
gathered the pine-needles together with his hand.
Nor did Othomar speak again; he imbibed his
last moments of relaxed repose in careful draughts:
each draught was a delight that would never
return. In the wood a stillness reigned as of
death, as though the earth were uninhabited;
the melancholy of things that finish hung among
the trees.

Suddenly Othomar took Herman's hand and
pressed it.

" Thank you," he said.

" What for ? " asked Herman.

" For the pleasure we have had together.
Mamma was right : I did not know you,
Herman. . . ."

" Nor I you, dear fellow."

" They were pleasant days. How delightfully we travelled together, like two tourists. How deliciously great India was, eh ? and Japan, how curious. I never cared very much for hunting, but when I was with you, I understood it and felt the excitement of it : I shall never forget our tiger-hunt! The eyes of the brute, the danger facing you : that invigorates you. At a moment like that, you feel yourself becoming primitive, like the first man. The look of one of those tigers drives away a lot of your hesitation. That's another danger, which Mamma always fears so ; oh, how enervating it is, it eats up all your energy. . . . And the nights on the Indian Ocean, on board our *Viking*. That huge wide circle around you, all those stars over your head. How often we sat looking at them, with our legs on the bulwarks. . . . Perhaps it is not right to dream for so long, but it rests one so, it rests one so. I shall never forget it, never. . . ."

" Well, old fellow, we must do it again."

" No, one never does anything again. What is done is done. Nothing returns, not a single moment. Later on it is always different. . . ."

He looked round about him, as though something might be listening; then whispered :

" Herman, I have something to tell you."

17

" What is it ? "

" Something to confide to you. But first tell me : that time with the tiger, you thought me a great coward, did you not ? "

" No, certainly not ! "

" Well, I am a coward all the same. I am frightened, always frightened. The doctors don't know it, because I never tell them. But I always am. . . ."

" But of what, old fellow ? "

" Of something inside myself. Look here, Herman, I am so afraid . . . . that I shall not be able to bear up. That at a certain moment of my life I shall be too weak. That suddenly I shall not be able to act, and then, then . . . ."

He shuddered ; they looked at one another.

" It is not right," he continued, mechanically, as though strengthened by Herman's look. " I shall fight against it, against that dread. . . . Do you believe in presentiments ? "

" Yes, in a contradictory sense : mine always turn out the opposite ! "

" I hope then that mine also won't come true."

" But what is it ? "

" That within the year . . . . one of us . . . . will be dead . . . . at Lipara."

Herman looked at him with a stare. In spite

of his robustness and his physical strength of muscle, there lay deep down within him a certain heritage of the superstition that murmurs from the sea as with voices of distant prophecy; superstition lulled by the beautiful legends of their Gothlandic sea, which like a syren sings strange, mystic fairy-tales. Perhaps he had never felt, until this moment, that some of it flowed in his rich blood, and he tried to shake it off, as nonsense.

" But Othomar, do be rational ! "

" I can do nothing to prevent it, Herman ; I don't think about it, but I feel little sharp stings, like thoughts suddenly springing up. And lately . . . . oh, lately, it has been worse ; it has become a dream, a nightmare. I was walking through the business street of Lipara, and from all the shops there came black people, and they measured out piles of black crape, with yard-measures, and to such an extent that the streets were filled with it, and the crape lay in the town as though in clouds, and surged over the town like a mass of black gauze. It made everything dark ; the sun could not shine through it, and shadow lay above all things. The people did not seem to recognize me, and when I asked what all that crape was for, they whispered in my ears : ' Hush, hush,

it is . . . . for the Imperial!' . . . O Herman,
then I woke, and I was damp with perspiration,
and it was as though I could still hear echoing
after me: ' For the Imperial, it is for the
Imperial ! ' "

Herman got up, he was a little nervous.

" Come," said he, " shall we go in ? . . .
Dreams, don't pay attention to dreams, Othomar!"

Othomar also rose.

" No, I ought to pay no attention to them," he
repeated strangely; " I never used to."

" Othomar . . . ." began Herman, decidedly,
as though he wished to say something.

" Don't talk to me for a minute ; let me be for
a moment," he interrupted, quickly, anxiously.

They walked through the wood in silence.
Othomar looked about him strangely over the
ground. Herman compressed his lips tightly
together, and puckered up his forehead : he was
annoyed. But he said nothing. After a few
moments Othomar's strange glances grew calmer;
they quieted down into their usual gentle melancholy.

Then he sighed gently, as if he were catching
his breath.

" Don't be angry," he said, putting his arm in
Herman's.

His voice had resumed its usual tone.

"Perhaps it is a good thing that I have told you : now perhaps it will leave me. So don't be angry, Herman. . . . I promise you, I shall not talk like that again, and I shall do my best too not to think like that. But when I have anything on my mind, I must tell it. And surely that is much better than for ever keeping silent about it ! And then, you see, soon I shall have no more time to think of such things . . . . to-morrow we shall be at Copenhagen, and then life will resume its usual course. How can I have talked so strangely? How did I take it into my head ? I can't remember, myself. . . . It seems very insane, even to me, now."

He gave a little laugh, and then, seriously :

"I am glad after all that we have had a talk alone, that I have been able to thank you. We are friends now, are we not ?"

"Yes, we are friends," replied Herman, laughing in the midst of his annoyance ; "but all the same I shall never be able to know you thoroughly ! "

"Don't say that just because of a solitary presentiment which I think foolish myself. What else is there in me that is enigmatical . . . ? "

Herman looked at him.

"No, nothing else ! " he assented. "You're a

good chap.   I don't know how it has come about,
but I like you very much. . . ."

They passed out of the wood; the sea lay
before them.   Like life itself, it lay before them,
with all its mysterious depths, in which a mani-
fold soul seemed to move and to round wave
upon wave.   Nameless and innumerable were its
changes of colour : its moods of unceasing movement ; and high up it spewed a foam of passion
on its savage crests.   But that passion was its
most superficial manifestation : merely the exu-
berance of its endless vitality; from its depth
there murmured, in the ultimate melodies of its
millions of voices, the mystery of its soul, as it
were a glory that the sky above alone knew.

VII

To His Most Gracious Imperial Highness
   Othomar, Duke of Xara, at Osborne
   House, Isle of Wight.

                    Imperial, Lipara,
                         —— *Sept.,* 18—.

Dear Son,—It was with much pleasure that
we received your letter, telling us of the cordial

welcome which you received first at Copenhagen and now in England. We must however express to you our surprise at what Aunt Olga wrote to us, and our regret that you did not act according to our wishes; the Emperor of Austria and the Archduke Albrecht express the same regret in their letters to us. We presume that we did not express ourselves definitely enough in our letter to Aunt Olga : otherwise we cannot imagine why she did not urge you more distinctly to obtain an interview with the Archduchess Valérie, and to speak to her of the important matter that we have all at this moment so much at heart. You would then have been able to announce your engagement confidentially at the courts which you are now visiting, and the betrothal could have been celebrated at the end of your journey at Sigismundingen. Whereas now you have doubtless placed yourself in a false position towards our friends, Their Majesties of Denmark and England, seeing that all the newspapers speak of a possible betrothal to the Archduchess Valérie, and the press is so kind as already to discuss vociferously the *pros* and *cons* of this alliance. Your journey would nevertheless have had to take place *in any case*, as it had already been so long announced— your illness intervened to postpone it—and as it is therefore nothing more than an act of politeness towards our friends.

Once again, that you did not act in this according to our wishes causes us great regret. We perceive in you a certain tendency towards a bourgeois hyper-sensitiveness, Othomar, which we hope you will learn to master with all the strength you possess. A sorrow such as Prince Von Lohe-Obkowitz has caused your future bride few of us have in this life escaped, but it remains an entirely personal and subordinate feeling, and should not be allowed to interfere *in the least* with affairs of such great political importance as the marriage of a future Emperor of Liparia. The Archduchess will doubtless learn to look at this in the same light, when she is older, and we hope that she will very soon realise that her inclination for Prince Lohe could never have brought her happiness, as it would have caused a rupture with His Majesty her uncle and with all her relations.

Master yourself, Othomar, we ask and urge. You sometimes have ideas and entertain proposals which are not those of a ruler. We have already noticed this frequently: amongst other occasions, when you visited *Zanti* at Vaza. We would not reproach you with this, as we were otherwise very much satisfied with you. Your dearest wish will no doubt be that we shall always remain so.

We hope therefore to see you again in three weeks at Sigismundingen, where the Archduchess Valérie will by that time have returned from Altseeborgen in order to meet you, and where we shall also meet the Emperor of Austria.

We cordially hope that the long voyage with Herman will have done you much good, and that your wedding will be able to take place at Altara *as soon as possible*. This glad prospect is for us a pleasant diversion from the difficulties about the Army Bill, which is meeting with such stubborn resistance in the House of Representatives, although we hope nevertheless to be able to carry it through, as our army must be augmented.

We cordially embrace you.

OSCAR.

CHAPTER V

I

IT was after the state banquet at the castle of
Sigismundingen, where the Imperial Families of
Liparia and Austria were assembled to celebrate
the betrothal of the Duke of Xara and the Archduchess Valérie. It was in September: the day
had been of a sultry heat, and in the evening it
still remained brooding in the air.

Dinner was just over, and the Imperial procession returned through a long corridor to the
reception-rooms. All the balcony windows of
this illuminated gallery stood open; beneath, as
in an abyss of river landscape, flowed the Danube,
rolling on towards the clouds, while above it
towered the castle with its innumerable little
pointed turrets. The mountain-tops were defined
in a sombre violet amphitheatre against the paler
sky, which was being incessantly lit up with

electric gleams of noiseless lightning. The wood stood gloomy and black, shadowy, sloping up with the peaked tops of its fir-trees against the mountains; in the distance lay small houses confused in the night, like some straggling hamlet, with here and there a yellow light.

The Emperor of Liparia gave his arm to the mother of the bride, the Archduchess Eudoxie; then followed the Emperor of Austria with the Empress of Liparia, the Archduke Albrecht with the Empress of Austria, Othomar with Valérie . . . . Valérie lightly pressed Othomar's arm, and withdrew herself with him out of the procession.

" It was so warm in the dining-room : you will excuse me," she said to Othomar's sister, the Archduchess of Carinthia, who was following with one of her Austrian cousins, and her smile begged the Archduchess to go on. The others followed : the august guests, the equerries, the ladies-in-waiting : they smiled to the betrothed Imperial couple, who stood in one of the open window-recesses to let them pass.

They remained alone in the gallery, standing before an open window.

" I need air," said Valérie, with a great sigh.

He made no reply. They stood silently together, and gazed at the evening landscape.

He wore the Uhlan uniform of the Austrian regiment which he commanded, and a new order glittered amongst the others on his breast: the Golden Fleece of Austria. She seemed to have grown older than she was at Altseeborgen, in her pink silk evening-dress, with wide puffed sleeves of very pale green velvet, a tightly-curled border of white ostrich-feathers edging the low-cut bodice and the train.

"Shall I leave you alone for a little, Valérie?" he asked, gently.

She shook her head, smiling sadly. An irrepressible emotion seemed to make her bosom heave nervously up and down.

"Why, Othomar?" she asked. "I am lonely enough at nights, with my thoughts. Leave me as little alone with them as you can. . . ."

She suddenly held out her hand to him.

"Will you forgive your future Empress her broken heart?" she asked, suddenly, with a great sob.

And her pale, shrunk face turned full towards him, with two eyes like those of a wounded doe. An irrepressible feeling of compassion caused something to well up suddenly in his soul; he squeezed her hand, and turned away, so as not to weep.

He looked out of the window, with an air of sombre romance; some of the pointed towers, visible from here, rose up against the sky, which was luminous with electricity. Below them, romantically, murmured the Danube. The mountains resembled the landscape in a ballad. But no ballad, no romance echoed between their two hearts. The prose of necessity and of the inevitable was the only harmony that bound them together. But this harmony also bound them in reality, brought them together, made them understand each other, feel and live at one with each other. They were now for a minute alone, and their eyes frankly sought the depths of each other's souls. There was no need for pretence between those two; each saw the other's sorrow lying shivering and naked in the other's heart.

It was not the riotous passion of despair that they saw. They saw a gentle and tremulous melancholy; they looked at it with great staring eyes of anguish, as children look who think they see a ghost. For them that ghost issued from life itself: life itself became for them a ghostly existence. They were spectres, although they felt themselves to be tangible, with bodies. What were they? Dream-beings with crowns;

they lived and bowed and acted and thought as in a dream, because of their crowns. They did not exist: a vagueness did indeed suggest in their dream-brains that something might exist, in other laws of nature than those of their sphere, but in their sphere they did not exist. . . .

His hand mechanically played with some papers that lay near him, on the gilt console of a mirror between two of the window recesses; they were illustrated periodicals, doubtless forgotten by some chamberlain. He took one up, to alleviate her sad silence, and opened it. The first thing he saw was their own portraits.

"Look," he said.

He showed them to her. They now turned over the leaves together, saw the portraits also of their parents, a drawing of the castle, a corner of the park of Sigismundingen. Then together they read the announcement of their engagement: to begin with they were each described, their talents cried up to the skies: he, an accomplished Prince, who did much good, very popular in his own country, and cordially loved by the Emperor of Austria; she, every inch a Princess, born to be the Empress of a great Empire, with also her special accomplishments. The eyes of all Europe

were at this moment fixed upon them. For their
marriage would not only be a Princely alliance
of political significance, but would also tie a knot
of real harmony: their marriage was a love-
match. There had been attempts to make it
seem otherwise, but this was not correct. In
Gothland, in the family circle at Altseeborgen,
the young Princes had learnt to know one another
well, their love had sprung like an idyll from the
sea, and the Duke of Xara had even once saved
the life of the Archduchess, who had ventured
out too far in stormy weather in a rowing-boat.
Their love was like a novel with a happy ending.
The Emperor Oscar would rather have seen the
Grand Duchess Xenia as Crown Princess of
Liparia, and attached great importance to an
alliance with Russia, but he had yielded to his
son's love. . . . And the article ended by saying
that the wedding would take place in October in
the Old Palace at Altara.

They read it together, with their mournful
faces, their wide, fixed eyes, which still smarted
with gazing into each other's souls. No single
remark came from their lips after reading the
article; they only smiled with their two heartrending smiles; then they laid the paper down
again. And she asked, with that strange calm

with which this betrothed pair endeavoured to learn to know each other:

"Othomar, do you . . . . care for nobody?"

A flush suffused his cheeks. Did she know of Alexa?

"I did once think that I . . . . was in love," he confessed; "but I do not believe that it was really love. I now believe that I do not possess the capacity to concentrate my whole soul upon a feeling for one other soul alone; I should not know how to find it, that one soul, and I should fear to make a mistake, or to deceive myself. . . . No, I do not believe that I shall ever know that exclusive feeling. I rather feel within me a great, wide, universal affection, an immense compassion, for our people. It is strange of me perhaps. . . ."

He said it almost shyly, as though it were something abnormal, that universal feeling, of which he should be ashamed beside her.

"A great love," he explained once more, when she continued to look at him in silence, and he made an embracing gesture with his arms, "for our people. . . ."

"Do you really feel that?" she asked, in surprise.

" Yes. .   ."

" But, Othomar," she said ; " that is very good. It is very fine to feel like that ! "

He shrugged his shoulders.

" Fine ! How do you mean ? I cannot but feel it when I see all the misery there is . . . . among our people, the lower orders, the very lowest especially. If they were all happy and enjoyed abundance, there would be no need for me to feel it. So why is there anything fine in it ? "

She gave a little laugh.

" I can't argue against that, that is too deep for me. I can't say I have ever thought over those social questions ; they have always been so, and . . . . I have not thought about them. But I can feel, with my feminine instinct, that it is fine of you to feel like that, Othomar."

She took his hand and pressed it, her face lit up with a smile. Then she looked, pensively, into the dark landscape beneath them, and she shivered.

" It is turning cold," he said. " Let us go in, Valérie ; you will catch cold here."

She just felt at her bare neck.

" Presently," she said.

They glanced down, at the murmuring Danube.

18

A mist began to rise from the river, and filled the valley as it were with light strips of muslin.

" Come," he urged.

" Look," she said; " how deep that is, is it not ? "

He looked down.

" Yes," he replied.

" Don't you feel giddy ? " she asked.

He looked at her anxiously.

" No, not giddy; at least not so soon. . . ."

" Othomar," she said, in a whisper. " I once sat here for a whole evening. I kept on looking down; it was darker than now, and I saw nothing but blackness, and it kept on roaring away through those black depths. It was the evening after our engagement was decided on. I felt such sorrow, I suffered so! I thought that I had already won a victory over myself, but they left me no peace, and I was only victorious in order to have to do battle once more. That I was to become your wife came as unexpectedly . . . . as my great sorrow came! Then I felt so weak because it overwhelmed me so, because they left me no peace. Oh, they were so cruel, they did not leave me a moment to recover my breath. I had to go on again, on! Then I felt weak. I thought that I should never overcome

that weakness. I sat here for hours, looking at
the Danube. It made me giddy. . . . At last
I thought that I had made up my mind: to throw
myself down. . . . I saw myself already floating
away, there, there, down there, right round the
castle. . . . Why did I not do it? I believe
because of . . . . him, Othomar. I still loved
him, I still love him now, although I ought to
have more pride. I would not punish him by
committing suicide. He is so weak, I know him,
it would have haunted him all his life . . . !
Then . . . . then, Othomar, I ran away, and I
prayed! I no longer knew what to do!"

She hid her face full of anguish in her hands,
with a great sob. His eyes had filled with tears;
he saw how she trembled. He threw a side-
glance full of terror at the deep stream beneath,
which roared as though calling. . . .

"Valérie," he stammered, in alarm; "for
God's sake let us go in. It is too cold here, and,
and . . . ."

She looked at him anxiously too, with wild
eyes.

"Yes, let us go, Othomar!" she whispered.
"I am getting frightened here; we have that in
our family; there is still so much romance in our
veins. . . ."

She took his arm, they went. But before they entered the suite of ante-rooms that led to the reception-rooms, she still detained him a moment :

" I don't know whether we shall see each other alone again, before you return to Lipara. And I still wanted to thank you for something. . . ."

" For what ? " he asked.

" For . . . . something Aunt Olga told me. For . . . . sparing me . . . . at Altseeborgen. Thank you, Othomar . . . ."

She threw her arm round his neck and gave him a kiss. And he too kissed her.

And they exchanged their first caress.

II

The next day the Imperial Family of Liparia travelled back from Sigismundingen to Lipara. The reception at the Central Station was most hearty ; the town was covered with bunting ; in the evening there were popular *fêtes*. The officers of the various army corps offered the Crown Prince banquets in honour of his betrothal. The Archduchess Valérie's portraits were exposed in the windows of all the picture shops ; the papers contained long articles full of jubilation.

It was a few hours before the dinner given by the officers of the Throneguards to their Princely colonel that Othomar was suddenly, as it were, overcome by a strange sensation. He was in his study, he felt rather giddy, and had to sit down. The giddiness was slight, but lasted a long time; for a long time the room seemed to be slowly endeavouring to turn round him and not to be able, and this gave a painful impression of resistance on the part of its lifeless furniture. One of Othomar's hands was resting on his thigh, the other on the ruff of the collie, which had laid its head upon his knee. He remained sitting, bent forward.

When the giddiness had passed, he retained a strange lightness in his head, as though something had been taken out of it. He let himself drop carefully backwards; the collie, half dozing in sleep, dreamily opened its eyes, and dropped off again, its head upon Othomar's knee, under his hand. An irresistible fatigue crept up Othomar's limbs, as though they were sinking in soft mud. It surprised him greatly, this feeling, and looking sideways at the clock, without moving his head —so as not to bring on the giddiness again—he calculated that he had still an hour and a half before dinner. This prospective interval relieved

him, and he remained sitting, as though calcu-
lating his fatigue : whether it would pass away,
depart from his body.

It lasted long, so long indeed, that he doubted
whether he would be able to go. When three-
quarters of an hour had passed, he pressed his
hand upon the bell, which stood near him on the
table. Andro entered.

"Andro . . . ." he began, but did not continue.

" Does Your Highness wish to dress? Everything is ready. . . ."

Othomar just patted the dog's head, as it still
lay motionlessly dozing upon his knee.

" Is Your Highness unwell ? "

"A little giddy, Andro; it is passing away
already."

" But had Your Highness better go : had I not
better send for Prince Dutri ? "

Othomar shook his head decidedly, and rose.

" No, it is already late, Andro. Come, help
me. . . ."

And he entered his dressing-room.

He appeared at the dinner, but nevertheless excused himself to the officers for his evident languor.
He only joined in the toasts by raising his glass,
with a smile. It struck them all that he looked
very ill, emaciated, with hollow eyes, white as

chalk in his uniform of white and gold. Immediately after dinner he returned to the Imperial, without accompanying them to the Imperial Jockey Club, the club of the *jeunesse dorée*.

He slept heavily; a vague dream hovered through his night. The man who had tried to kill him at Zanti's grinned at him with clenched fists; then the scene changed to the Gothlandic Sea, and he rowed Valérie, but however much he rowed, the three towers of the castle always drew further away, unapproachable. . . .

When he awoke, it was already past eight. He reflected that it was too late for his usual morning ride, and remained lying there. He rang for Andro.

" Why did you not wake me at seven o'clock ? "

" Your Highness was still sleeping so soundly; I dared not; Your Highness was not well yesterday. . . ."

" And so you just let me sleep ? . . . Very well then. . . . Let Her Majesty be told that . . . . I am not well."

The man looked at him anxiously.

" What is the matter with Your Highness ? "

" I don't know, Andro . . . . I am a little tired. Where is Djalo ? "

" Here, Highness. . . ."

The collie ran in noisily, put its great paws up on the bed, shook its haunches wildly to and fro as it wagged its tail. . . .

Then, suddenly, it went and lay quietly beside the bed.

The Empress sent back word that she would come at once; she was not yet dressed. . . . With quiet, open eyes Othomar lay waiting for her.

She entered at last, a little excited with anxiety. She questioned him, but learnt nothing from his vague, smiling replies. She laid her hand on his forehead, felt his pulse, and could not make up her mind whether he had fever. There was typhoid fever about: she was afraid of it. . . .

The physicians-in-ordinary were called and relieved her mind: there was no fever. The Prince seemed generally tired; he had doubtless over-exerted himself lately. He must take rest. . . .

The Emperor was astonished : the Prince had just rested and had remained weeks at Altseeborgen. What had been the use of that then !

The report went through the palace, the town, the country, through Europe, that the Duke of Xara was keeping his room on account of slight indisposition. A simple and very reassuring bulletin was issued by the physicians.

However, in the afternoon Othomar got up, and even dressed himself, but not in uniform. He lunched in his room, and now went to Princess Thera's apartments. She sat drawing; with her was a lady-in-waiting, the young Marchioness of Ezzera.

The Princess was surprised to see her brother.

"What, is that you? I thought you were in bed. . . ."

"No, I am feeling a little better. . . ."

He bowed to the Marchioness, as she rose and courtesied.

"Won't you paint?" asked Othomar.

Thera looked at him.

"You are looking so pale, poor boy. Perhaps I had better not. It tires you so, that sitting, does it not?"

"Yes, sometimes, a little. . . ."

They were now standing in front of the portrait; the Marchioness had retired, as she always did when the brother and sister were together. The painting was half covered with a silk cloth, which Thera pulled aside: it was already a young head full of expression, in which life began to gleam behind the black melancholy eyes; painted with broad, firm brush-work, with much reflection of outside air, which fell upon one side of the face, and brought it out in relief, throwing it forward out of the shadow of the background.

" Is it almost finished ? " asked Othomar.

" Yes, but you have kept me waiting so long for the last touch: just think, you have been away for four months. I haven't been able to work at it all that time. But you know .... you have changed. If only I sha'n't have to leave it like this. It is no longer like you. . . ."

" It will begin to look like me again, when I look a little better ! " answered Othomar ; but the Princess became rather nervous ; she suddenly pulled the silk cloth over it again. . . .

Othomar did not appear at dinner ; he went to bed very early. The next day the physicians found him in a very listless condition. He was up but not dressed ; he lay in his dressing-gown on the sofa in his study, with the collie at his feet. He complained to the Empress that he felt so strange in his head, as though it were about to open, and all the contents pour out.

For days this condition remained unchanged : a total listlessness, a total loss of appetite, a visible exhaustion. . . . The Empress sat by his side, as he lay on his sofa, staring through the open rooms into the green depths of the park of plane-trees. The birds chirruped there ; sometimes Berengar's small, shrill voice sounded there, as he played with a couple of little friends. The Empress read aloud, but it tired Othomar, it made his head ache. . . .

After a long interview which the three doctors had with the Emperor and Empress, Professor Barzia was summoned from Altara for a consultation: the Professor was an European specialist for nervous diseases.

In the Emperor's study the Emperor, the Empress and Count Myxila sat waiting for the result of the examination and the subsequent consultation. It lasted long. They did not speak while they waited; the Empress sat staring before her with her quiet, resigned expression; the Emperor walked to and fro in irritation. The old Chancellor, with his stern, proud face and bald head, stood pensively near the window.

Then the doctors were announced. They appeared, Professor Barzia first; the others followed. The Empress thought she read the worst on the Professor's pale, rigid features; one of the physicians, however, compassionately nodded to her from behind him with his kind, big head to reassure her.

"Well!" asked the Emperor.

"We have carefully examined His Imperial

Highness, Sir," began the Professor. " The Prince is quite free from organic disease, although he is generally of a frail constitution."

" But what is wrong with him then ? " asked Oscar.

" The Prince's nervous system seems to us to be alarmingly strained, Sir."

" His nerves ? But he is never nervous, he is always calm," exclaimed the Emperor, stubbornly.

" We should appreciate the Prince's self-restraint all the more, Sir. His Highness has evidently long kept himself up, and this last exertion has been too much for him. He is indeed calm now, as Your Majesty says. But this calm does not alter the fact that his nerves are completely run down. His Highness has clearly taxed himself too much lately."

" And what has that too much consisted in ? " asked the Emperor, haughtily.

" That would doubtless be better known by those at Court than by me, fresh from my study and my hospitals, Sir. Your Majesty will be able to answer that question yourself. I can only give you a few indications. His Highness told me that he remembered sometimes feeling those fits of giddiness and exhaustion even before the great floods in the North. That was in

March. It is now September. I presume that
His Highness has in the meantime led a life of
much activity?"

The Emperor made movements with his eyebrows as if he could not understand; tremulous
motions of his energetic head with its fleece of
silvering hair.

"The journey to the North may indeed have
affected His Highness, Professor . . . ." began
the Empress.

She sat haughtily upright, in her plain dark
dress. Her face was expressionless, her eyes
were cold. She spoke in a matter-of-fact tone,
as though she were not a mother.

"His Highness is very sensitive to impressions," she continued; "and at that time he
received some very shocking ones at Altara."

The Professor made a light movement of the
head.

"I remember seeing His Highness at the
identification of the corpses in the meadow,
Madam," he said; "His Highness was in fact
particularly affected . . . ."

"But to what does all this tend?" asked the
Emperor, still recalcitrant.

"That His Highness has presumably allowed
himself no rest since that time, Sir. . . ."

" His Highness has allowed himself months of rest ! " exclaimed the Emperor.

" Will Your Majesty just permit us to look back ?　After the very fatiguing journey in the North, the Prince came at once into excitement of a political nature—Lipara was at the time in state of siege—and afterwards came the bustle of a festival time, when the King and Queen of Syria were here. . . ."

The Emperor shrugged his shoulders.

" After that, the Prince, on the advice of my esteemed colleagues, went and undertook a sea-voyage in order to restore his health.　No doubt His Highness then had some days of rest ; but the great hunting excursions in which he took part with Prince Herman were doubtless too much for His Highness.　Now, recently, His Highness has been betrothed ; this may have caused him some excitement.　I am casually mentioning some of the principal facts, Sir.　I know nothing of the Prince's intimate life ; if I knew something about that, it would make certain things much easier for me.　But this is certain : His Highness has led from day to day a too agitated existence, whatever they may have been, great agitations or small.　That His Highness did not collapse earlier is undoubtedly due to an extraordinary power of self-control, of which I believe the Prince himself to be unconscious, and an extraordinary sense of duty, which is also quite spontaneous in His Highness. These are high qualities, Sir, in a future ruler. . . ."

A slight flush dyed the Empress's cheeks ; a softer expression suffused the coldness of her features.

"And what is your advice, Professor ? " she asked.

"That His Highness takes indefinite rest, Madam."

"His Highness's marriage was fixed for next month," resumed the Empress, inquiringly.

Professor Barzia's features became quite white and rigid.

"It would be simply unpardonable, if His Highness's marriage were to take place next month," he said, with his even, oracular voice.

"Must it be postponed, then ? " asked the Emperor, with suppressed rage.

"Without doubt, Sir," answered the Professor, with cool determination.

"My good Professor . . . ." the Emperor growled out between his teeth, with a pretence of geniality ; " you speak of rest, and of rest again. Good God, I tell you, the Prince has had

rest, months of it, long months. . . . Do I ever
rest so long? Life is movement, and government
also is movement. We can't allow ourselves to
rest. Why should a young man like the Prince
be always resting? I never remember having
rested, when I was Crown Prince! He may not
be so strong as I, but yet he is of our race!
Excitement, you say! Good God, what excitement? Excitement of a political nature? That
fell to *my* share, not to the Prince's! And I had
no need of rest after it. And is it necessary for
a Prince to go and rest when he gets engaged to
be married? Really, Professor, that is carrying
hygiene too far!"

"Sir, Your Majesty has done me the honour to
desire to know my opinion of the Prince's condition. I have given that opinion to the best of
my knowledge."

"So he must rest?"

"Undoubtedly, Sir."

"But for how long do you want him to
rest?"

"I am not able to fix a date, Sir."

"For how long do you want his marriage to be
postponed?"

"Indefinitely, Sir."

The Emperor walked up and down the room:

something strange passed over his energetic features : anguish. . . .

"That is impossible," he muttered, curtly.

All were silent.

"That is impossible," he repeated, hollowly.

"In that case His Highness will marry, Sir," said Barzia.

The Emperor stood still.

"What do you mean?" he asked, fiercely.

"That nothing can prevail with Your Majesty in this most important matter . . . . except your own sentiment and reasonableness."

The Emperor's breath came in short gasps between his full sensual lips ; his veins swelled thick on his low Roman forehead ; his strong fists were clenched. No one had ever seen Oscar like that before ; nor had any one ever yet dared so to address him. . . .

"Explain yourself more clearly . . . ." he thundered into the Professor's rigid face.

The latter did not move a muscle.

"If His Highness is married next month . . . . it will be his death."

The Empress remained sitting stiff and upright, but she turned very pale, quivered, closed her eyes as though she felt giddy.

"His death?" repeated the Emperor, in consternation.

19

"Or worse," rejoined Barzia.

"Worse?"

"The extinction of Your Majesty's posterity."

The Emperor shouted out a fierce oath, and struck his fist on the huge writing-table. The bronze ornaments on it rang. Myxila drew a step nearer.

"Sir," he said; "there is nothing lost. If I understand the Professor, His Highness's illness is only temporary and curable."

"Certainly, Excellency," replied Barzia. "So long as it is not compelled to become incurable and chronic."

Oscar convulsively bit his lips. His gleaming eyes stood out small and cruel. It struck Myxila how at this moment he resembled a portrait of Wenceslas the Cruel.

"Professor," he hissed. "We thank you. Remain till to-morrow at Lipara, so that you may diagnose His Highness once more."

"I obey Your Majesty's command," said Barzia.

He bowed, the physicians bowed, they withdrew. Left alone with the Empress and the Chancellor, Oscar no longer restrained his rage. Like some wild beast, he walked fiercely up and down with heavy steps, he screeched as though

the breath refused to come through his con-
stricted throat.

"Oh!" he gnashed out between his teeth,
bursting out at last. "That boy, that boy. . . .
He is not even fit to get married! His Duchess
—he was able to get married to her! And that
boy, oh! that boy is to succeed me, me. . . ."

A furious laugh grated out scornfully from
between his large white teeth, with biting irony.

The Empress rose.

"Count Myxila," she said, trembling. "May
I beg Your Excellency to follow me?"

She turned towards the door. Myxila, hesitating, was already following her.

"What for?" roared the Emperor. "What's
the reason of that? I have something more to
say to Myxila."

The Empress gave the Emperor a look as cold
as ice.

"It is my express wish, Sir, that Count Myxila
should follow me," she said, in the same quivering
voice. "I think Your Majesty requires solitude.
Your Majesty says things which a father may not
even think, and which a sovereign may certainly
not say in the presence of one of his subjects, not
even one of his loftiest subjects. . . ."

The Emperor tried to interrupt her.

" Your Majesty," continued the Empress, with a tremor of haughtiness, cutting the words away from him with her icy-cold quivering voice as though with a knife, "says those things of the future Emperor of Liparia . . . . and I do not desire that one subject, not even Count Myxila, should hear such things, and Your Majesty at the same time says those things of *my son* : therefore I do not desire to hear them myself, Sir! Excellency, I request you once more to follow me."

" Go then," roared the Emperor like a madman, " Go, both of you, yes, leave me alone, leave me alone ! "

He walked furiously up and down, threw the chairs against each other, roared like an irritated caged lion. He took up a bronze statue from a console in front of a tall mirror that rose to the ceiling in gilt arabesques.

" There then ! " he lashed out with his voice, and his passion seemed to seethe like a cloud in his bewildered brain, to shoot red lightning-flashes from his bloodshot eyes, to drive him mad because of his impotence against those stupid fatal powers of the logic of circum-stances.

Like an athlete he swung the heavy statue with his arm through the air; like a child he hurled it at the great mirror, which fell down, clattering in a flicker of sherds.

The Empress and Myxila had left the room.

III

The ordinary life of the Court continued; the Empress's first Drawing-room took place. The reception-rooms leading to the great presence-chamber were illuminated, although it was day-time; the ladies entered, handed their cards to the High Chamberlain, signed their names, and waited until their titles were called out by the Masters of Ceremonies. They stood in low-necked dresses; the long white veils fell down from the feathers and the jewelled tiaras, in misty folds of gauze. It was the first display of the new toilettes of the season: the fashion which had sprung into life, and now moved and had its being; but the crowded reception-rooms seemed but the ante-chambers of that display, and the uplifted trains gave an impression of pre-paration for the solemn moment: that momentary appearance before Her Majesty.

The Duchess of Yemena stood waiting, her train also thrown over her arm, with the two

Marchionesses her stepdaughters, whom she was about to present to the Empress, when she saw Dutri, bowing, apologizing, twisting through the expectant ladies, so as to make way for himself through the crowded room.

"Dutri," she beckoned to him, because he did not seem to perceive her.

He reached her after some difficulty, bowed, paid his compliments to the little Marchionesses. They stood with rigid little faces, frightened round eyes and compressed mouths, and their small, youthful figures were outlined with the shyness of novices; constantly, with graceful awkwardness, they arranged their heavy court-trains over their arms. They just smiled at Dutri's words; then they looked stiff again, compared the dresses of the other ladies with their own.

"Dutri," whispered the Duchess, "how is the Prince?"

"Always the same," the equerry whispered back; "terribly melancholy. . . ."

"Dutri," she murmured still lower; "would there be no chance for me to see him?"

Dutri started in dismay.

"How do you mean, Alexa? When?"

"Presently, after the Drawing-room. . . ."

"But that is impossible, Alexa! The Prince sees no one but Their Majesties and the Princess; he talks to nobody, not even to his chamberlains, not even to us. . . ."

"Dutri," she insisted, with her hand on his arm. "Do your best. Help me. Ask for an interview for me. If you help me . . . . I will help you too . . . ."

He looked at her expectantly.

"What do you think of Hélène?" she asked.

"I think Eleonore prettier," he smiled.

"Well, come to us oftener, to my special days; we never see you, I will prepare the Duke. . . ."

She dangled the rich match before his eyes: he blinked them, continued to watch her with a smile.

"But you must help me too . . . ." she continued, with a gentle menace.

"I will do my best, Alexa, but I can promise nothing . . . ." he just had time to reply.

"Wait for me after the Drawing-room, in one of the other rooms," he whispered to her, accompanying her a few steps.

All this time the titles were being cried, impressively, slowly; the ladies went, dropped their trains, blossomed out.

"Her Excellency the Duchess of Yemena,

Countess of Vaza; Their Excellencies the Marchionesses of Yemena. . . ."

The Duchess went, the girls followed her, crimson, with beating hearts. They passed through a long gallery, dropped their trains; at the door of the presence-room, before they entered, lackeys arranged the heavy court-mantles.

"Her Excellency the Duchess . . . ." was heard for the second time, this time through the presence-chamber, with a resonance of greater reverence, because the titles resounded in the listening ears of receiving Majesty.

The Duchess and the Marchionesses entered. Between the broad billows of dark-blue velvet, on which was displayed the cross of St. Ladislas, and under the canopy propped up by gilt pillars, sat the Empress, like an idol, glittering in the shadow in her watered silver brocade, the ermine Imperial mantle falling in heavy folds to her feet, a small diadem sparkling upon her head. To the right of the throne sat the Princess Thera on a low stool; on the left stood the Grand Mistress, the Countess of Threma; round about on either side a crowd of court-ladies, court officials, equerries, ladies-in-waiting, grooms of the bed-chamber. . . .

The Duchess made her courtesy, approached the throne, with great reverence, as though with diffident lips, touched the jewelled finger-tips, which the Empress held out like a live relic. Then the Duchess took two steps backwards, the Marchionesses, one after the other, followed her example, surprised everybody by the attractive freshness of their first courtly movements, in which the touch of awkwardness became a charm. Then the bows in a long ritual of withdrawal. They disappeared through other doors, found themselves in a long gallery, entered other reception-rooms, where people stood waiting for their carriages. And the young girls looked at each other, seeking each other's impressions, still crimson with the excitement in their vain little hearts, and strangely surprised at the incomprehensible shortness of this first and all-important moment of their lives as grown-up people: as ladies who accompanied their Mamma to the Imperial, where they would in future live out their lives. For how many months beforehand they had thought and dreamed of this moment; now, suddenly, with surprising quickness, it was over. . . .

The Duchess tapped Hélène's chin, arranged Eleonore's veil, said that they had bowed beauti-

fully, that she had even herself noticed how
pleased the Countess of Threma had looked with
them. Then she chatted busily with the other
ladies, introduced the little Marchionesses, promised visits. Then she turned to a lackey.

" Go and see where my carriage is, and let it
leave the rank and drive up last. Here. . . ."

She gave him a small gold coin, the lackey went.
A nervous impatience seized the Duchess; she
looked out anxiously for Dutri. At last her eye
discerned him; he came up to her with his
fatuous fussiness :

" Alexa, it's impossible. . . ."

" Have you asked the Prince ?"

" No, not yet; there is the question to begin
with whether he will see *me*. But then: how am
I to take you to him ? There are always lackeys
walking about in the doorways, to say nothing of
the guards and halberdiers ; in the ante-rooms you
may run up against a chamberlain at any moment.
Really, it is impossible."

She grew angry.

" Begin by asking him. We shall see later on
how we can get to him."

Dutri made elegant gestures of despair.

" But, Alexa, can't you really understand that
. . . it is impossible. . . ."

She made no reply, not wishing to reflect, her head filled with her stark, fixed idea to see the Prince, to insist on seeing him. And suddenly, turning towards him:

" Very well, if you don't care to do anything for me, you need not think that I shall help you in any way."

Her nervous, angry voice sounded louder than her first whispered words: the two girls heard her.

" Alexa," he besought her, gently.

" No, no," she resisted, curtly.

He thought of his debts and of Eleonore.

" I will try," he whispered, in despair.

She promptly rewarded him with a smile; he went, hurried away again, with his eternal air of fussy importance, because of his young Imperial master who was so sadly ill. In the anteroom he found the chamberlain on duty.

" Would the Prince be willing to see me?"

The chamberlain shrugged his shoulders.

" I'll ask," he said.

He speedily returned: the Prince sent word that Dutri might come in.

Dutri entered. Othomar lay on a couch of tiger-skins in front of his writing-table. He had grown thinner; his eyes were hollow, his complexion was wan; his neck protruded frail and

96MAJESTY

The page.

slim from the loose turn-down collar of his silk shirt, over which he wore a velvet jacket. In his hand he held an open book. Djalo, the collie, lay on the floor.

Dutri the voluble began to press his request with rapid sentences, which followed close upon each other's heels. . . .

"The Duchess?" repeated Othomar, faintly. "No, no. . . ."

Dutri galloped on, simulated melancholy, employed words of gentle, insinuating sadness. Othomar's face assumed an expression which was strange to it and quite new; it was as though the melancholy of his features was crystallizing into a stubborn obstinacy, a silent doggedness.

"No," he said once more, and his voice, too, sounded doggedly obstinate: "make my excuses to the Duchess, Dutri. And where . . . where would she wish to see me?"

"I did not fail to point out this difficulty to Her Excellency, but perhaps if Your Highness would be so gracious . . . one might nevertheless . . ."

Othomar closed his eyes, and threw his head back; his hand fell loosely upon the collie's head. He made no further reply, and his lips were compressed tightly together.

Dutri still hesitated : what could he do, what should he tell Alexa. . . .

But the door opened, and the Empress entered. The Drawing-room was over; she had put off the robes and the crown, but she still wore her stiff, heavy dress of silver brocade. She looked coldly at Dutri, and just bowed her head for him to go : the equerry beat a confused retreat, without showing his usual tact.

Othomar half rose from his couch.

" Mamma ! . . ."

She sat down by his side, stroked his forehead with her hand.

" How do you feel ? "

He smiled, and blinked with his eyes, without replying.

" What was Dutri doing here ? "

" He asked me . . . Oh, Mamma, never mind, don't ask. . . . How beautiful you look! May I, too, kiss your hand ? "

Winningly, jestingly he took her hand and kissed it. She took his book from between his fingers, read the treasonable title.

" Are you reading again, Othomar. . . . You know you must not read so much. And why all those strange books . . . ? "

On the table lay Lassalle, Marx, works by

Russian Nihilists, a pamphlet by Bakounine, pamphlets by *Zanti*. . . . The little work that he was reading was by a well-known Liparian Anarchist, and entitled, " Injustice by the Grace of God ; " it overthrew everything : religion and the state ; it addressed itself directly to the crowned tyrants in authority ; it addressed itself directly to Oscar.

" Is it to get better that you read things like those, Othomar ? " she asked, with pained reproach.

" But, Mamma, I must see what it is that they want. . . ."

" And what do they want ? "

He looked pensively before him.

" I don't know what they want, I can't understand them. They give you very long phrases, and the same phrases always repeated, with the same words always repeated. I only understand that they disapprove of everything that exists and want something different. But yet sometimes . . ."

" Sometimes what ? "

" Sometimes they say terrible things, terrible because they sound so true, Mamma. When they speak of God, and prove that He does not exist, when they describe our whole system of government as a monstrosity, and reject all authority, our own included. . . . They sometimes speak like children who have suddenly learnt to talk and to judge, and then sometimes they suddenly speak clearly, and then very crude thoughts spring up within me: if God exist, why is there injustice and misery, and our authority, by what right? O God, Mamma, what right have we to reign over others, over millions? Tell me, but argue from the beginning, don't argue backwards; don't begin with us, begin with our first rulers, our usurpers; what right had they, and does ours only flow from theirs? Oh, those problems, those simple problems, who can solve them, my God, who can solve them. . . ."

Elizabeth suddenly turned pale: she stared at him as though he had gone mad.

"Who gives you those books?" she asked harshly, hoarsely, anxiously.

"Dutri, Leoni; Andro has also fetched me some."

"They are mad!" exclaimed the Empress, rising. "Why do you ask for them?"

"I want to know, Mamma . . ."

"Othomar," she cried. "Will you do what I ask?"

"Yes, Mamma," he replied, gently; "but sit

down again, and . . . and don't be angry. And
. . . and don't say Othomar. And . . . and go
and change your dress, oh, I can't see you in that
dress; you are so far from me; your voice does
not reach me, and I dare not kiss you, you are
not my mother, you are the Empress. Mamma,
O Mamma . . . ."

His voice appealed to her. A powerful emotion
was aroused in her.

"O my boy!" she cried; a half sob broke in
her throat.

"Yes, yes, call me that. . . . Mamma, let us
be quick and find one another again, let us not
lose each other. What is your request?"

"Give me all those books."

"I will give them to you; they make me no
happier, after all!"

"But then why are you unhappy, my boy, my
boy?"

"Mamma, look at the world, look at our
country, see how they suffer, see how they are
oppressed! What shall I ever be able to do for
them! I shall always be powerless in spite of all
our power! Oh, it grows so dark in front of me, I
can see nothing more, I have no hope, none but
Utopians have any more hope, but I . . . I no
longer hope, for I can do nothing, nothing . . . !

O God, Mamma, the whole country is falling upon me and crushing me : and I can do nothing, nothing. . . . I shall have to reign, and I shall not be able to, Mamma. What am I ? A poor sickly boy : how can I become Emperor? I don't know why it is, Mamma, nor what it comes from, but I don't feel like a future Emperor, I feel like a feeble child ! I feel like your child, your boy, and nothing more. . . ."

He seemed about to throw himself into her arms, but on the contrary he flung himself backwards, as though he were frightened by her brilliant toilette ; his head dropped nervelessly on to his chest, his arms fell loosely down. She saw his movement : her first feeling was one of regret that she had come to him in court-dress, longing as she did to see him, not allowing herself the time to change. But this regret passed through her as a transient emotion, for it was followed by an intense dizziness, as though an abyss opened yawning at her feet, the earth retreated, and black nothingness gaped. A despair as of utter impotence enveloped her soul. Vaguely she stretched out her arms, and threw them round his neck as though she were feeling out into the darkness, with wandering eyes.

" My boy, don't talk like that any more, be-

20

cause . . . when you talk like that, you take away my strength too ! " she whispered, in alarm. " For how can it be helped ? You must, we all must . . ."

" Forgive me, Mamma, but I, I shall not be able to. Oh, I see it clearly now. I am not excited, I am calm. I see it, I prophesy it, it can never be. . . ."

" But Papa is still so young and so strong, my boy; and when you grow older . . ."

" The older I grow, the more impossible it will be, Mamma. I was always frightened of it as a child, but I never realized it so desperately as now. No, Mamma, it cannot be. Now that I am ill, I have plenty of time to reflect, and I now see before me what the end of all our trouble must be. . . ."

His eyes gazed at the floor in despair; she still half hung on to him helplessly; a menacing shiver seemed to float through the room.

" Mamma. . . ."

She made no reply.

" I must tell you of my resolve. . . ."

" What resolve . . . ?"

" Will you tell it to Papa ? "

" What, what, Othomar, my boy ? "

" That I can't marry . . . Valérie, because . . ."

" Later, later, you need not marry now. . . ."

" No, Mamma, I never can, because I . . ."

She looks at him beseechingly, inquiringly.

"Because I want to abdicate . . . my rights . . . in favour of Berengar. . . ."

She made no reply; feebly she drooped against him, not knowing how to console and cheer him, and softly and plaintively she began to sob. It was as though her soul was being flooded with anguish, slowly, but persistently, until it brimmed over. She reproached herself with it all. He was her child : the future Emperor of Liparia had derived this weakness from her. And the manifestation of this agonizing mystery of heredity before her despairing eyes deprived her of all her strength, all her courage, all her capacity for resignation.

"Mamma . . ." he repeated.

She sobbed on.

" Do not despair so. . . . Berengar will be better than I. . . . You will tell Papa, won't you ? . . . Or no, never mind, if it costs you so much : I shall tell him myself. . . ."

She started up nervously from her despair.

"O God, no ; Othomar, no, don't talk to him about it, he is so passionate ; he would . . . he would murder you ! Promise me that you will not talk to him about it! *I* will tell him, O my God, *I* will tell him. . . ."

But a tremor of hope revived within her.

" But, Othomar, I ask you, why do you do this; you are ill now, but you will get better, and then . . . then you will think differently ! "

He gazed out before him; his presentiment quivered through him : he saw his dream again : the streets of Lipara, that were filled with crape, right up to the sky, where they veiled the sunlight. And over his features there passed again that new air of hardness, of dogged obstinacy which made him unrecognizable ; he shook his head slowly from side to side, from side to side.

" No, Mamma, I shall never think differently. Believe me, it will be better so."

When she saw him like that, her new hope collapsed again, and she sobbed once more. Sobbing, she rose ; amid her sorrow yawned a void ; she was losing something : her son.

" Are you going ? " he asked.

She nodded yes, sobbing.

" Do you forgive me ? "

She nodded yes again. Then she gave him a smile, a smile full of despair, lacking the strength to kiss him, and she went out, sobbing still.

He remained alone, and rose. He stood up in

the middle of the room; his eyes stared at the collie.

"Why need I give her pain!" he thought.

Everything in his soul hurt him.

"Why did I go on that voyage with Herman?" he asked himself again. "It was in those first days of rest that I began to think so. And yet Professor Barzia says: rest. . . . What does he know about me? What does one person know about another . . . ?"

"Djalo!" he cried.

The collie ran up, wriggling, joyfully.

"Djalo, what is right, how should the world be? Must there be Kings and Emperors, Djalo, or had we better all go away?"

The dog looked at him, wagging his tail violently; he suddenly jumped up and licked his face.

"And why, Djalo, need one man always make the other unhappy? Why need Princes make their people unhappy? Will life then always remain the same, for centuries . . . ?"

Othomar sank into a heap on the couch; his hand dropped down upon the dog, who licked it passionately. "Oh!" he sobbed. "My people, my people . . . !"

.   .   .   .

In the front square of the Imperial at that moment the last carriages were driving away; the staring crowd, behind the Grenadiers, peeped curiously at the pretty ladies glistening through the glass of the equipages. That of the Duchess of Yemena was the last of all.

IV

A spirit of gloom seemed to haunt the resounding marble halls of the Imperial; a faded melancholy seemed to tone down the cadences of the voices and their echoes, and to hang from the ceilings as it had been a heavy web of air. It was autumn ; the first entertainments were to take place; the first court ball was given. But it seemed to be given because there was no help for it : it was a slow, official, tedious function. The more intimate circles of the Imperial, those of the Duchess of Yemena and of the diplomatic body, regretted the more select reunions in the smaller rooms of the Empress. They looked upon those great balls as necessary inflictions. The smaller dances of the Empress, however, were always favoured as the most charming festivities. But the Empress had decided that they should not take place, because of the illness of the Crown Prince. At this first great ball their Majesties only appeared for a short moment, to take part in the Imperial quadrille. . . .

Gray ashes hovered down over the glittering mood of regal festivity which so short a time ago had been the common atmosphere of the palace. The dinners, formerly the glories of the day, were shortened; only the most necessary invitations were given. The Emperor himself remained in a constant frowning mood: the Army Bill for the augmentation of the active forces still continued to be attacked in principle in the House of Representatives, and the Emperor was resolved at all costs to uphold his Minister of War; withal, thanks to the dash of childishness that filtered through his energy, he had not yet recovered from his disappointment at the postponement of the Duke of Xara's marriage. He seemed to be in a continual state of irritation because his Liparian world would not go as he wanted it to go.

Neither the Empress nor the Prince himself considered the moment favourable to communicate to the Emperor the mournful resolution. But just for this reason the Empress quietly began once more to cherish a hope. Nothing

had been said as yet: the humiliating secret
existed only between her son and herself.
Humiliating, because why need he resign his
dominions? What pretext would have enough
probability to conceal that true motive of weakness and impotence? And yet he was her child
and Oscar's. It seemed out of the question to
make Othomar's wish known to his father, and to
tell him that his own son had no capacity for
government. Oh, what would she not sacrifice
to be able to spare her child this humiliation!
But was he really so impotent to master himself
and to hold himself proudly erect, under the
weight of what was as yet no more than a Prince's
coronet? Had she but had a reply to his discouragement; but she had only been able to sob,
only to give way before his despair; in vain had she
sought the secret spring in his soul which should
cause him to rise from the impotence in which
the languor of his reflections had made him sink.
. . . And yet she felt that there must be a secret
spring, because she instinctively divined its presence in the souls of all her equals in rank: it
was the mystery of their sovereignty, the reason
that they were sovereigns, the reason of their
privilege. She had that adorable, ingenuous
belief, that in them, the crowned heads, there was

one common quality of distinction by reason of which they were above the crowd—that single drop of sacrosanct blood in their veins, that single atom of inherited divinity, which shed lustre through their souls. She believed in their high exclusive right of Majesty. Because she believed in it as, at the same time, she believed in her sinfulness as a human being and in the absolution of her confessor, the Archbishop of Lipara, she would never for a single instant be able to doubt their right divine as monarchs. Whatever people might think, or write, or want different, theirs was the right; of this she was as certain as of the Trinity. That Othomar had doubted the existence of God had struck her as impious, but had not overcome her so much as his disbelief in their own right. Was he alone then lacking in that quality of distinction, that sacred golden drop of blood, that divine atom? And if he lacked it, if he, the Crown Prince, lacked Majesty, was this monstrous deficiency her fault then, the fault of the mother who bore him?

The suspicion of this weakness crushed her, and before she even dared to speak to Othomar, she humbled herself before the Archbishop. The Prelate, alarmed at these portents in the mysterious melancholy of the Imperial,

had scarcely known how to comfort her. After
that, she remained prostrate for hours before her
crucifix. She prayed with all her soul, prayed
for light for herself and for her son, prayed for
strength and that the spark might descend upon
Othomar. When she had prayed thus, so long
and with such conviction, there came over her,
like an afflatus of the Holy Ghost, a sense of
peace. She became herself again, she awaited
events, regained her superstitious fatalism, her
conviction that nothing happens but what must
happen and is right. What was wrong did not
happen. If it were fated that Othomar were to
receive that spark, that would be right; if it were
fated that he were to abdicate, that would be
right too, O God, right with a strange, inscrutable
rightness . . . !

Since the days had gone by without the
Empress's having yet spoken to the Emperor,
she hoped anew; she hoped that Othomar would
be his old self again, and no longer seek his
own degradation. But it was as though she
hoped in spite of everything, for each time that
she saw Othomar again, she found him duller
and more exhausted, more helpless beneath the
certainty of his weakness. Professor Barzia,
who treated the Prince personally, and twice a

day gave him his cold-water douche in the palace, seemed to be least uneasy about his physical weakness. The Prince was not robust, but the Professor divined in his delicate constitution the presence of the quality that had sprung from the first sensual, rough strength of the Czyrkiski race : the Slavonic element, which had become enervated through its Roumanian mixture, but had lingered on : a secret toughness, an indestructible element of unsuspected firmness, that lay deep down, like a foundation, upon which there seemed to be built up much that was very frail and fragile. What had once been rude strength the Professor believed he had discovered in a certain toughness ; what had been cruelty and lust, in a certain enervation, which had hitherto been kept in equilibrium by self-restraint and a spontaneous sense of duty, but which now suddenly revealed itself in this excessive lassitude. Barzia distinctly discovered in Othomar the descendant of his ancestors, and he considered that although the rich physical vigour of the blood of the first rulers had been refined—though it might flow more thinly now through his veins—yet that blood was not so impoverished that the delicacy of this future Emperor need be ascribed to exhaustion of race. Possibly

Barzia's sudden sympathy for the Prince tinged this physiological diagnosis with too much optimism; however this might be, the Professor was not in the least afraid of his fragility, or even of his weakness of nerves; what he did fear was lest those spiritual qualities which had so suddenly endeared the Prince to him, should not be able to maintain themselves during this period of fatigue and exhaustion. Spontaneous, unreflected, uncalculated, he knew those virtues to be in the Prince, as it were a treasure unknown to himself; would they be lost, now, in these mournful days, or would they remain, become developed perhaps, refine themselves, make up to Othomar in moral strength for what he lacked in physical strength, and in that way cure him? For the Professor knew: these qualities alone could cure him. . . .

Othomar himself thought neither of his virtues nor of his blood: he thought of his future, and thought of it with an hourly increasing dread. When the Empress asked Barzia whether that resting would be good for the Prince, and whether distraction would not be better, the Professor asserted that the Prince had lately had distraction enough. He must first get the better of his fatigue, and entirely; it mattered less with what the Prince at this moment kept his brain occupied. . . .

But Barzia did not mean this altogether, and would doubtless have been very far from meaning it, had he known of what the Prince thought, or been able to judge of the latter's utter spiritual flaccidity.

And the days passed by. Othomar did not speak again to the Empress of his resolve, desiring to give her as little pain as possible ; neither did the Empress allude to it ; she hoped on.

But in Othomar's meditations it revolved unceasingly like a wheel : he was able to do nothing for his people, and yet he loved them ; he did not know how to govern them, he would abdicate his rights and his Crown-Princely title : Berengar should become Duke of Xara. . . .

The small Prince came and paid his brother a short visit every morning; he always wore his little uniform, looking like a sturdy little general in miniature, and Othomar watched him with his smiling scrutiny.

Did no desire for government go through the child's little mediæval brain, was there no jealousy in his passionate little heart ? Othomar remembered in the history of Liparia, in the cruel times of their early middle ages, that terrible drama—they still showed at St. Ladislas the chamber where it had been enacted—that second son stabbing his elder brother in his lust for power, and throwing the corpse from an oriel window into the Zanthos which flowed at the foot of the fortress. What was left in the child of this rivalry? And although this rivalry had been refined away in less violent feelings, would not an immeasurable happiness enter Berengar's small Princely soul if he were to learn that he might be Crown Prince, and that he would one day become: Emperor! But what would the child think of him, Othomar, who gave up all his magnificence voluntarily? Would he despise him, while yet feeling grateful to him, or would he suspect a lurking mystery behind all this greatness which Othomar cast from him, and cherish mistrust. . . . Then he would draw the little chap to him with silent compassion, yet feeling with pleasure the firm flesh of his sturdy little limbs, listening with delight to his short, sharp little sentences. Then Berengar rode away, and Djalo was allowed to run with him through the park: in an hour he would bring the dog back to Othomar and talk importantly of his lessons which were just beginning.

And when Berengar had gone, Othomar lay thinking about him in his long hours of reverie, looked already upon his brother as entirely the

Crown Prince, and erased himself from the cata-
logue of future sovereigns, thought of what he
should do when he was cured and had shaken off
all his purple, remembered his Uncle Xaverius,
who was the abbot of a monastery, pictured
himself studying, writing works on history and
sociology. . . .

V

They were autumn days; the sunny blue of the
sky was often clouded over with gray; in the
morning the winds blew from the North, blew
across the sea till it became steel-coloured; then
the sun broke through and shone very warmly for
a couple of hours, with an occasional cold blast,
suddenly and treacherously bursting out at the
corners of the streets; then at about four or half
past the sun was extinguished, and the blank sky
was left breathing out its chilliness, ice-cold on
the open harbour, between the white palaces, in
the streets and squares.

It was a time of dangerous weather: the
Empress and Berengar had both caught cold
driving in an open carriage; they both kept
their rooms, and Othomar in his turn went to visit
them; the Empress coughed, the little Prince

was feverish ; there were never so many illnesses
at one time the doctors declared.   And a melancholy continued to brood through the halls of the
Imperial, through the whole town, where one no
longer saw the Imperial Family at the Opera and
at entertainments.   Never had the daily dinners
at the Imperial been so short, with so few guests,
and it gave an insurmountably mournful impression not to see the Empress seated next to the
Emperor, delicate, distinguished, august, but in
her stead the Princess Thera, who seemed quite
incapable of lighting up Oscar's frowning, peevish
features.

Othomar did not even know that people were
getting anxious about the Empress; she always
received him with all the cheerfulness that she
could muster, in spite of the pain on her chest ;
the doctors told him nothing, no one gave him
the bulletins, they wished to spare him ; and
besides there was less anxiety in the Imperial
than in the town, throughout the country.

But the small Prince received Othomar with
less meekness than the Empress, and every day
there were dumb passions, sulks with the doctors
for keeping him in his little bed.

Once, when the Crown Prince came to see
Berengar, the doctors were with him ; the fever

had increased, but the little Prince wanted to get out of bed; he was naughty, called names, had even struck the good-natured, big-headed doctor, and pummelled him with his little clenched fist.

"So soon as you are better, Berengar," said Othomar, after first reproving him, "I shall make you a present."

"What of?" asked the boy, eagerly. "But I am better now."

"No, no, you must do what the doctors tell you, and not vex them."

"And what will you give me then?"

Othomar looked long at him.

"What shall I have then?" repeated the child.

"I mustn't tell you yet, Berengar; it is really still rather too big for you?"

"What is it then: a horse?"

"No, it is not so big as a horse, but heavier; don't ask any more about it, and also don't try and guess what it is, but be obedient; then you will get better, and then you shall have it."

"Heavier than a horse and not so big . . . " pondered Berengar, with glowing cheeks.

With his head leaning on his breast, dragging his footsteps along, Othomar returned to his room. He stayed there for hours, sitting quietly, gloomily,

21

in the same position ; as usual he did not appear at dinner, and hardly ate what Andro brought him. Then he went to lie down on his couch, took up a book to read, but put it down again and raised himself up, as though with a sudden impulse.

"Why not now?" he thought. "Why continually postpone it . . . ?"

Night fell, but the upper corridors of the palace were not yet lighted ; dragging his fatigue through this dusky shadow, Othomar went to the Emperor's ante-rooms. The chamberlain announced him.

Oscar sat at his writing-table, a pen in his hand.

"Am I disturbing you, Papa? Or can I speak to you?"

"No, you're not disturbing me. . . . Have you been to see Mamma?"

"Yes, this afternoon ; she was pretty well, but Berengar was feverish."

The Emperor looked up at him.

"Worse than this morning?"

"I don't know : he was very hot."

The Emperor rose.

"Do you want to talk to me?"

"Yes, Papa'"

"Wait a moment, then. I haven't been to Berengar yet to-day."

He went out, left the door open.

Othomar remained alone. He sat down. He looked round the great study, which he knew so well from their morning consultations with the Chancellor. Lately, however, he had not attended these. He thought over what he should say; in the meanwhile his eyes wandered around; they fell upon the great mirror with its gilt arabesques; something seemed strange to him. Then he got up and went towards the glass.

"I was under the impression there was a flaw in it there," he thought; "I can't well be mistaken. Has it been renewed?"

He was still standing by the looking-glass, when Oscar returned.

"Berengar is not at all well; the fever is growing worse," he said, and the tone of his voice hesitated. "Mamma is with him. . . ."

Absorbed as he was in his own meditations, it did not strike Othomar that the little Prince must doubtless have become worse for the Empress, who was herself ill, to be with him.

"And about what did you want to talk to me?" asked the Emperor, as the Prince remained silent.

"About Berengar, Papa."

"About Berengar?"

"About Berengar and myself. I have been

contrasting myself with him, Papa. We are brothers, we are both your sons. Which of us, do you think, takes most after you . . . . and . . . . our ancestors ? "

" What are you driving at, Othomar ? "

" At what is right, Papa—right. Nature is sometimes unjust and blind ; she ought to have let Berengar be born first, and then me . . . . or me even not at all."

"Once more, what are you driving at, Othomar?"

"Can't you see, Papa? I will tell you. Is Berengar not more of a ruler than I? Is that not the reason why he is your favourite? And ought I to deprive him of his natural rights for the sake of my traditional rights? I want to abdicate in his favour, Papa. I want to abdicate everything, all my rights."

" The boy is mad," muttered Oscar.

" All my rights," repeated Othomar, dreamily, as though he foresaw the future : his little brother crowned.

" Othomar, are you raving ? " asked the Emperor.

" Papa, I am not raving. What I am now telling you, I have thought over for days, perhaps weeks ; I don't know, time passes so quickly. . . . What I am telling you I have talked over with

Mamma; it made her cry, but she did not oppose me. She understands it too. . . . And what I tell you holds good; I have resolved, and nothing can change my mind. . . . I am fond of Berengar: I am glad to give up everything to him, and I shall pray that he may become happy through my gift. I am convinced—and so are you—that Berengar will make a better Emperor than I. What talents do I possess for it . . . ? "

He helplessly shrugged his shoulders, with a nervous shudder, that jolted them.

"None," he answered himself. "I have none, I can do nothing. I do not know how to decide—as now—I do not know how to act; I shall always be a dreamer. And why then should I be Emperor, and he nothing more than the Commander-in-Chief of my army or my fleet? Surely that cannot be right; that cannot have been intended by Nature . . . . Papa, I give it him, my birthright, and I . . . . I shall know how to live as is right. . . ."

The Emperor, his elbows on the table, his hands under his chin, had listened to him, sat staring at him with his small, screwed-up eyes.

" Do you mean all that ? " he asked.

" Yes, Papa."

" You're not delirious ? "

"No, Papa, I'm not delirious."

"Then you're mad."

The Emperor rose.

"Then you are mad, I tell you. Othomar, understand that you are mad, and return to your senses; don't go quite out of your mind."

"Why do you call me insane, Papa? Can you not agree with me that Berengar would be better than I?"

His father's cruel glance stabbed Othomar.

"No, you are not insane in that; you are right there. . . ."

"And why, then, am I insane because I wish, for that reason, to abdicate in favour of him?"

"Because it's impossible, Othomar."

"What law prevents me?"

"My will, Othomar."

The Prince drew himself up proudly.

"Your will?" he cried; "your will? You acknowledge that I am nothing of a Prince except by birth? You acknowledge that Berengar does possess your own capacity to rule, and you will not, you *will* not have me resign? And you think that I shall fall in with that will . . .?"

He broke out into a hoarse laugh.

"No, Papa, I shall pay no heed to that will. You can carry through your will in everything, but not in this. Although you called all your army together, you could not prevail here. There is a limit to the power of human will, Papa, and nothing, nothing, nothing, can prevent me from considering myself unfit for government and from not *willing* to wear a crown!"

The Emperor seized Othomar's wrists; his hot breath hissed in Othomar's face.

"You damned cub!" he gnashed out between his large, white teeth. "You nincompoop! You are right, there is nothing of the Emperor in you; there never will be. If I did not know better, I should say you were the son of a lackey. You are right, you are incompetent. You are nothing, our crown does not fit you. And yet, though I were compelled to lock you up in a prison, so that no one might hear of your baseness, you shall not resign your rights. The extent of my will reaches further than you can see. Do you hear? You shall not do it, you shall not resign, although from this moment I have to hide you, as a disgrace, from the world. Your slack brain can't understand that, can it? You can't understand that I am more attached to Berengar than to a poltroon like you, and that nevertheless I will not have him as my successor in your stead? Then I shall have to tell you. I will not allow it, so that I need not betray to the world the degeneration of our race. I will not have the world know how pitiably weak it is grown in you, and I would rather . . . I would sooner murder you than permit you to abdicate!"

Fiercely Oscar took the Prince by his shoulders, pushed him backwards upon a couch, on which he sat down, sank into himself; he continued to hold him like a prey in the grip of his strong hands.

"But I tell you," continued the Emperor; "I tell you, you are *not* the son of a lackey, you are my son, and I shall not murder you, because I am your father. I will only say this to you, Othomar: you might have spared me this. I believe you have a high opinion of your own delicacy of feeling, but you have not got the very least feeling. You do not even feel that you have contemplated a baseness, the baseness of a proletarian, a slave, a pariah, a wretch. You have not even felt for an instant what pain you would cause me by such an infamy. You saw that I was fonder of your brother; you thought that I should approve of your cowardly proposal. Not for an instant did it suggest itself to you, that with that cowardice you would give *me* the greatest pain that it would ever be possible for me to experience . . .!"

Othomar, crushed, had fallen back upon the couch. He was no longer able to distinguish what was just and what was true; he no longer knew himself at that moment; his father's words lashed his soul like whips. And he felt no strength within him to resist them; the insulting reproaches kept him down, as though he had been thrashed. Baseness and disgrace, insanity and degeneration, he collapsed beneath them; he gulped down the mud of them, until he choked in it. And that he did not choke in them, and continued to breathe, continued to live, that the daylight was bright around him, that things remained unchanged, that the world outside knew nothing, all this was despair to him. For a moment he thought of his mother. But he wished for darkness, death, to hide himself, himself and his shame, his degeneration, the leprosy of his pariah-temperament. . . . It flashed through him in the second after that last lash of reproach, flashed across his depressed soul. He knew that Oscar always kept a loaded revolver in an open pigeon-hole of his writing-table. His brain grew tense in the effort of thinking how to reach it. He rose, approached the pigeon-hole; suddenly he sprang towards it, stretched out his hand and seized the pistol. . . .

Did Oscar believe that his son had been confounded by his last words, and now wanted his father's life? Did he see through this ecstasy of suicide in his child, was his quivering brain penetrated by that horrible thought that self-destruction . . . . would be the last refuge of the pariah? However this might be, he rushed at Othomar. But the Prince lightly sprang out of his reach, pointed the revolver, with wild eyes, with distorted features, in senseless despair upon himself, upon his own forehead, on which the blue veins swelled up. . . .

"Othomar!" roared the Emperor.

At this moment hurried footsteps were heard outside, confused words sounded in the ante-room, and the Marquis of Xardi, the Emperor's aide-de-camp, alarmed, confused, threw wide open the door. . . .

"Sir!" he exclaimed; "the Empress asks if Your Majesty will come this instant to Prince Berengar. . . ."

The shot had gone off, into the wall. Blood dripped from Othomar's ear. The Emperor had caught hold of the Prince and torn the revolver, still loaded in five chambers, away from him; the second shot also went off in that short moment of struggle, into the ceiling. Othomar remained standing inanimately.

"Marquis!" the Emperor hissed out at Xardi. "I don't know what you think, but I tell you this: you have seen nothing, you think nothing. What happened here before you came in . . . . has not happened."

He pointed his finger threateningly at Xardi.

"Should you ever forget, Marquis, that it has not happened, then I too shall forget who you are, although your pedigree goes back further than ours!"

Xardi stood deathly pale before his Emperor.

"My God! Sir . . . ."

"What do you mean by coming into your Sovereign's cabinet in this unmannerly fashion? The Duke of Xara himself lets himself be announced, Marquis!"

"Sir . . . ."

"What? Speak up . . . !"

"Her Majesty . . . ."

"Well, Her Majesty . . . ?"

"Prince Berengar . . . . the fever has increased: he is delirious, Sir, and the doctors . . . ."

The Emperor turned pale.

"Is he dead?" he asked, fiercely. "Tell me so at once."

"Not dead, Sir, but . . . ."

"But what?"

" But the doctors . . . . have no hope. . . ."

With an oath of anguish the Emperor thrust the aide aside, and rushed forward, out of the room.

The Prince remained standing. Life returned to him; a reality full of anguish, born of nightmare. His eyes swam with tears.

" Xardi . . . ." he implored ; " your house has always been loyal to our House; swear to me that you will keep silence."

The Marquis looked at the Crown Prince in consternation.

" Highness . . . ."

" Swear to me, Xardi."

" I swear to you, Highness," said the aide, subdued, and he stretched out his fingers to the crucifix that hung on the wall.

Othomar pressed his hand.

" Did Prince Berengar . . . ."

He could scarcely speak.

" Did Prince Berengar become so ill suddenly . . . ? "

" The fever is increasing every moment, Highness, and he is delirious. . . ."

" I will go to him," said Othomar.

He wiped the blood from his ear with his pocket-handkerchief, and held the cambric, which was at once soaked through, against it.

In the last ante-room he passed the chamberlain, and looked at him askance. Xardi stood still a moment.

" The Duke of Xara has hurt himself slightly," he said. " He was examining something in the Emperor's pistol when I came in, and he started : two shots went off."

" I heard them," whispered the chamberlain, growing pale.

" There might have been an accident . . . ."

They were silent for a moment, their glances understood each other. A shudder crept down their spines. The night seemed to be descending coldly over the palace, as with clouds of ill-omen.

" And . . . . the little Prince . . . ? " asked the chamberlain, shivering.

Xardi shrugged his shoulders; his eyes grew moist, through innate, immemorial love for his sovereigns.

" He is dying . . . ." he replied, faintly.

VI

The Crown Prince passed through the ante-room : one of the doctors stood there, dipping poultices in a basin of ice ; a valet was bringing in a pail of fresh ice. The door of the bedroom was open, and Othomar remained standing at the door. The little Prince lay on his camp-bed, and talked away in a low, sing-song tone; the Empress, pale, suffering, bearing up in spite of everything, sat next him with the Princess Thera.

The Emperor exchanged brief words with the two other doctors, whose features were overcast with a rigid hopelessness; a mordant anguish distorted Oscar's face, which became furrowed with deep wrinkles.

"My God, he does not know me, he does not know me!" Othomar heard the Emperor complain.

"Nor me," murmured the Empress.

"What can it be? what, what, what can it be?" sang the little Prince, and his usually shrill little voice sounded soft as a bird's melody: it was as though he were playing by himself.

"I'm to have a present from my brother, from my brother, something nice!" he sang on; and the Empress could distinguish his words, but she did not understand, and when he went on to sing the name of the Crown Prince, with his title:

"Othomar, O Othomar of Xara, of Xara . . . ." she turned to the door, and gently implored:

"Othomar, he is calling your name; come, perhaps he will know you!"

Othomar approached; he went past the Emperor, he knelt down by the bed; a smile lit up Berengar's little face.

"He is becoming calmer," said the good-natured doctor, whose tears were running down his face, to Oscar. "Does Your Majesty see: the Prince recognizes His Highness the Duke. . . ."

Gladness resounded in his voice.

A violent jealousy distorted the Emperor's features.

"No, no," he said.

"Certainly, Sir, only look," urged the doctor, his hope reviving.

"O Othomar, O Othomar of Xara," sang the little Prince: he had recognized his brother, but did not see him in the flesh, saw him only in his waking dream, through the mist of his fever.

"What do you bring me that's nice? Smaller than a horse, but heavier? Heavier? Oh, how heavy it is, how heavy, heavy, heavy. . . ."

His little voice came as though with an effort, as though he were lifting something; his convulsive, small, broad hands made a gesture of lifting with difficulty.

"Berengar," said the Crown Prince, and his voice broke, his heart sank within him. . . .

"Othomar," replied the child.

A cry of anguish escaped the Emperor.

"Yes, you're always so kind to me," continued the little Prince in his sing-song. "You always give me such nice things. You know, those lovely cannons on my birthday? And that pistol? But Mamma's so afraid of that. . . . Are you dying, Othomar? Look, there's blood on your ear. . . . But when people bleed they die! Are you dying, Othomar? Look, blood on your coat. . . ."

The Empress remained rigidly sitting; she looked from Berengar to the bleeding wound of her eldest son. . . .

"Blood, blood, blood!" sang the child. "Othomar is dying! Yes, he always gives me so many nice things, does Othomar. I have so many already, many more than all the other children of Liparia! And what am I to have now . . . . still more? That nice thing? What is it? I can feel it: it's so heavy, but I can't see it. . . ."

The doctor had come from the ante-room, and approached with the poultices.

"I can't see it . . . . I can't see it . . . !" the child sang out, painfully.

When the doctor applied the poultices, he struggled against it, he began to cry, as though a great sorrow were springing up in his little heart.

" I can't see it ! " he sobbed. " I shall never see it . . . ! "

A violent paroxysm succeeded the sobbing; he hit out wildly with his arms, pulled off the poultices, threw the ice off his head, stood up with little mad eyes in his bed, flung away the sheets. . . . Othomar rose, the Empress also. The Emperor sat in a chair, his face covered with his hands, and sobbed by the Princess Thera's side. The doctors approached the bed, endeavoured to calm Berengar, but he struck them : the fever mounted up in his little brain in madness.

At this moment Professor Barzia entered; he did not live in the palace ; he had been sent for at his hotel.

" What is Your Highness doing here ? " he said, straight out to Othomar.

The Crown Prince made no reply.

" Your Highness will retire immediately to your own rooms," commanded the Professor.

" Save my boy ! " exclaimed the Emperor, broken, sobbing.

22

"I am saving the Crown Prince first, Sir; he is killing himself here!"

"Very well, but next save him!" shouted Oscar, fiercely.

The other doctors had given orders; a tub was brought in, filled with tepid water, regulated by a thermometer. . . . But Othomar saw nothing more, he rushed away, driven out by Barzia's stern glances. He rushed along the corridors, through a group of officers and chamberlains, who stood together anxiously whispering, and made way for him. He plunged into his own study, which was not lighted. In the dark, he thought he was flinging himself upon a couch, but bumped down upon the ground. There he remained lying. Then, as though crushed by the darkness, he began to croon, to moan, to sob aloud with sharp, hysterical cries.

Andro entered; his foot knocked against the Prince. He lit the gas, tried to lift up his master. But Othomar lay as heavy as lead; fierce and prolonged, his nervous cries started from his throat. Andro rang, once, twice, three times; he went on ringing for a long time; at last there appeared a lackey and a chamberlain together at different doors.

"Call Professor Barzia!" cried Andro to the

lackey. "Excellency, will you help me lift His Highness . . . !" he implored the chamberlain. But when the lackey turned round, he ran up against the Professor, who could do nothing for the little Prince, and had followed the Crown Prince. He saw Othomar lying on the floor, moaning, screaming. . . .

"Leave me alone with His Highness," he commanded, with a glance around him.

The chamberlain, Andro, the lackey obeyed his command.

The Professor was a tall old man, heavily built and strong; he approached the Prince and lifted him up in his arms, notwithstanding the leaden heaviness of hysteria. So he held him, merely with his arms round him, upon the couch, and looked deep into his eyes, with trenchant glances. Suddenly Othomar ceased his cries; his voice was hushed. His head fell feebly upon Barzia's shoulder. The latter continued to hold him in his arms. The Prince became calm, like a quieted child, without Barzia's having uttered a word.

"May I request Your Highness to go to bed," said the Professor, with a gentle voice of command.

He helped Othomar to get up, and himself lit

the light in the bedroom, assisted the Prince to take off his coat.

"What has made Your Highness's ear bleed?" asked Barzia, whose fingers were soiled with clotted blood.

"A shot . . . ." Othomar began, faintly; his reversed face and closed eyes told the rest.

The Professor said nothing more; as though Othomar were a child, he went on helping him, washed his ear, his neck, his hands, with a mother's gentleness. Then he made him lie down in bed, covered him over, arranged the room like a servant. Then he went and sat by the bed, where Othomar lay staring with strange, wide-open eyes; he took the Prince's hand, and stayed so for a long time, looking softly down upon him. The light behind, turned down low, threw Barzia's large head into the shadow, and only just glanced upon his bald skull, from which a few gray locks hung down to his neck. At last he said, gently:

"Your Highness wishes to get well, do you not?"

"Yes," said Othomar, in spite of himself.

"How does your Highness propose to do so?" asked the Professor.

The Prince made no reply.

" Does your Highness not know? Then you must think it over. But you must keep yourself very calm, will you not, very calm. . . ."

And he stroked Othomar's hand with a gentle, regular motion, as though anointing it with balsam.

" For Your Highness must never give way again to a nervous attack. Your Highness must consider how to prevent them. I am giving Your Highness much to consider," continued Barzia, with a smile. " I am doing this because I want to let Your Highness think of other things than of what you are thinking. I want to clear your brain for you. Are you tired and do you wish to go to sleep, or shall I go on talking? "

" Yes, go on," whispered the Prince.

" Days of great trouble are in store for the Imperial . . . ." the doctor began again, gently. " Your Highness must think of those days without permitting yourself to be overcome by the trouble of them. . . . The little Prince will probably not recover, Highness. Will you think of that, and think of your parents, Their poor Majesties? There are days like that for a nation or for a single family, upon which trouble seems to pile itself up. For does not this day, this night seem to be the end of your race, my

Prince? Be still, be still, do not move; let me talk on, like a garrulous old man. . . . Does Your Highness know that the Emperor to-day, for the first time in his whole life, cried, sobbed? His younger son is dying. Between this child and the father is a first-born son, who is very, very ill. . . . Is not all this the end?"

"Yet if God wills it so . . . ." whispered Othomar.

"It is our duty to be resigned," said Barzia. "But does God will it so?"

"Who can tell. . . ."

"Ask yourself, but not now, Highness, to-morrow, to-morrow. . . . After the most painful nights . . . . the mornings come again. . . ."

The Professor rose and mixed a powder in a glass of water.

"Drink this, Highness. . . ."

Othomar drank.

"And now lie quiet and close those wide eyes."

"I shall not be able to sleep though. . . ."

"That is not necessary, only close those eyes. . . ."

Barzia stroked them with his hand; the Prince kept them closed. His hand again lay in the hand of the Professor.

A hush descended upon the room. Outside, in
the galleries, perplexed steps sometimes approached, from the distance, in useless haste ;
then they sounded away, far away, in despair. A
world of sorrow seemed to fill the palace, there,
outside that room, until it held every hall of it
with its dark, tenebrous woe. But in this one
room nothing stirred. The Professor sat still,
and stared before him, absorbed in reflection ; the
Crown Prince had fallen asleep like a child.

VII

The next morning the day rose upon the mourning of an Empire. Prince Berengar had suc-
cumbed in the night.

Othomar had slept long, and woke late in a
strange calm. When Professor Barzia told him
about the young Prince's end—the apathy of the
last moments, after a raging fever—it seemed to
him as if he already knew this. The great sorrow
that he felt was singularly peaceful, without
rebellion in his heart, and surprised himself.
He remained lying calmly, when the Professor
forbade him to get up. He pictured to himself
without emotion the little Prince, immoveable,

202

with his closed eyes, on his camp-bed. Mechanically he folded his hands, and prayed for his
brother's little soul.

He was not allowed to leave his room that day,
and only saw the Empress, who came to him for
an instant. He was not at all surprised that she
too was calm, with dry eyes: she had not yet
shed tears. Even when he raised himself from
his pillows, and embraced her, she did not cry.
Nor did he cry, but only his own calmness
astonished him: not hers. She only stayed for
a moment; then she withdrew with mechanical
steps, and he was left alone. He saw nobody
else that day, except Barzia: even Andro did not
enter his room.

Outside the chamber the Prince could divine
the sorrow of the palace, judging from certain
steps in the corridors, certain sounds of voices—
the little that penetrated to him; he pictured to
himself the rumour of sorrow going through the
country, through Europe, and causing the people
to stand in consternation in the presence of Death,
which had surprised them. Life was not secure:
who could tell that he would be alive to-morrow!
Vain were the plans of men: who could tell what
the hour would bring forth! And he remained
thinking of this calmly, in the singular peace-

fulness of his soul, in which he saw the futility of struggling against Life and against Death.

Not till next day did Barzia give him leave to get up, late in the afternoon. After his shower-bath, he dressed quietly, in his lancer's uniform, with crape round the sleeve. When he saw himself in the glass, he was surprised at his resemblance to his mother, at seeing how he now walked with the same mechanical step. Barzia allowed him to go to the Empress's salon. He there found her, the Emperor, Thera, and the Archduke and Archduchess of Carinthia, who had arrived at Lipara the preceding evening. They sat close together; now and then a low word was exchanged.

Othomar went up to the Emperor and would have embraced him; Oscar, however, only pressed his hand. After that Othomar embraced his sisters and his brother-in-law. Then he sank down by the Empress, took her hand in his, and sat still. She looked attenuated and white as chalk in her black gown. She did not weep: only the two Princesses sobbed persistently, again and again.

The family dined alone in the small dining-room, unattended. A depression had sunk down upon the palace, which seemed to be entirely

silent at this hour, with only now and then the
soft footsteps through the galleries of an aide-de-
camp carrying a funeral wreath in his hand, or a
lackey bringing a salver full of telegrams.   After
the short dinner, the family withdrew once more
to the Empress's salon.   The hours dragged on.
Night had quite fallen.   Then the Archbishop of
Lipara was announced.

The Imperial family rose ; they went through
the galleries, unattended, to the great Knights'
Hall.   Halberdiers stood at the door, in mourning.   They entered.   The Emperor gave his hand
to the Empress, and led her to the throne, whose
crown and draperies were covered with crape.   On
either side were seats for Othomar, the Princesses,
the Archduke.

In the middle of the hall, in front of the throne,
rose the catafalque, under a canopy of black and
ermine.   On it lay the little Prince in uniform.
Over his feet hung a small blue Knight's robe
with a great white cross ; a child's sword lay on
his breast, and his little hands were folded over
the jewelled hilt.   By his little head, somewhat
higher up, shone, on a cushion, a small Marquis's
coronet.   Six gilt candelabra with many tall
candles shone quietly down upon the child, and
left the great hall still deeper in shadow : only,

outside, there rose the moon in the distant blue, nocturnal sky; here and there it tinged with a white glamour the armour, the trophies that hung or stood like iron spectres in niches and against the wall. At the foot of the catafalque, on a table like an altar, with a white velvet cloth, a great, gilt crucifix spread out its two cross-arms, between candelabra, compassionately.

With drawn swords, motionless as the armour on the wall, stood four Knights of St. Ladislas, in their blue robes, two and two, at either side of the catafalque.

A soft perfume of flowers was wafted about. All round the catafalque the wreaths of every kind of white blossom were heaped up in piles; the aroma of violets predominated.

They sat down: the Emperor, the Empress, and their four children. Slowly the Archbishop entered with his priests and acolytes. Then the Imperial party knelt down on cushions before their seats. The Prelate read the requiem, and the Latin of the *Kyrie Elcison* and the *Agnus Dei* implored for Berengar's little soul amongst the souls in Purgatory, quivered gently through the vast hall, was wafted with the perfume of the flowers over the motionless, sleeping face of the Imperial child. . . .

The rite came to an end; the Prelate sprinkled the holy water, went sprinkling around the cata-falque. The Princes left the hall, but Othomar stayed on.

" I want to place my wreath . . ." he said, softly, to the Empress.

The priests also departed, slowly; the Crown Prince expressed to the four Knights, who were waiting to be relieved by others, his desire to remain alone for a moment. They too went. Then he saw Thesbia appear at the door, with a large white wreath in his hand. He went towards the aide-de-camp, and took the wreath from him.

Othomar remained alone. The hall stretched itself out long, broad, with dark boundaries. The moon had risen higher, seemed whiter, cast a ghostly glamour over the suits of armour. In the centre, as though it were something holy, between the pious gleams of the tall candles . . . rose the catafalque, lay the Prince.

The Crown Prince ascended two steps of the catafalque, and deposited his wreath. Then he looked at Berengar's face; no fever distorted it now; it lay peacefully, white, as though it were sleeping. All sounds had died away in the hall; a deadly silence supervened. Here the world of sorrow which had filled the palace and the nation seemed to have become sanctified in an ecstasy of calm. And Othomar saw himself alone with his soul. The uncertainty of life, the vanity of human intentions were again revealed to him, but more clearly; it was no black mystery, and it became harmony. It was as though he saw the whole harmony of the past; in the whole of Liparia's historical past, in the whole past of the world there sounded not one false note. All sorrow was sacred and harmonic, brought nearer to the lofty End, which would again be Beginning, and never anything but harmony. Resignation descended upon his mood like a spirit of holiness; his strange calmness became resignation. It was as though his nerves were relaxed in one great alleviation.

And in his resignation there was only the melancholy thought that he would never again hear the lofty, commanding little voice of the child of whom he had been fond. That this little life had lived its course, so soon, and for ever. In his resignation there was only mingled the astonishment that all this was so ordered, and not as he had imagined it. He himself would have to wear the crown which he had wished to resign to Berengar. And it seemed to him now as though he were receiving it back from the little dead one himself. For this reason no doubt he felt an absence of rebellion in his soul, he felt this peace, this conception of harmony. His gift returned to him again as an heritage.

Long he stood thus, thinking, staring at his motionless little brother, and his thought was simplified within him; he saw lying straight before him the road which he should follow. . . .

Then he heard his name:

"Othomar. . . ."

He looked up and saw the Empress at the door. She approached.

"Barzia was asking where you were," she whispered. "He was becoming uneasy about you. . . ."

He smiled to her, and shook his head to say no, that he was calm.

She came close, climbed the steps of the catafalque, and leant against his arm.

"How peaceful his little face is . . ." she murmured. "O Othomar, I have not yet given him my last kiss. And to-morrow he will no longer belong to me: all those people will then be filing past."

"But now, Mamma, he still belongs to us, to you. . . ."

" Othomar. . . ."

" Mamma. . . ."

" Shall I not have . . . to lose you also ? "

" No, Mamma, not me. . . . I shall continue to
live . . . for you. . . ."

He embraced her ; she looked up at him, surprised at his voice. Then she looked again at
her child. She released herself from her son's
arms, raised herself still higher, bent over the little
white face and kissed its forehead. But so soon
as the stony coldness of the dead flesh met her
lips, she drew back, stared stupidly at the corpse,
as though she now for the first time realized it.
Her arms grew stiff with cramp; she wrung
her fingers ; she fell straight back upon Othomar.

And her eyes became moist with the first tears
that she had shed for Berengar's death, and she
hid her head in Othomar's arms, and sobbed,
sobbed. . . .

Then he led her carefully, slowly down the
steps of the catafalque, led her out of the hall.
In the corridor they came across Barzia; the
Prince's quiet, calm face, as he supported his
mother, put the Professor at ease. . . .

So soon as the Empress and the Crown Prince
had left the Knights' Hall, four Knights of St.
Ladislas entered in their blue robes. They took

up their position on either side of the catafalque,
and remained standing motionless in the candle-
light, staring before them, watching in the night
of mourning over the little Imperial corpse, upon
which the blue light of the moon now fell. . . .
The priests too entered, and prayed. . . .

The palace was silent. When Othomar had
consigned his mother at the door of her apartments to the care of Hélène of Thesbia, he went
through the galleries to his own rooms. But on
turning a corridor, he started. The great state-
staircase yawned, faintly lighted, at his feet, with
beneath it the hollowness of the colossal entrance-
hall. Upholsterers were there occupied in draping
the banisters of the staircase with crape gauze,
for the time when the coffin should be carried
downstairs. With wide arms they measured out
the mists of black, threw black cloud upon cloud ;
the clouds of crape heaped themselves up with a
dreary lightness, up, and up, and up, seemed to
fill the whole staircase, and to rise stair upon
stair as though about to conquer the whole palace
with their gloom.

The upholsterers did not perceive the Crown
Prince, and worked on, silently, in the faint light.
But a cold thrill passed through Othomar. In
deathly pallor he stared at the men who at his

feet measured out the crape and sent the clouds up towards him. He called to mind his dream: the streets of Lipara overflowing with crape till the very sun reeled. . . . His blood seemed to freeze in his veins. . . .

Then he made the sign of the Cross.

"O God, give me strength!" he prayed in consternation. . . .

VIII

The next day, through the guard of honour of the Grenadiers, the people filed past the body of the little Prince. The following morning, it was removed to Altara, and interred in the Imperial vault in the Cathedral of St. Ladislas. The Princes Gunther and Herman of Gothland had come over for the ceremony, but the Duke of Xara was forbidden by Professor Barzia to take part in it: he stayed on at Lipara.

The Gothlandic Princes and their suite returned with the Emperor Oscar to the capital, where, at her sister's pressing request, Queen Olga had also come, with Princess Wanda. And in the mourning stillness of the Imperial, the family drew together in a narrow circle of inti-

23

macy. After her first tears, the Empress
Elizabeth had lost her unnatural calm; she
constantly gave way to violent fits of sorrow,
which Queen Olga or Othomar with difficulty
succeeded in allaying. The Emperor was inconsolable, submitted with childish vehemence
to his grief. Nobody had ever seen him like that
before, nobody recognized him. The fact that he
had lost his favourite child aroused his soul to
rebellion against God. In addition to this, he
had very much taken to heart his last conversation with Othomar, in which the latter had
spoken to him of abdicating. The Emperor
had not returned to the subject, but it was
never out of his thoughts. He feared that he
would have to go into it with Othomar again.
He was furious when he felt how impotent he was
to forbid the Crown Prince to take this desperate
resolution. And he pictured to himself the constitutional results if the Prince were to persist:
the Archduchess of Carinthia Empress, the Archduke Prince Consort, and the House of Czyrkiski
no longer reigning on the throne of Liparia in the
male line. The possibility of this occurring, taken
together with his sorrow on account of Berengar's
death, made the Emperor Oscar suffer with that
very special suffering of a monarch in whose blood

still flows all the inherited attachment to the
greatness of his ancestors, and who hopes to see
this maintained for all time. And he was also
inconsolable for the loss of the child whom he
loved best, more profoundly, but also more
silently, in greater secrecy—as he did not speak
about it—and on this occasion his grief was
probably more poignant at this idea, the future
which he saw imaged before him. He had not
even spoken of it to the Empress, from a certain
fear and superstition.

And to this mental sorrow—that his valiant
soul, which had always retained a touch of childishness, allowed itself to grow weak, as though it
were the soul of any other mortal rather than his :
that of a monarch—there was mingled his sub-
stantial annoyance about the Army Bill. There
would be three hundred millions necessary; one
hundred millions had already been granted for the
increase of the infantry; the other two hundred
for the artillery Count Marcella, the Minister for
War, had not yet succeeded in obtaining. The
majority of the Army Committee was against this
colossal arming of the frontier fortresses; in the
House of Representatives the Minister already
suspected a violent opposition, was prepared for
his overthrow. Neither Oscar, Myxila nor

Marcella were willing to make the least com-
promise. And Oscar moreover was prepared to
support his minister to the point of impossibility.

It was at this period that Othomar made
General Ducardi acquaint him thoroughly with
this question, studied the staff-charts, and
military statistics, and reports of the committee,
followed the parliamentary discussions from out
of his solitude. He held long deliberations with
the General. He had, however, not for months
attended the morning conferences in his father's
study. But one morning he dressed himself—as
was now no longer his wont—in uniform, and
sent a chamberlain to ask Oscar whether the
Emperor would permit him to be present at the
audience of Count Marcella. The Emperor was
surprised, shrugged his shoulders, but combated
his antipathy and sent his son word that he
might come. So soon as the minister and the
Imperial Chancellor were with the Emperor,
Othomar joined them. He had grown still more
slender, and the silver frogs of his Lancer's
uniform barely sufficed to lend breadth to his
slimness; he was pale and a little sunk in the
cheeks, but the glance of his eyes had lost its
former feverish restlessness and recovered its
melancholy calm, together with a certain rigid

haughtiness. He refrained at first from taking part in the discussion, let the Emperor curse, the Chancellor shrug his shoulders and rely on impossibilities, the Minister declare that he would never give in. Then, however, he asked Oscar for leave to interpose a word. He took a pencil in his hand; with a few short, decided lines of demonstration on the maps, with a few simple, correct indications on the registers, with a few figures which he quoted, accurately, by heart, he showed that he was quite conversant with the subject. He expressed the opinion that, in so far as he could gather from the reports of the committee, from the mood of the House of Representatives, it remained an undoubted fact that the two hundred millions would be refused. That the Minister would fall. He repeated these last words with emphasis, and then looked firmly first at his father, and then at Count Marcella. Then, in his soft voice, which tone upon tone rose and fell logically with serene words of conviction, he asked why one should not submit to circumstances, and make the most of them. Why not accept the one hundred millions for the infantry as so much gained, and—for this would after all be possible without immediate danger—endeavour to distribute the other two hundred over a period of

four or five years.   He was certainly of opinion
that an increase of twenty millions or so a year
would not meet with such violent opposition.
With such an arrangement Count Marcella would
be able to maintain himself in office and to be
supported by the Emperor. . . .

When he had ceased, a silence succeeded his
words.   His advice, if not distinguished by genius,
was at least practical, and made the most of this
critical situation.   Count Myxila slowly nodded his
head, approvingly.   The Emperor and Count Marcella could not at once adhere to Othomar's idea,
were stubborn, as though they still hoped to force
through the Army Bill unchanged as conceived
at first.   But the Chancellor took the same view
as the Crown Prince, proved it still more clearly
that an arrangement of this sort would be the
only one by which His Majesty would be able to
retain Count Marcella.   And the end of the
consultation was that the Duke of Xara's proposal should be taken into consideration.

When Myxila and Marcella had gone, the
Emperor asked the Prince to wait a moment
longer.

"Othomar," he said; "it gives me great
pleasure that you are again occupying yourself
with the affairs of our country. . . ."

He hesitated an instant, almost anxiously.

"What conclusion may I draw from this . . . for the future?" he continued at last, slowly.

The Crown Prince understood him.

"Papa," he said, gently. "I have had my moments of discouragement. I shall perhaps have them again. But forget . . . . what was said between us so shortly before Berengar's death. I have given up all thought of abdicating. . . ."

The Emperor drew a deep breath.

"I am religious, Papa, and I have faith," continued the Prince. "Perhaps an almost superstitious faith. I plainly see, in what has happened, the hand of God. . . ."

He passed his hand over his forehead, with a meditative gaze.

"The hand of God," he repeated. "I have had a presentiment of the death of one of us within this year. I thought that I myself should be the one to die. That is perhaps why, Papa, I did not see how monstrous it was of me to resolve as I did. I did not think of myself, who was bound in any event to die; I only thought of Berengar. But now he is dead and I live, and I shall now think of myself. For I feel that I do not belong to myself. And I feel that it is this that should make us hold ourselves up through life: this feeling that we do not belong to ourselves but to others. I have always loved our people, and I have wished to help them vaguely, in the abstract; I threw out my hands, without knowing why, and when I did not fulfil, it drove me to despair. . . ."

He suddenly stopped, looked shyly towards his father, as though he had gone too far in the delivery of his thoughts. But Oscar sat calmly listening to him, and he continued:

"And I now know that this despair is not right, because with this despair we retain ourselves for ourselves, and cannot give ourselves to others. You see," and he rose and smiled, "I cannot succeed in curing myself of my philosophy, but I hope now that it will teach me how to strengthen myself, instead of enervating me, as it now flows from quite a different principle."

The Emperor lightly shrugged his shoulders.

"Every one must work out his own theory of life, Othomar; I can only give you this advice: do not fanaticize, and keep your point of view a lofty one. Do not analyze yourself quite away, for such abnegation is not lasting and is sure later to resume the old rights. I do not reflect so much; I am more spontaneous and impulsive. But I do not wish to condemn you for being different; you cannot help it. You are perhaps more of this age than I am. I only wish to look at the result of your meditations, and that result is that you give yourself back to the ordinary life and to the interests of your country. And this rejoices me, Othomar. Nor do I wish to look too far into the future; I dare say that later too you will not have my ideas, I dare say that later you will reign with a brand-new constitution, with an elected Upper House. I dare say that you will receive great opposition from the Authoritative party among the nobles. . . . But, as I say, I do not wish to penetrate too far into that, and only rejoice over your moral convalescence. And I am very grateful to you for the advice you gave us just now. It was quite simple, but of ourselves we should never have thought of it. We are too tenacious for that. I think now that what you propose will be the best thing to be done, that it cannot be done otherwise. . . ."

He held out his hand, Othomar grasped it.

"And," he continued with the great loyalty which, in spite of his despotic haughtiness, lay at the root of his soul, "do not bear any malice because of . . . . the words I used to you,

Othomar. I am violent and passionate, as you
know. I was fonder of Berengar than of you.
But you yourself loved that child. Bear me no
malice, for his sake. . . . You are my son too,
and I am attached to you, if only because of
the fact that you are my son and the last of
my race . . . . forgive my candour."

Then he pressed Othomar in his arms. It
struck him painfully to feel the fragility of the
Prince in his firm embrace so immediately upon
his words : the last of my race. . . . A strange,
bitter despair went through his soul, but yet he
clearly divined the mystery of this fragility: an
unknown moral spring, which he himself lacked
in the simplicity of his methodical nature, but
which, to his great surprise, he discerned in his
son. When the Prince was gone and Oscar,
alone, thought of this, and sought this spring in
what was known to him of his son, he did not find
it, yet felt that, whatever it might be, it was something enviable : a strength that was tougher than
muscular strength. He looked about him ; his
eyes fell upon a portrait of the Empress on his
writing-table. How often had he not stared at it
in annoyance because of their successor, who was
so wholly her son. But as it were a gleam of
light passing before his eyes, he now looked at

the delicate features without his old peevishness, and a grateful warmth began to irradiate within him. Whatever it were, Othomar had derived this mysterious strength from his mother. It saved him, and spared him for his country, for his race. And—who knew?—perhaps this mystery was just the element that their race needed, a necessary constituent of its new lease of life . . . . He did not penetrate farther into this; the future — even although it was now emerging more clearly from out of its first dimness—had no attraction for him. He loved the past, those iron centuries with their heroes of Emperors. But he felt that everything was not lost. In his pious belief in the Highest, he thought, as did his son, of the hand of God. If it must be so, it was right. God's will was inscrutable.

And grateful to the Empress, grateful that it grew clear to him, he bent his knees before the crucifix upon the wall and prayed for his two sons, he prayed long for the son who was to bear his crown, but longer for the soul of the child of his own blood, whose loss would be the grief that would always be as wormwood in the depths of his soul, which was now poured out. . . .

IX

From the Journal of Alexa, Duchess of Yemena, Countess of Vaza.

—— Nov., 18—.

The Crown Prince has not accompanied the Emperor. Professor Barzia forbade him, because he considered that the big hunting-parties with which the Emperor wishes to divert his thoughts from his sorrow for our little Prince would be too fatiguing for my sweet invalid. I hear nevertheless from Dutri that he is making remarkable progress towards recovery, and has already resumed his daily morning ride.

It is over with me. Poor sinful heart within me, die. For after this last flower of passion that blossomed in you, I wish you to die to the world. For the sake of the purity of my Imperial flower, I wish you now to die. Nothing after this, nothing but the new Life which I see lifting before me. . . .

And yet, I am still young; I look no older in my glass than I did a year ago. I should not need, did I not wish it, to abdicate my feminine powers at all. And that is how every one looks at it, for I know that they whisper of the Duke of Mena-Doni, as though he would be glad to replace my adored Crown Prince in my heart. But it is not true, it is not true. And I am so glad of it, that they do not know me, and do not know it. That they do not understand, that I want to let my Imperial love fade purely away, and wish to cherish no earthly love after it.

Dear Love of my heart, you have raised me to my new Life! You were still sin, but yet you purified, because you yourself purified by the contact of that sacred something that is in sovereignty. Oh, you were the last sin, but already you were purer than the one before. For I have been a great sinner; I have offered up all my sinful woman's life to consuming passion, and it has left nothing behind it in my heart but ashes! Great scorching love of my life for him who is now dead—may his soul rest in peace—I will not deny you, because you have been my most intense earthly pleasure, because through you I first learnt to know that I had a soul, and because you thus brought me nearer to what I now see before me; and yet, what were you but earthliness! And my pure, Imperial love, what were you too but earthliness! Gentle sovereign of my soul, what will God have you be but earthly. An Empire awaits you, a crown, a sceptre, an Empress. God wills it thus, and therefore it is good, that you are earthly, while your earthliness is yet at the same time consecrated by your pious belief. But I, I have been more than merely earthly : I was sinful. And now I wish that my heart should entirely die within me, because it was nothing else than sin. Then shall my heart be born again, in new Life. . . .

I have prayed. For hours I lay on the cold marble of the oratory, till my knees pained me and my limbs were stiff. I have confessed my sinful life to my holy confessor, Monsignor of Vaza. Oh, the sweetness of absolution and the ecstasy of prayer ! Why do we not earlier feel the blessed consolation that is to be found in the fulfilment of our religious duties ! Oh, if I could wholly lose myself in that sweet mystery, in God ; if I could go into a convent ! But I have my two stepdaughters. I must bring them into Society ; it is my duty. And Monsignor says that it is my penance and my punishment : never to be able to withdraw myself into hallowing seclusion, but to have to continue to breathe the sinful atmosphere of the world.

I will give my castle in Lycilia, where we

never go, my own castle and patrimony, to our
Holy Church for a convent for Ursulines of gentle
birth. I went there recently with Monsignor.
Oh, the great sombre rooms, the frescoes in
shadow, the gloomy park! And the chapel, when
the new windows shall have been put in, through
which the light will fall down in a mystical confusion of colour. My dearest wish is to be able
to grow old there, and to be able to die entirely
from the world : but shall I ever be permitted,
Holy Mother of God, shall I ever be permitted !

.   .   .   .   .   .

Am I sincere ? Who knows, what do I myself
know ? Do I in reality feel this purification of
my soul, or do I still remain what I am ? A
fearful doubt rises within me ; it is Satan entering
into me! I will pray ; Holy Virgin, pray for me!

.   .   .   .   .   .

I have become calmer ; prayer has strengthened
me. Oh, full of anguish are the doubts which
tear me from my conviction. Then Satan says
that I am deluding myself into this conviction, in
order to console myself in my destitution, and
that I have become religious for want of occupa-
tion. I then see myself in the glass, young : a
young woman. But when I pray, the doubts

retire again from my sinful mood, and I look back
shuddering upon my wicked past.   And then the
new Life of my future again lights up before
me. . . .

Beloved Prince, lord of my soul, here in these
pages which none shall ever read, I take farewell
of you, because it was not vouchsafed me to
bid you farewell in the moment of tangible
reality.   Oh, I shall often, perhaps from day
to day, still see you in the confusion of the world,
in the ceremony of palaces, but you will never
again belong to me, and therefore I take farewell
of you.   Whatever I may be—a twofold sinner
perhaps, longing only for Heaven because the
earth is no longer mine—I have been true to you,
as I always have been, in love.   I have seen you
bowed down, you so frail, beneath your heavy yoke
of empire, and I have felt my heart overflow with
pity for you.   I have tried to give you my poor
sinful consolation as far as I could.   May Heaven
forgive me!   I met you at a moment when the
tears were flowing from your dear eyes with
bitterness because people hated you, and had
dared with traitorous hands to strike at your
Princely body, and I tried to give you what I
could of sweetness, so as to make you forget this
bitterness.   Ah, perhaps I was even then not

quite sincere; perhaps I am even not so now! But that would be too terrible; that would make me despise myself as I cannot do! And I will at least retain this illusion, that I was sincere. That I did wish to comfort you. That, sinful though it was, I did comfort you. That I did, in very truth, love you. That I still love you now. That I shall no longer love you—because I may not—as your mistress, but that I shall do so as your subject. The blood of my veins loves yours, your golden blood! And when I myself shall have found peace, and shall no longer doubt and hesitate, my last days shall be spent only in prayer for you, that you also may receive peace and strength for your future task of government. I feel no jealousy of her who is to be my future Empress. I know that she is beautiful, and that she is younger than I. But I do not compare myself with her. I shall be her subject, as I am yours. For I love you for your own sake, and I love everything that is yours. You are my Sovereign; you are my Sovereign even more than Oscar! Farewell, my Prince, my Crown Prince, my Sovereign! When I see you again, you will be nothing more to me than my Sovereign, and my Sovereign alone!

To His Most Gracious Imperial Highness
Othomar, Duke of Xara, Lipara.

Castel Vaza,
—— *Nov.*, 18—.

My beloved Prince,—Pardon me, if I ven-
ture to send you the accompanying pages. I
intended at first to send you a long letter, a letter
of farewell. And I did write you many, but did
not send them to you, and destroyed them. Then
I wrote to you only for myself, took leave of you
for myself. But can I trace what goes on within
me, what I think from one moment to the other ?
I did miss it so : my sweet farewell, which would
still bind me in some intimate way to you. And
so I could not refrain—at last, after much vacilla-
tion of mind — from sending you these pages,
which I had only written for myself. At your
feet, I beg of you, graciously accept them,
graciously read them. Then destroy them ;
through them you will learn the last thoughts
that I have dared to consecrate to the mystery
which had been our love. . . .

I press my lips to your adored hands.
Alexa.

CHAPTER VI

I

THE Empress Elizabeth rode with Hélène of
Thesbia in a victoria, preceded by an .outrider,
from St. Ladislas to the Old Palace, which, together with the Cathedral and the Episcopal,
formed one gigantic building; there, at Altara,
the Archduke Albrecht and the Archduchess
Eudoxie, with the Imperial bride, had the preceding day taken up their abode. From the
lofty fortified castle, which in a broad mass of
stone blocks looked over Altara with its crenulated plateaus and squat towers, the road wandered down, indistinguishable beneath the old
chesnut-trees, with somewhat tortuous zig-zags.
The dust flew up from the wheels; on both sides
lay villas with terraces, gay with vases, and
flowers and statues, sloping down lower and
lower towards the town. The villas blazed with

bunting; the blue-and-white flags with the white
crosses revelled in all their gaudy freshness beneath the dusty foliage of the old trees and
acacias.

It was June, six months after the death of the
little Prince, but the mourning had been softened
because of the approaching nuptials of the Duke
of Xara, which the Emperor wished to see celebrated as early as possible. The Empress, however, wore heavy mourning, which she would not
lay aside until the day of the wedding; Hélène
was in gray; the liveries were gray.

Many pedestrians, horsemen, equipages passed
along the road, stopped respectfully; the Empress
bowed to left and right; she received salutations
from the balconies of the villas. In this warm
summer weather there reigned a mellowness, a
soft gaiety all along the road; the road, with its
villas where the people sat in groups, breathed
out a friendliness which affected the Empress
pleasantly and made her heart swell within her
breast with a gentle melancholy. Children ran
about and played in white summer suits; then
stopped suddenly and, after the fashion of well-
bred children, accustomed to seeing the members
of the Imperial Family pass every day, they
bowed low, the boys awkwardly, the little girls

with newly-learnt courtesies. Then they went on
playing again. . . . And the Empress smiled at
a large family, old and young people together,
who sat on a terrace, doubtless celebrating a
birthday, and laughed and drank, with many
glasses and decanters before them : the children
with their mouths full of cake. So soon as they
saw the outrider, they stood up and all saluted,
some with their glasses still in their hands, and
the Empress, laying aside her usual stiffness,
bowed back with an amiable smile.

And it was as though she were driving through
a huge, luxurious village ; for a moment she forgot
the light obsession that depressed her, she forgot
why she was to-day going to Valérie, and allowed
herself to be rocked by her delight in the love
that she divined all round her. It was the love
of the old Liparian patrician families—noble or
not noble—for their sovereigns. It was a caress
which she never received at Lipara. And she
remembered Othomar's letter, at the time of the
inundations of last year : " why are we not oftener
at Altara . . . ? "

She could not for a moment desist from bowing.
But the town was now approached; the old houses
shifted like the wings at a theatre ; the whole
town shifted nearer, gay with flags, which threw

an air of youth over its old stonework. The streets were full; thousands of visitors, provincial or foreign, were at Altara; in the hotels there was no room to be had. And the Empress could scarcely speak a word to Hélène; she could do nothing but bow, bow perpetually. . . .

In the fore-court of the Old Palace, the infantry composing the guard-of-honour of the Austrian bride were drawn up, and presented arms as the Empress drove in. The Archduchess Eudoxie was awaiting the Empress.

" How is Valérie?" asked Elizabeth immediately.

" Better, calmer," replied the Archduchess; " I had not dared to hope it. But she will receive no one. . . ."

" Do send word whether I can see her. . . ."

The Archduchess's lady-in-waiting went off: she returned with the message that Valérie was expecting the Empress.

Elizabeth found the young girl in a white lace tea-gown, lying on a sofa, pale, with great, dark, dull eyes; she rose, however.

"Forgive me, Madam," she said, apologetically.

Elizabeth embraced her with great tenderness; the Archduchess said:

" I was not well, I felt so tired. . . ."

But then her eyes met those of the Empress, and she saw that the latter did not expect her to exhibit any superhuman endurance. She pressed herself up against the Empress, and cried softly, as a person cries who has already wept long and passionately, and is now exhausted with weeping, and has not the strength to weep except very softly. The Empress made her sit down, sat down beside her, and caressed her with a soothing movement of her hand. Neither of the two spoke; neither of the two found words in that difficult relation which at that moment they bore towards one another.

Two days ago, the day before that on which the bride was to set out on her journey to Altara, it had become known that Prince Von Lohe-Obkowitz had shot himself dead in Paris. The actual reason of this suicide was not known. Some thought that the Prince had taken very much to heart the disfavour of the Emperor of Austria and the disagreement with his family; others that he had lost a fortune at baccarat, and that his ruin was completed by the Bohemian extravagances of his wife, the notorious Estelle Desvaux, who herself had more than once been ruined, but had always come to the surface again by means of a theatrical tour and the sale of a few diamonds. Others again maintained that Prince Lohe had never been able to forget his love for the future Duchess of Xara. But whatever was asserted in Vienna court-circles, nothing was known for certain. Valérie had, accidentally, read the news, which they had endeavoured to conceal from her, in the same newspaper in which, now almost a year ago, she had also read, on the terrace at Altseeborgen, the news of Prince Lohe's proposed marriage and abdication of his rights. Her soul, which had no tendency towards mysticism, nevertheless, in the shock of despair that passed through it, became almost superstitious because of this repetition of cruelty. But when, months ago, she had combated and worn out her sorrow, it had been followed by an indifference for any further suffering that it might still befall her to experience in life. The death of her illusions was a final death ; after her betrothal she had found herself again, as with a new soul, hardened and girt round with indifference. It was strange, that in this indifference the only thing to which she continued sensible was that something exquisite in Othomar's character : his delicacy in sparing her at Altseeborgen, against Oscar's desire ; his broad feeling of universal love for his people ; his whole character of gentleness, his simple sense of duty. . . .

But however indifferent she might, for the rest, think herself, this second incident struck her cruelly, as though a refinement of fate had chosen the moment for it. The official journey from Sigismundingen to Altara had been a martyrdom. Valérie had endured like an automaton the receptions on the frontiers, the reception at the Central Station at Altara, with the greeting of her Imperial bridegroom, who had there kissed her, and the addresses of the authorities, the offering of bread and salt by the Canons of the Chapter of St. Ladislas. She had swallowed it down, their bread and salt. And the drive through the town, gay with bunting, and with triumphal arches erected from street to street, to the Old Palace, in the open landau with the Emperor and her bridegroom, right through the cheering of the people, that cut her ears and her over-excited nerves as it were with sharp-edged knives! Then, at the Palace, it had struck Othomar how like some hunted creature she looked, with her frightened eyes. Prince Lohe's death was known also at Altara, and though the people had cheered, cheered from true sympathy for the future Crown Princess, they had stared at her on that account, inquisitively, eager to see an august anguish shuddering in the midst of their festivities, pursued through arches of green and gala-flags. They had seen nothing. Valérie had bowed, smiled, greeted them with her hand from the balcony of the Old Palace by Othomar's side ! They had seen nothing, nothing, for all their tense curiosity, for all their inward imaginations. But presently Valérie's strength had come to an end. Her part was played, let the curtain fall. Othomar left her alone with a pressure of the hand. For hours she had sat lifelessly ; then night had come ; she could not sleep, but she had been able to sob.

Now it was the next day ; she lay down exhausted, but really she had cried, fought her last, recovered her indifference : no sorrows that were in store for her could ever hurt her again !

But the tender embrace of Othomar's mother softened her, and she again found her tears.

They barely exchanged a few words, and yet they felt a common sympathy passing between them. And through the midst of her sorrow Valérie could see her duty, which would at the same time be her strength ; no bitter indifference, but an acquiescence in what her life might be. Oh, she had imagined it differently in her dreams as a young girl : she had pictured it to herself as more agreeable and smiling and finding its

expression more naturally, more spontaneously
and without so much calculation. But she had
awakened from her dreams, and where else
should she seek her strength but in duty . . . !
And she conquered herself, whatever might be
destroyed in her soul, by a vitality she had not
suspected—her real nature—even more than by
her thoughts. She dried her eyes, spoke of the
fact that the time was approaching when a deputation of young Liparian noblewomen were to
come and offer her a wedding-present, and the
Empress left her alone, so that she might
dress.

She appeared shortly after, in a white toilette
worked with dull gold, in the drawing-room where
her parents sat with the Empress and with Hélène
of Thesbia and the Austrian ladies-in-waiting.
Shortly after came Othomar too, with his sisters
and the Archduke of Carinthia. And when the
deputation of young ladies of rank was announced, and appeared, with Eleonore of Yemena
in their midst, Valérie listened with her usual
smile to the address of the little Marchioness,
with a gracious gesture accepted from the hands
of two other girls the great case which they
caused to spring open, showing, upon light velvet,
a threefold necklace of large pearls. And she was

able to find a couple of pretty phrases of thanks;
she uttered them in a clear voice, and no one
who heard her would have suspected that she
had passed a sleepless night, bathed in tears,
with the lifeless body of a young man with
shattered temples before her eyes.

The young ladies of the deputation were permitted to see the wedding-presents, which were
displayed in a large room; Princess Thera and
the ladies-in-waiting accompanied them. There,
in that room, it was like a sudden gleam of
brilliancy, in the daylight streaming in on the
long tables, on which the presents stood surrounded by flowers : the heavily gilt candelabra,
gilt and crystal table and tea services, gilt and
silver caskets of various towns, a silver Cathedral
of Altara, silver ships with delicate, swelling sails
from naval institutions, and jewelled gifts from all
the Royal friends and relations of Europe. On
a satin cushion lay, like a fairy trinket, a sparkling Duchess's diadem of large sapphires and
brilliants, one of the presents of the bride's future
parents-in-law. And very striking was the present
of Princess Thera : the Duke of Xara's portrait,
a work of art that had already become known at
exhibitions in both of the capitals. But there
was little likeness left, and it was therefore the

despair of the Princess. It was younger, more indecisive, feebler than the Prince looked now : a little thinner than of old, but with a thicker stripe of moustache, and a lightly curling beard on his cheeks. The melancholy eyes had got more of the look of the Empress Elizabeth; for the rest too Othomar resembled his mother, and more than before. But what was still noticeable in the young Prince, in his nervous refinement, was the look of race, his trenchant distinction, his air of righteous haughtiness. He had lost much of his angularity, his stiff tactlessness, and had acquired something more certain and decided ; and in spite of his colder look, it inspired more confidence in a Crown Prince than his always sympathetic but somewhat feeble presence of former days. Thought seemed to be more sharply defined within him, the words to come more pointedly from between his lips ; he seemed to have more self-reliance, to care less for what others might think of him. It was, although not yet quite consciously, that unique Princely feeling that was awakening within him : his naïve, haughty, innate confidence in that single drop of golden blood which ran through his veins, and gave him his rights. . . .

It was Professor Barzia especially, who, attached

as he was to Othomar, and treating him personally
every day, had aroused this self-confidence with
his words, which were due both to his knowledge
of mankind and his love for the dynasty as well as
to a personal affection for the Crown Prince. The
cold-water douches had braced the Prince up,
but the suggestions of the Professor, who had
awakened Othomar's latent practical qualities as
it were from their lurking-place, had probably
been a still more efficacious remedy. The Prince
had learnt to govern himself, and he had become
dearer to the Professor and dearer. . . .

This devotedness, born of a discovery of what
others did not know—high qualities of temperament—was strengthened by Barzia's foster-
ing of those qualities, and, when the Prince's
marriage could be fixed, the Professor looked
down with as much pride as affection upon his
patient, whom he declared to be physically cured,
and considered, in his own mind, to be cured
morally. . . . .

II

Two days later was the day of the Imperial
wedding. The town was swarming from the
early morning with the people who had streamed

in from the environs, and who noisily crowded through the narrower streets. For already at an early hour the main thoroughfares had been closed by the infantry, from the Fortress to the Old Palace and the Cathedral. And Altara, otherwise gray, old, weatherbeaten, was unrecognizable, multi-coloured with flags, fresh with festoons of green, adorned with draperies and tapestry hanging from its balconies. A warm, Southern, May sun shed patches of light over the town, and the red and the blue and the white and the green of the expectant uniforms, with the even flash of the bayonets above them, drew broad lines of colour through it, with almost floral gaiety, up to the Fortress of St. Ladislas.

Through the closed streets court-carriages drove to and fro, blazing with uniforms : Royal guests who were being carried to St. Ladislas or the Old Palace. There were to be seen Russian, German, English, Austrian, Gothlandic uniforms ; briskly, as though preparing for the ceremonial moment, they flashed through Altara, through its long, empty streets hedged with soldiers.

Beneath the chesnuts on the Castle Road, the villas also thronged with spectators, who walked or sat in the gardens and terraces, and in the sunbeams that filtered through the foliage, the light summer-costumes of the ladies, their coloured sunshades made variegated patches; it was as though garden-parties were being given from villa to villa, while people waited for the procession of the bridegroom, who, in accordance with Liparian etiquette, left St. Ladislas to fetch his bride from the Old Palace.

Eleven o'clock. From the Fort of St. Ladislas booms the first shot, other shots come continually thundering after it. A buzz of excitement passes over the whole of the Castle Road. On the almost imperceptible incline of the road appear trumpeters and kettle-drums, heralds on horseback. Behind them come the slashing Throneguards, round the gilt and crystal gala-carriages. The High Chamberlain, the Count of Threma, in the first; in the second, with the Imperial crown and the plumed team of eight: grays caparisoned in scarlet—and the cheering from the villas rises higher and higher—the Emperor and the Duke of Xara himself by his side; in the following coaches the assembled majesties and highnesses from all Europe: the Empress of Liparia, the German Emperor and Empress, the King and Queen of Gothland, Russian Grand-Dukes, the Duke of Sparta and the Prince of Naples. . . . The Imperial Chancellor, the ministers, the robed

members of the House of Nobles. . . . And the
endless procession passes slowly amid the roar of
the cannon down the Castle Road through the
main streets and into the heart of the city. There,
in the Old Palace, the bride is waiting with all
her Austrian relations : the Emperor and Empress, the Archduke Albrecht and the Archduchess
Eudoxie. . . .

It is there that the marriage treaties are signed,
on the gilt table, covered with gold brocade, upon
which the Emperors and Empresses of Liparia
have written their signatures since centuries,
upon which, after the Crown-Princely couple, the
august witnesses sign the acts. . . .

Now the whole procession goes through gallery
after gallery to the New Sacristy. It is a ceremonious parade of some minutes : the trumpeters,
the heralds, the masters of ceremonies ; the blue-
robed Knights of St. Ladislas : the white-and-
gold Throneguards ; the Emperor Oscar with the
Duke of Xara, the Emperor of Austria with the
bride. . . . Slowly she walks by her uncle's side,
her head a little bent, as though beneath the
weight of her Princess's crown, from which the
blonde veil floats down, gently irradiating her bare
neck, which is studded with drops of brilliants.
Her gown is of stiff, heavy satin brocade, em-

25

broidered in front with silver and smothered beneath arabesques and emblems of pearls; great, white velvet puffed sleeves bourgeon up at her shoulders; the train of silver brocade and white velvet is so long that six maids-of-honour carry it after her, swaying from its silver loops. Behind the maids-of-honour follow the bridesmaids, dressed all alike with the same bouquets: they are the Princess Thera, the Princess Wanda, German, English and Austrian Princesses. And the Majesties and Highnesses follow; the procession flows into the New Sacristy; here the Cardinal-Archbishop, Primate of Liparia, with all his mitred clergy, receives the bridegroom and bride. . . .

In the Cathedral waits the crowd of invited guests. In spite of the glow of the summer sun, a mystic twilight of shadow hovers through the tall and stately arches of the Cathedral, and the daylight blossoms only on the multi-coloured windows of the side-chapels; in the vaultings it is quite dark. But the high altar is one blaze of innumerable candles. . . .

The Imperial Chancellor, the ministers, the ambassadors, the whole diplomatic body, the members of the House of Nobles and Representatives, members of the High Court have entered;

they fill the tiers that have been erected to right
and left. And the whole Cathedral is filled; one
great swarm of heavy rustling silks—the gala-
dresses of the low-necked ladies, whose jewels
sparkle—a blaze of gold on the glittering uniforms
and gala-coats, which like great sparks light up
the twilight of the Cathedral.

Then sound the trumpets, the organ peals out
its jubilant tones in the solemn festival march;
the first cortège enters through the Sacristy: the
German Emperor with the Empress Elizabeth of
Liparia and the Archduchess Eudoxie, and a long
train of followers. . . . Now the trumpets sound,
the organ peals unceasingly, and the invited
Majesties with their suites, the representatives of
the Powers enter in procession after procession.
The canopies to right and left of the choir begin
to fill up. Soon the second cortège follows: the
dignitaries in front, with the insignia of Empire;
the Emperor Oscar, leading the Duke of Xara:
both wear over their golden uniforms the long,
draped blue robes of the Knights of St. Ladislas,
with the large white cross gleaming on the left
arm; four Crown Princes follow as the four
witnesses of the bridegroom: the Duke of
Wendeholm, the Czarevitch, the Duke of Sparta,
and the Prince of Naples; the Knights of St.

Ladislas, the officers of the Throneguards, grooms and pages follow after. . . .

And suddenly, a choir of high voices vibrates with a crystal shrillness, and proclaims a blessing on the bride, who comes in the name of the Lord. . . . The third cortège has entered : the Emperor of Austria and the Archduke Albrecht, leading the bride, with her maids-of-honour and her bridesmaids, and she seems to be one white opulence of high-born maidenhood among her white and fragrant retinue. And the song scatters its sounds as with handfuls of silver lilies before her feet ; her solemn advent arouses an emotion that quivers through all that confused splendour, through the whole cathedral. Now, at last, appears the fourth cortège : the Cardinal-Archbishop, Primate of Liparia, with his Bishops and Canons and Chaplains; the high ecclesiastics take their seats in the tall sculptured stalls of the choir ; the rite begins. . . .

The sun seems to have waited until this moment to come shooting down, through the tall, multi-coloured, pointed windows, upon which the life of St. Ladislas sparkles with its small, square jewel-coloured tableaus, shooting down with a gleaming mass of rays upon the choir, upon the priests, upon the canopies where the Majesties are

sitting, upon the bridegroom and bride. . . .
And all the colours—the old gold of the altar, the
new gold of the uniforms, the brocades, and the
jewels of the crowns—all flame up as though the
sun were setting them on fire: one conflagration
of changing sparks which, together with the
numberless candles on the altar, suddenly irradi-
ates the church. The diadems of the Princesses
are like crowns of flame, the orders of the Princes
like stars of a firmament. The acolytes swing
incense that clouds up misty blue, delicate, transparent in the sunshine; the sunshine powders
through the blonde veil of the kneeling bride,
lights a glowing fire over her white-and-silver
train, illuminates her as with an apotheosis of
light that reflects a maiden paleness upon her.
Her bridegroom kneels beside her: his blue robe
enfolds him entirely; on his arm, the pure sheen
of the white cross. Both now hold tall candles
in their hands. And the Primate, with his
jewelled mitre and his stiff gold dalmatic covered
with jewelled arabesques, raises his eyes, spreads
his hands on high, and stretches them in benedic-
tion above the bent Imperial heads. . . .

The chant swells high again; the *Te Deum
Laudamus*, as though the waves of the voices
were rising upon the waves of the organ, higher

and higher, up through the cathedral to the sky in one ecstasy of sacred music. The old, stone, giant building seems to quiver with emotion, as though the music became its soul, and it sends out over Altara from all its bells a swelling sea of sound, bronze in the depths, and molten out of all metals into gold of crystal purity, in the highest heighth of audible sound. . . .

An hour later. On the closed Cathedral Square movement begins again, among the waiting gala-carriages. Now the procession returns to St. Ladislas, but behind the Emperor Oscar's carriage Othomar and Valérie now sit together. And the city cheers, and echoes out its vivats; the houses groan with it through all the flags and trophies. The guards present arms, and in the festal intoxication it passes unnoticed how yonder in the smaller streets fighting goes on, arrests are made, a well-known anarchist is almost murdered by the Imperialist populace. . . .

With its costly pageant, now heightened by the white presence of the young Duchess of Xara and her own retinue, the endless and endless procession returns, through the town, up the Castle Road, and there, too, the villas now see Valérie, and cheer to her, endlessly.

It is in the White Throne-room that Othomar

and Valérie hold their court: all defile before
them : the ministers and ambassadors, the
members of both Houses, of the Courts of
Justice, corporations and deputations. After the
court, the *déjeuner*, at which the table glitters
with the ceremonial gold and jewelled plate,
which is only used at the Imperial marriages.
After the *déjeuner* the last observance: in the
Gold Hall—a vast low hall, Byzantine in archi-
tecture and decoration, ages old and unchanged—
the torch-dance ; the procession of the ministers,
who carry tall, lighted links in gilded handles,
while Othomar and Valérie keep on inviting the
Highnesses according to rank, invite all the
Highnesses in turns, and march round behind the
ministers. . . . It is a monotonous ceremony,
continually repeated : the ministers with the
torches, Othomar with a Princess and crowded
about by the Knights of St. Ladislas, Valérie with
a Prince and all her white suite ; and it is a relief
when the function is finished and the newly-
married couple have withdrawn to change their
dress. Then they appear: Othomar as commanding officer of the Cuirassiers of Xara,
Valerie in her white cloth travelling-dress and
hat with white feathers, and they pay their
adieus ; an open landau awaits them, and with

a compact escort of the Cuirassiers of Xara they
ride anew through the town, ride in every
direction, show themselves everywhere, bow to
every one, and at last drive out to the castle
where they will spend the first days of the
honeymoon : Castle Zanthos, near the town, on
the broad river. . . .

And the old weather-beaten capital, which
remains full of majesties, which still flutters with
pennants, which in the evening is one yellow
flame and red glow of fireworks and illumination,
seems no less, without the newly-married couple,
to have lost the attraction which turned it into
the centre of festivity and splendour and Imperial
ceremony ; and in the evening, despite the
illuminations and fireworks and gala-perform-
ances, the Central Station is besieged by
thousands leaving. . . .

III

It was months after the wedding of the Duke
of Xara that the Emperor Oscar, entering his
study very early in the morning, and moving
towards his writing-table, caught sight of a piece
of cardboard with large, black letters affixed,

that lay on the floor by the window. He did not pick it up; although he was alone, he did not turn pale, but on his low forehead the thick veins swelled with rage to feel that he was not even safe in his own study from their treason. He rang and asked for his valet, a trusted man.

"Pick up that thing!" he commanded, and thundered through the silence: "How did it get here?"

The valet turned pale. He read the threatening words of abuse, with their big, fat letters, as it lay on the ground; stooped, and held the placard in his trembling hand.

"How did it get here?" repeated the Emperor, stamping his foot.

The valet swore that he did not know. In the morning no one was permitted to enter the study but he himself; half an hour ago he had come in to open the windows, and then he had seen nothing.

"The only explanation is, Sir, that some one stole in through the park and flung it through the window. . . ."

This doubtless was the only explanation, but it was an explanation that annoyed the Emperor exceedingly. It was not the first time that the Emperor had found such placards in the intimacy

of his study.   The result was that sudden arrests
were made in the Imperial of servants, of soldiers
of the various guards, but these arrests and
inquiries had brought nothing to light, and therefore made an impression all the more painful.
The guards of the palace, the guards at the gilt
railings of the park, where this merged into the
Elizabeth Parks—the public gardens of the
Capital—were already increased ; the secret
police, the Emperor's own police, even kept a
sharp watch on the guards themselves.

The Emperor Oscar looked fixedly at the valet ;
the thought rose in him for a moment to have this
man himself examined, but he immediately afterwards saw the absurdity of such suspicion : the
man had been for years and years in his personal
service, was entirely devoted to him, and stood
answering Oscar's long gaze with the calm,
respectful eyes, evidently pondering over the
mystery of the strange riddle.

" Burn that thing," ordered the Emperor ;
" and don't talk about it."

Subsequently Oscar had a long interview with
the head of his secret police, with whom he had
recently had every reason for satisfaction : secret
printing-presses of Anarchist papers, that were
continually being distributed, had been dis-

covered ; a plot to blow up the Imperial train on its way from the summer-palace in Xara, Castel Xaveria, to Lipara had been frustrated; suspicions of being connected with Anarchist committees had fallen upon a clerk at one of the government offices and even upon a young officer, and it was proved that these suspicions were correct. Quite recently a workshop had been discovered in which was taught the manufacture of dynamite-bombs and infernal machines. But who the insolent miscreants were who had succeeded in flinging their threatening letters into the very Imperial cabinet, it had not been possible to discover. For a whole week the study windows had been watched from the park, and all that time nothing had been seen; it was now a couple of days since that secret watch had been given up. The head of the secret police felt convinced that the guilty ones were lurking in the Imperial itself, and acquainted with the intimate habits of the Emperor. Silent, sudden domiciliary visits were paid to all the servants of the Imperial of whom there was any doubt, and when an anarchist leaflet was discovered in the possession of a groom, on which stood insulting words directed against the Emperor, this man was relegated to the quick-silver mines in the East.

This banishment was the beginning of numberless other banishments; they followed one another in quick succession—soldiers, sailors, many smaller departmental officials: the newspapers did not even render an account of all the banishments. The censorship was rendered more severe; newspapers were continually being seized; editors fined and imprisoned; the Imperialist papers, the organs of Count Myxila, almost despotically indicated the tone which was required. A meeting of Socialists was dispersed with sword-cuts by the Hussars; serious disturbances followed in the capital, and infected the other large towns, Thracyna, Xara, even Altara. A strike of dock-labourers filled Lipara for weeks with rising insubordination; police-constables were cruelly murdered in the harbour in broad daylight.

The Duke of Mena-Doni was during this period the Emperor Oscar's right hand, and his rough displays of force kept the capital so far in submission that no riot burst out, that the every-day life of sunny, laughing luxury went on, that the elegant carriages continued every afternoon at five o'clock to stream to the Elizabeth Parks, where the Empress or the Duchess of Xara still showed themselves every day for a moment. But thousands of protecting eyes were secretly cast upon this apparent carelessness; the troops were confined to barracks; blazing escorts of Cuirrassiers accompanied the Imperial landaus.

The Empress also had requested Othomar to desist from his solitary morning rides, and never to show himself unattended. The Duke and Duchess of Xara inhabited the Crown Palace, a comparatively new erection on the quays, where they kept up an extensive court, and in this palace of his son the Emperor also caused domiciliary visits to be made, and it transpired that there were anarchists lurking among the household.

This treason within their very palaces kept the Empress in a constant shudder of terror: she lived in these days an unceasing life of dread, whenever she was separated from the Emperor. For she was least terrified when she showed herself by Oscar's side, at exhibitions, at ceremonies, at the Opera, and this was strange: she did not then think of him, but, if they were not with her, of her children, as though the catastrophe could only happen at some place where she should not be present.

The Empress saw in Othomar so very much her own son that, in the intimacy of their morning conversations—for the Crown Prince still came every morning for a moment to his mother—it surprised her that she did not find again in him her own dread, but on the contrary all her own resignation, which was the reverse side of it. But since his marriage she had found him altogether changed; no longer, in these short moments of their private intercourse, complaining, hesitating, searching, but speaking calmly of what he ought to do, full of an evident harmony that gave a restful assurance to his words, his gestures, and even to his actions. With this assurance he retained a quiet, dignified modesty; he did not thrust himself violently into prominence; he continued to possess that receptiveness for what comes from other people which had always to such a high degree and so sympathetically characterized him. He was undoubtedly old for his young years; any one who did not know would have given him more than his twenty-three years, now that he also grew a crisp beard on his cheeks. . . . And yet, yet, especially in these troubled days, his old fears would often well up within him, he could remain sitting alone for minutes at a time, staring at a vague point in his room, listening to the murmur of the future, as he had listened in that night of the phantoms of his forefathers at Castel Vaza. He then felt that, suddenly, as with a garment, all his new resignation in life was slipping from him, fell from his shoulders. But he had learnt so to govern himself that nobody, not his father, not his mother, not even the Crown Princess, noticed anything of this dizziness of soul, which left him ice-cold in his short periods of solitude, doubting his right, full of strange, feeble compassion for his people. . . .

It was, actually, the old illness which thus, periodically, fermented again within him like an evil sap, flowed through his arteries, enfeebled his nerves, crushed him internally, as though he would never be cured again. But he grew accustomed to it, felt no despair any more because of it, even knew, during the minutes that the sickness lasted, that it would pass, and afterwards regained that sense of harmony which above all was his acquiescence.

It was in these days of silent fermentation that there was a talk of a marriage between Princess Thera and the Prince of Naples; nothing, however, was as yet decided on between the two families, but the young Prince was invited to Lipara to attend the great autumn manœuvres. Hunts were arranged; different entertainments followed one upon the other. Othomar had, especially in these days, more than ever to combat these sudden weaknesses ; a strange feeling, a shivering, a mysterious terror, remained with him and no longer left him : a terror which he dared not analyze, for fear of discovering motives which would cause him altogether to lose his calm. There revived within him the memory of the fact that shortly after his marriage he had dreamt a dream more or less similar to his former dream : the sinister capital filling with crape. . . . It happened while he was still residing with his young wife at Castel Zanthos, and he had attached no importance to it, because he considered that this second dream was only the silhouette of the former one, only the remembrance of what had already happened, and nothing more. But now, in these days of busy festivity in honour of the Prince who was visiting their Court, with the ferment of popular discontent like a turgid, gloomy element beneath the surface brilliancy of all their Imperial display, the memory of it revived, and the terrors and shudders drew round it always plainer and plainer outlines in his imagination, and at one moment he felt his former nervous weakness coming over him to such an extent that he found an excuse to summon Professor Barzia from

Altara, and had a long interview with that learned man of which he did not even speak to the Duchess of Xara. When the Professor had gone, Othomar felt relieved, strengthened : only the thought remained hesitating within him that it was not right that a future sovereign should be so much under the influence of a stronger mind as he was under that of Barzia ; and he proposed to himself the next time not again to call in Barzia's suggestions, but to cure himself, in the entire secrecy of his own soul. This plan of always relying on his own strength made him find himself wholly again. . . .

The day succeeding his interview with the Professor, he spent the whole morning and afternoon in the company of the Prince of Naples, with whom he visited different places with a gaiety and liveliness which were rarely witnessed in the Duke of Xara. The suite was astonished at this radiant merriment on the part of the Crown Prince, in whom they had grown used to perceiving always a grain of melancholy. That evening there was a great state-banquet at the Imperial. After the dinner, the Imperial Family were to accompany their guest to the Opera, where a state performance was to be given, and a renowned tenor was to sing.

In those days, whenever the Imperial Family
went out, for all the semblance of glittering display, severe precautionary measures were taken.
A compact and strong escort of Cuirassiers
pranced around the carriages that drove that
night to the great Opera-House. The street at
the side of the building, where the Emperor's
private entrance stood, was closed off; a guard-of-
honour stood on the staircase; the secret police
mingled with the expectant public: the whole
great world of the capital. . . .

The Imperial box, with its dark violet draperies
and gold tassels, was just over the stage of the
colossal theatre; the first act was finished—they
were giving " Aïda "—when the trumpet-blasts
clanged out from the orchestra, and the august
personages appeared : the Emperor, the Empress,
the Prince of Naples, the Duke and Duchess of
Xara, Princess Thera. . . . And their entry seemed
to electrify the dull, expectant, nervously indifferent mood of the crowded house, as though, upon
their entry, the light in the lustres shone more
brilliantly, the house blazed out with all the
changeful flickerings of its jewels, all its flashing
gilt, all the curiosity of the bright eyes that gazed
at the Imperial centre-group; as though the
toilettes of the ladies had suddenly blossomed out

with one rustling sound of heavy silken stuffs, the fans unfolded, waved to and fro as though a breeze were blowing through many flowers, in much light. . . .

Then the rising of the curtain : the second act with all its melodrama of Royal Egyptian state : the victory after the war and the consequent dances : the hero's love for the Ethiopian slave, and the jealous daughter of Pharaoh, and the procession of the gods with the sackbuts : all sung, orchestrated, swelling up with music in a square frame against a painted background : a stirring picture of Princely Egyptian antiquity chanted before the eyes of modern sovereignty, of a modern audience, indifferent to the rest so long as they met, wherever the great world decided that at that moment they should meet : under the eyes of the Emperor and his family and their august young guest. . . . The passions on the stage unbridling themselves in swelling and swelling bursts of music, a world of music, love and despair, and war and triumph, and priestly ambition in music, everything music, as though life were music, music the soul and essence of the world. . . . And beneath the illumination of that music and of that factitious life, the visible pantomime of the actors, the glory of the renowned

tenor with his too modern head, his dress in its
splendour so unsuited for war, his bows and his
smile for the real world outside his small stage-
world frame : for the public that applauded after
the Emperor had deigned to clap his hands. . . .

It was at this moment, this moment of ovation,
this moment of lustrous triumph for the tenor :
his applause led by the Imperial hands.   It was
at this moment : the Emperor Oscar turning
round to his aide-de-camp, the Marquis of Xardi,
behind him ; the aide listening respectfully to the
command of His Majesty that he should summon
the singer to the withdrawing-room of the
Imperial Box . ; . the Empress Elizabeth and
the Duchess of Xara, gleaming in their gala, their
jewels, in smiling conversation with the young
foreign Crown Prince who was their guest. . . .
Othomar still with his gaiety of the afternoon,
jesting with Thera and the ladies-in-waiting. . . .
The whole house gazing, now that the curtain had
fallen for the last time, at all of them, in their
blaze of luxury and light. . . .

At this moment : in the topmost gallery a
sudden tumult, a struggle of soldiers and police
with one man. . . . A sudden rough scrimmage
up there in the midst of the most mundane expan-
sion of aristocratic pageant.   And all eyes no

longer directed to the Imperial box, but upwards.
. . . Then, the man, struggling free with superhuman strength from the grasp of his assailants,
surging forwards, from out of their throng, like a
black lightning-flash of fate : dark, woolly head,
eyes flashing hatred, fixed and fanatical, one arm
suddenly stretched out towards the Imperial
grandeur beneath, as though at a target with an
inexorable aim. The whole house one tumult,
shouting, shrieking ; wide gestures of helpless
arms, all this very quick, lasting barely a second.
. . . A shot, and yet another shot. . . .

The Emperor is hit in the breast, he falls up
against the Empress, whose bare, jewelled bosom
he suddenly soils with blood, which immediately
soaks his golden uniform through and through.
Not golden blood : rich red blood. . . . But the
Empress throws up her arms in despair ; her
strident scream penetrates the house. She falls
back into the embrace of the Duchess of Xara.
The Emperor has sunk into the arms of Xardi
and of Othomar ; a furious oath forces its way
through his tight-clenched teeth, while he tears
open his gory uniform so fiercely, that the buttons
fly around him. . . .

IV

Outside, the great Place de l'Opéra, brightly
lighted with many-armed, monumental lamp-
posts, had at once become dark and swarming,
filled with a mass of people; the whole town
poured into it from every street; the alarm drew
all the inhabitants there, as though with a
magnet. Detachments of Hussars were already
moving through the town, keeping the excited
populace in order; the Duke of Mena-Doni was
to be seen everywhere at once, trampling down
the revolution with the military at his command
in whatsoever corner it seemed to lift its head.
Overhead the sky was dark and frowning. It
began to rain. . . .

The rumour sped, that the Emperor had died.
It was not true. Wrestling for breath, the Sovereign lay in the foyer of the Opera-House, amidst
the panic of his family, of his suite, of the doctors
hurrying up. He must not be moved, they said.
He insisted. He would not die there. He was
set on returning to the Imperial. And straining
the springs of his energy, he commanded, he drew
himself up, with the blood jetting from his throat:
Othomar and the aides supported him. . . .

Outside, in the square, the mass of people grew in numbers, the panic increased, the riot seethed up from the darkness of those clusters of people. Continual fights burst out between groups of men, dock-labourers, and the guard in front of the building, the police. The court-carriages returned empty, under escort, to the palace.

Other carriages, cabs, endeavoured here and there to force a way through the people; they were surrounded by Cuirassiers, who protected them with drawn swords. Volumes of curses and abuse spattered up against them, against the vaguely transparent windows, behind which were patches of light colours, shooting sparks of jewels. Women's terrified eyes peered out fixedly, askance, without moving.

In the corridors, on the huge, monumental staircase of the Opera-House, they hustled each other, fought to get through; then, suddenly, all eyes, staring wide, looked up above: the Emperor was passing, bleeding, panting for breath, surrounded by his kin. . . . A feeling of awe stopped the crush for a moment; then they pressed on again. . . . Ladies fled till they found themselves behind the scenes, where they mingled their aristocracy with the bohemianism of the actors, the actresses, all mixed up, confused, amidst the terrified, murmurous crowd of ballet-girls, priestesses of Isis. Gratuities were lavished, carriages were begged for, cabs. . . .

The Duchess of Yemena stood there with her daughters; they were looking out for their carriage, which they had already sent for ten times . . . . A stage-carpenter shrugged his shoulders indifferently: he did not know where he was to get a carriage from.

" I won't wait any longer," said the Duchess, shuddering: the young girls fastened on her, sobbing hysterically.

From an actress she obtained a leather bag; she hastily took off her jewels, ordered the girls to do the same. They put them into the bag. She asked a dresser, in return for a piece of gold, to pin up their trains, high up, asked her to find them some black shoes. Other ladies, half-swooning with fright, waiting, looked at her, saw her thus, strangely practical. She succeeded in purchasing from a couple of chorus-girls three long black cloaks, with three black hats, flung one cloak over herself, flung the others over the sobbing little Marchionesses.

" I am frightened, Mamma! " sobbed Eleonore.

The Duchess was determined.

" Come, come along . . .' she urged, and she

drove the young girls before her; the other ladies, in alarm, watched them disappear through a back-door into a side-street. . . .

The Duchess pressed the bag with the jewels to her.

"For God's sake, don't cry, be calm," she ordered her daughters. "Walk quietly on, and not too fast. Keep your cloaks well round you."

She walked on, tall and erect between the two little trembling Marchionesses, in the choristers' clothes; the rain poured down. Clusters of people ran up against them; they mingled with them; for a moment she lost Hélène. . . .

"Wait a moment!" she said to Eleonore.

And they remained standing amid the press of people; troops came jogging on, socialistic songs of triumph carolled up coarsely. . . . Then she went back with Eleonore, pushing, shoving, giving Hélène an opportunity to reach her again. . . .

"Now both give me an arm: here. . . ."

They did as they were told; thus, seemingly calm, slowly, slowly, as though they were sight-seers who had also come to look, they approached the Place de l'Opéra, where the people were swarming up against the guards. Carriages passed, at a walking-pace, escorted. A wretched old hired growler, with a gaunt hack, pushed a muddy wheel right up against her, grazed her knees; a Cuirassier of the escort raised his sword threateningly against her. . . .

"My God!" she cried, awe-struck, and clutched the children. She had first recognized the driver, in a dirty coat: a footman from the Imperial, whose face she recalled. Then, with a swift glance into the cab, she recognized—just close to a lamp-post with many decorative arms—the Emperor leaning against Othomar, and her own stepson, Xardi. But the Marquis did not recognize her, for, startled by the great light, he quickly turned his face away, bent, sombrely, protectingly, over the Emperor and the Crown Prince. . . .

The girls had seen nothing; the Duchess said nothing, afraid of betraying them. . . . She felt all her brave composure forsaking her; she shuddered from head to foot. She could not restrain her tears for her poor Emperor, who was dying, who was returning to his palace in such a guise. A great, heavy terror took possession of her. The rain trickled over her bosom. . . .

"Keep your cloaks round you!" she again admonished her daughters; then she proceeded, dragging herself along, and the girls as well, beside her, with legs that failed them. . . .

But a whirlwind of people swept across the

Place de l'Opéra; a fight seemed to be going on there. . . . A heap of men, surrounding a group of police-constables and soldiers, amid whom a madman wrestled with forcible gestures; a coarse clamour sounded up. At the lighted, open windows of the Opera-House, above the perystile, still in its bright illumination of festivity, appeared face after face, actors still in costume looked on. . . .

"Mamma, we shall never be able to get through!" sobbed Eleonore, softly.

The Duchess thought in despair of the great Empress Avenue in which their town-house stood; so far away . . .; how should they reach it . . .?

"They are murdering him, they are murdering him, they must not murder him!" vociferated the people round them.

Then the Duchess understood, then she saw, and the girls also saw: the people, furious, foaming at the mouth—avengers now, though at first malcontents, perhaps even Anarchists: such were the Liparians!—the people, pressing against the soldiers and constables, in the midst of whom the Emperor's assassin still made fight with his large, frenzied gestures. And the avengers stormed this circle of protecting police; they dragged the man out. . . . They dragged him

right under the eyes of the Duchess, of her
daughters. . . .

"Ugh, ugh, ugh!" they roared brutally, men
and women alike; they tore the clothes from his
body, beat him, and he howled back. They
struck him to the ground with cudgels, and they
trampled on him with coarse shoes; his blood
poured forth; his brains were spattered out from
his crushed skull. . . .

Then, at the sight of blood, they grew like
wild beasts; they grinned and smacked their lips
with delight. . . .

Eleonore fell back fainting against the Duchess,
but Alexa shook her by the arm.

"Keep up, keep up, for God's sake keep up!"
she cried out loud. "I can do nothing with you,
if you faint!"

Her strong hands goaded the little Marchioness
back into life, and again she dragged them on,
staggering. . . .

V

The Emperor, who refused to die, lived on out
of sheer energy for two days longer, with his
perforated lungs, panting for breath.

And such were the Liparians: the man, the

assassin, seized in the Opera-House, despite the police and the guard, had been battered into a shapeless mass by the malcontents themselves. . . .

And such is life: the Emperor of a great Empire was shot dead in the midst of his *entourage* by a fanatic, and yet life went on. . . . The Empire was as extensive as before; a rich, naturally beautiful, Southern Empire; tall, snow-clad mountains in the North; mediæval and modern towns, lying in broad governments; the residential capital itself, white in its golden autumn sunshine, with its Imperial, beneath a blue sky, close to the blue sea, round which circled the quays. . . .

And such is the life of rulers : the Emperor was lying dead, murdered with a simple pistol-shot, and the High Chamberlain was very busy, the Masters of Ceremonies were unable to agree ; the pomp of an Imperial funeral was being prepared in all its intricacy; through all Europe sped the after-shudder of fright ; all the newspapers were filled with telegrams and long articles. . . .

All this was because of one shot from a fanatic, a martyr of popular justice. The Empress Elizabeth stared with wide-open eyes at the fatality that had happened. It was not thus that she had ever pictured to herself that it would come, thus, so rudely, in the midst of that festivity and in the presence of their Royal guest. Thus, glancing past her, striking only her husband, and not crushing them all, at one blow, all their Imperial pride! It had come to pass, and . . . she still feared, she still went on fearing, more now than before : for her son . . . ! It seemed to her as though she had never feared before. . . .

It was the day before the funeral of the Emperor Oscar, when the Duchess of Xara, now the young Empress, was seized with indisposition, and the doctors declared that she was *enceinte*.

The Emperor's remains had already been removed in great pomp to Altara. At St. Ladislas the Altarians were to see him lying in state between thousands of flaming candles, with the brilliant insignia of highest sovereignty at his feet; after that he was to be removed to the Imperial vault in the Cathedral. . . .

On that day too at Lipara, whose whiteness took tones of sombre twilight beneath mourning decorations and black flags, the salutes from Fort Wenceslas resounded over the town, thundering out in dull tones their regular, heavy, monotonous bombardment of farewell. Lonely, majestically, amidst the town re-echoing with the salutes, stood the Imperial, empty, with its caryatides looking down with gloomy, rigid, down-cast eyes. The young Emperor, Othomar XII., was at Altara, leading the solemn procession. The Dowager Empress was at the Crown Palace, with the young Empress Valérie. . . . Over their lustre, which had for a moment been overclouded, there shone new lustres in life, which had gone on, which went on still. . . .

The Empresses sat together. Valérie held Elizabeth quietly in her arms: at regular intervals the cannon-shots boomed from the fort, through the palace. . . .

Then Elizabeth drew herself painfully up from the arms of her daughter-in-law, and in low, oracular tones:

"If it is a son . . . it will be a Duke of Xara. . . . He would so gladly have seen a Count of Lycilia. . . ."

The cannon-shots boomed; the two Empresses, in mourning, wept, sobbed. And now for the first time after a long interval—as there had also been a long interval at Berengar's death—Elizabeth realized all her loss, her sorrow, her misery, her despair, and she felt that this Emperor, to whom, as a very young Princess, now four-and-twenty years ago, she had been given in marriage, without love, she had come to love in that quarter of a century of their common life on his high pinnacle of sovereignty. . . .

That evening Othomar returned, and alone with his wife, with his mother, he sobbed with them, the young Emperor, whom no one had seen weeping in the Cathedral at Altara. For the Empress Elizabeth had repeated yet once more :

"If it is a son . . . it will be a Duke of Xara. . . ."

And then the Emperor of Liparia had lost his self-restraint. In one lightning-flash, one zig-zag of terror, he saw again his life as Crown Prince, he thought of his unborn son. What would become of this child of fate ? Would it be a repetition of him, of his hesitation, his melancholy, and his despair ?

And then with irrepressible sobs, suddenly overwhelmed by the menace of the future, he sobbed out his grief for his father, who had been, and his son who was to be ! He sobbed, with his head in the arms of his young Empress, who, suddenly realizing that she must comfort him, had grown calm, and looked calmly down upon him, taking their life of majesty upon her

shoulders as though it were an oppressive, heavy
mantle of purple and ermine and nothing more,
taking it up so valiantly because there flowed in
her veins, as in his : one single drop of sacred
golden blood, common to all of their order, their
might upon earth and their right before God. . . .

VI

To Her Imperial and Royal Highness Eudoxie
Archduchess of Austria, Sigismundingen.

St. Ladislas, Altara,
—— *May*, 18—.

My dear Mother,—I cannot tell you what
sorrow your letter caused me. For God's sake,
do not excite yourself so and say such terrible
things. We too regretted exceedingly that you
were not able to be present at our coronation,
and that your rheumatic fever compelled you
to remain at Sigismundingen; but why need
you, dear Mother, look upon that fever as a
punishment from God, and why need you look
upon it as a punishment from God that you did
not see your dearest illusion taking place and
were not able to be present in our old Cathedral

27

when Othomar, after being crowned by the Primate, with his own hands crowned me Empress of Liparia. You were not there, but yet it came about: your illusion is yet truth. And I tell you this without the least, oh, believe me, without the *least* bitterness! A punishment for forcing me, against my will . . . ! You must be ill indeed, ill in body and mind, poor Mother, to be able to write like that: it makes me smile a little, I no longer recognize you so. And let my smile bear witness that I am not unhappy: oh, far from it! Our happiness is hardly ever what we ourselves intend it to be, and what we regret that it is not. . . .

If you were to see me, you would see that I am not unhappy. It is May, the sun is shining, the oriel-windows are open. In the distance, when I look out, I can see the *Zanthos* winding away in a broad, gleaming expanse of water. Close by my writing-table stands your lovely, great silver cradle, and through the closed lace curtains I can see my little Duke of Xara slumbering. . . . I do not know how to write this to you, I have no command of words to be able to express it fully to you: but what I feel, with that wide view of river land before me and that small, precious child by my side, oh, Mamma, that is not unhappiness!

It is a feeling in which lurks a certain melancholy, but in which there is concealed nothing more sombre than that. And why should it really, in spite of that melancholy, not be even happiness? I am young, I am Empress, and I see life before me! Round about me, I see my country, I see my people: I want them to become the people of my heart, of my soul, entirely. I don't yet know how, but I want to live for that people, I want to live together with Othomar. Oh, I grant you, how I am to do that I don't yet know, but I shall find a way, together with him! And having a husband, and a child, and a people: an Emperor, a Crown Prince and an Empire, have I then no object in life, and having an object in life—and what an object!—have I not then also happiness? Is happiness anything else than to have found a lofty, a noble aim in life?

I would so gladly convince you. And if you saw me here, at our quiet St. Ladislas, now that all the agitation of the coronation festivities is past, you will believe me. Othomar likes St. Ladislas and proposes to come here every year for a month in the spring. It is considered a good omen that my child was born here, for you know the feeling of the Liparians, their wish to see the Crown Prince of their country born at St. Ladislas,

under the immediate protection of the Patron
Saint.

Othomar, however, is not here at this moment;
he has gone for a few days to Lipara—you know
this of course from the papers—; he writes to me
twice a day. I asked him to do so in order that
I might remain fully informed as to his state of
mind; the tragedy of his father's death, the two
days' agony of the Emperor Oscar! they affected
Othomar so violently, so violently; my God, how
can I find words to describe to you that terror!
How can I still live with hope after all that I have
already suffered in my short life, and have seen
around me in the way of terror! And yet, yet it
is like that, for youth is so strong, and I, I am
strong, I must be strong. . . .

I admired my young Emperor, in those terrible
days, for his outward calm, through which the
storm-flood of all his emotions never burst loose
before the eyes of the world. Directly after the
funeral, the ceremony of the Signatures under the
Five Holy Acts; the immediate agitation of the
accumulated affairs of State. . . . A month later,
the new elections, the Constitutional majority in
the House of Representatives, the resignation of
the Ministry. . . . All this you will have seen in
the papers. After that, the birth of our son, and

then our coronation, at the moment when Liparia seemed shaken to its foundations! And now Othomar is at Lipara, because of the new Constitutional Ministry. . . . Then Count Myxila, who does not agree with Othomar's modern ideas, and who has even ventured to reproach him with some vehemence for giving up all his father's ideas of government so shortly after his violent death, and he is now tendering his resignation. . . . Othomar would retain Myxila, but he realizes that it will not be possible. And the Revision of the Constitution in the immediate future, with so many encroaching changes; probably with the inauguration of the Upper and Lower Chambers, while the House of Nobles will continue outwardly to exist, but will be nothing more than an honorary consulting body. These are concessions, if you will have it so, but then, you know, Othomar has quite different ideas to his father's, and if he makes these concessions he undoubtedly makes them to the past and not to the future nor to himself. . . .

Life is cruel, cruel in its changes and cruel even in its renascences, and for us rulers all this is perhaps even more cruel, but the world belongs to the future. . . . The Empress Elizabeth is still here; she has suddenly grown so old, so

gray, and very dull and depressed, and she does
not know what to do, whether to remain with her
Household at the Imperial, to stay on here at St.
Ladislas, or to retire to Castel Xaveria. . . . All
the Imperial palaces and castles are now whirling
through her poor head : her private properties and
the Crown domains : she does not know where
she wants to go to : we of course continue to urge
her not to leave the Imperial : it is large enough
to enable her to retain almost all her own Military
and Civil Household. . . .

Dearest Mother, I will write to you again soon :
my head is still too much in a whirl now ; I have
touched on too many topics ; my feminine brain
is not capable of thinking that all out logically
and coherently, and of writing it down. . . . And
I have only been Empress for such a short time,
and I am only two-and-twenty, although I no
longer feel so young. . . . This letter is only a
hurriedly-written reply to your doleful self-re-
proach, which I now beseech you, in the name
of Heaven, to throw off from you *entirely*. Now
that I write this to you, the evening of my betrothal dinner at Sigismundingen rises anew
before my mind. We were such a strange betrothed couple, Othomar and I. I asked him—
smile at this, Mamma, and don't cry over it—

whether he loved anybody. He told me no. He told me he loved his people, and he stretched out his arms, as though he would have embraced them. His People! The dawn of a new idea—old no doubt to thousands and ages old, but new to me, as a new day is new—shone out before me, threw light over my gloomy sufferings, illuminated the road before me. . . .

That road, Mamma, I now see stretching before me clearer and clearer every day, and I mean to follow it with my husband and my child, with my Emperor and my Crown Prince!

My Crown Prince, who is waking and crying for me!

May God grant me strength, Mamma.

VALÉRIE.

THE END.